CHASING Vincent

Chasing Vincent

DOUGLAS SCOTT ROSS

Century West Publishing

For information contact:
douglasscottross@outlook.com
douglasscottrossauthor.com

Published by:
Century West Publishing

Cover design by: Ace Silva

Interior book design by Francine Platt • Eden Graphics, Inc.
edengraphics.net

Paperback ISBN 979-8-89454-093-1
eBook ISBN 979-8-89454-094-8

Library of Congress Control Number: 2025917618

Manufactured in the United States of America
First Edition

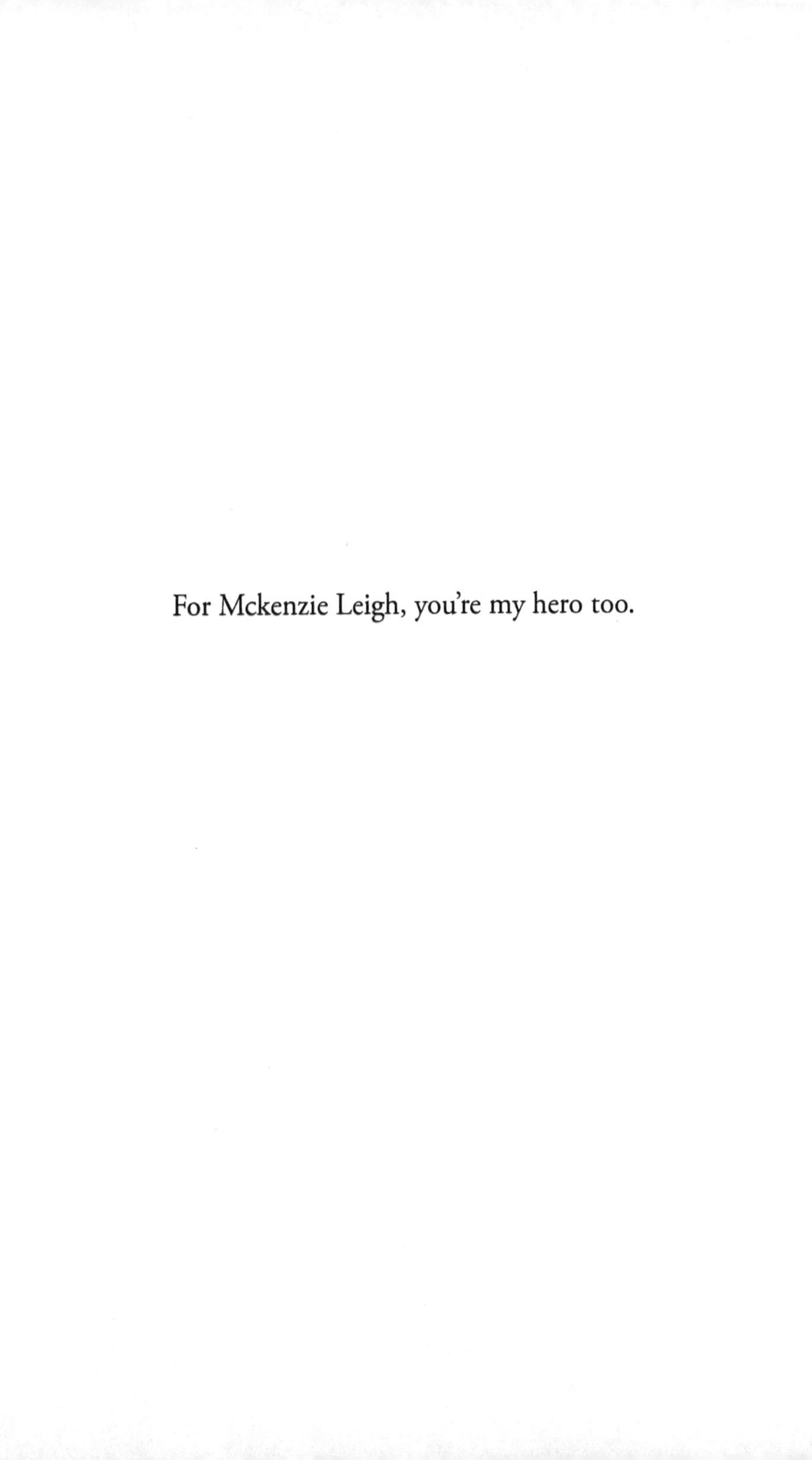

For Mckenzie Leigh, you're my hero too.

PROLOGUE

A bonfire is raging in the courtyard of the Louvre; they are burning us!

Arriving in Paris on a moonlit night in the back of a troop transport truck, rattling between ornate furniture, I can see the Sacré-Coeur Basilica on the Butte Montmartre towering above where my master lived and painted when he first came to Paris. I see the Seine, Notre Dame Cathedral, and of course, Eiffel's Tower. It is my first trip to The Cité.

Choosing some of us, the ones they hate, slashing our faces with razor knives and bayonets, they pitch us into the fire. WHOOSH! We burn fast—all canvas and oil, paper and paint. A hot flash. A flare of flame. And we are gone. Forever! Most of us are young, modern, a new generation, some only children, misunderstood as the young often are.

Pulling into the Jeu de Paume, I am impressed: a long,

tall museum, elegant and stout, part of the nearby Louvre. A new home for Moi? Of course I have heard of the great Paris art exhibitions, who has not? Gallery showings and museum exhibits. But I am from humble beginnings, from a humble master and of the countryside, not of aristocratic birth, not a portrait of a nobleman's mistress like a Leonardo. Carting me into the huge space, stacking me like cordwood, this is not a greeting but an offload by soldiers impersonating stevedores and supervised by Waffen-SS. The sight of them makes me tremble in my frame. It is they who arrested my family and ripped me from the wall of our home. Our home is in Provence, an estate of olive groves, fruit orchards, and vineyards. The flower garden is magical, tended by honey-bees and hummingbirds. The sounds of home: bees, birds, Louis Armstrong on the gramophone, Clara cooking in the kitchen—all ceased yesterday with unrelenting pounding on our door and the thud of jackboots in our home.

Tonight they undress me. I am disrobed, exposing all of me to their prurient inspection. Others are undressed too, a Monet, a Cézanne, a Fragonard. Stripped naked for them, they fawn over us with gleeful greed. Some of us they dismiss as "degenerate." Moi? They pay little attention to me. But a lady, a drab, mousy woman with round glasses, keeps looking at me with surreptitious, furtive glances. She likes me. I can tell.

This place is massive, crammed with paintings, statues, beautiful furniture, and tapestries. Some of us are still wrapped in burlap. Some of us are displayed on the walls. Oh my God, I see a Rembrandt *and* a Vermeer!

"*Heil Hitler!*" and jackboots echo throughout the hall, smelling of cigarette smoke and furniture polish.

I look for my place on a wall, a well-lit spot. There! Next to my master's friend Degas. Instead, my frame is hooked by a soldier muttering, "*Entartete kunst*—Degenerate art," and dragged to the basement into a dusty room where other paintings are hung haphazardly and stacked on wooden shelves. They are hiding Moi. Dumped on the dirty floor between Marc Chagall and Paul Klee, I am scared; this room is so dark.

What will happen to me?

I miss my family. What have they done with them? Husband Paul and his wife Clara arrested and shoved into the back of a black Citroën. Young Jacob escaping out the kitchen door, his pockets stuffed with money and his mother's jewelry. And the older sister—my sweet, pretty Eloisa— taken into a bedroom and, and… I cannot bear the thought of what they did to her. I think Eloisa's screams will forever echo inside of me.

I want to cry. I am not brave, not like my family. I don't want to burn.

She comes to me in the darkest part of the night—the mousy one, silently on worn shoes. Switching on her dim flashlight, she finds me. Seeing my reflection in her glasses, I look frightened. With no makeup, her hair rolled into a tight bun, and dressed to discourage any man's advances, she is the opposite of Moi. Where I am thought to be pretty, she is just the opposite. My Master could never paint her, well, maybe when he was younger and working in the north. But later in Paris and Provence, his palette no longer carried all the grays and browns it would take to capture her. Best left to Millet—painter of peasant farmers.

With the determination of an accountant or even a detective, not with the admiration of a connoisseur, she examines me, scrawling hurried notes. I see her notebook is filled with scribbles of other paintings. She flinches as gunshots report with sharp notes resonating through deserted streets—Frenchmen standing blindfolded against a stone wall of a nearby church. Just before leaving me, her countenance changes, and she touches me with gentle fingers upon my brushstrokes, a caress. She is no longer the impartial juror; I see something else in her eyes. And I know when I see it. I see love.

Locked away with the others they call "degenerate," I am stored with a Cézzane, a Picasso, and my dear friend, Émile Bernard. And across the wall is a Salvador Dali, but frankly, he scares me, and I am already living a nightmare. I don't care what they think. But I must. We will burn. All of us.

At dawn, I hear the scurrying of rats. And I am sitting on the floor! I know what rats do. They gnaw on wood and canvas. Claw and chew with sharp incisors. I shudder. Take Picasso or Paul Klee, not Moi! I must survive, somehow. I am not charitable in this endeavor. There is no honor in it. Not one shred of nobility. Every painting for itself. I am not proud of this feeling. Not a time for pride. A rat is sniffing around my edges, his whiskered nose appraising me. I feel his raspy tongue licking me—*eeew!*

As the door opens, rats scurry away. She comes to me

again. Ignoring Henri Matisse and Piet Mondrian and Marc Chagall, she lifts me up, holding me high, and we gaze at each other. Blowing a breath across my canvas to remove the settled dust, it feels like she is blowing me a kiss. Carrying me up to the great hall, she elicits help as I am one of my master's largest paintings, and she searches for open wall space. The whole building is in a bustle of cleaning and decorating. We hear that the boss is coming for a visit. Everyone, including us, is here to impress His Highness.

I learn her name is Rose Vallard, Assistant Curator. She is the only French person allowed inside. The Germans rely on her expertise. Side by side with an experienced eye, she works for them, directing soldiers using suggestions and not orders. They call her "Madame." She calls them "Monsieur Lieutenant," "Monsieur Capitaine," and "Monsieur Sergeant." Working for them seems traitorous.

Rose, please find me some good light where I can shine.

She hangs me next to a Van Dyck portrait of a Dutch nobleman, his high white collar an intricate masterpiece all in itself; to my left is a landscape by Claude Monet. I am pleased with my predicament. I hang next to masterpieces! And Moi? What am I? I don't know. I am unsure. People tell me I am pretty. But I have never been shown in a gallery or a museum or decorated a fine chateau in the Loire Valley.

I am a portrait of Marie Toledano, a friend to my master, only 16 years old. It was a good day for him, a rarity. A clear head. A day to unleash pent-up passion. Unbridled. I remember that day. We walked from the Asylum in Saint-Rémy back when I was a blank canvas. A brisk hike with an easel, brushes, and palette. My master's brother Theo had shipped a fresh supply of paints: tubes of ocher, yellows, reds, greens, and lapis. And on the way, he stops to pocket a sparrow with a broken wing.

I hear whispers in the museum's hall that Hermann Goering is coming—he is *their* master. We are to be "selected." Every officer is sharp in their uniform. Immaculate. Impressive. The hall is clean and ready for this special occasion, a presentation, an exhibition for one. He has been here before, I hear, every time there is a new shipment. Today, it is Paul Rosenberg's gallery and art pieces from the wealthy Rothschilds, both Jewish like my family, the Toledanos.

I get it. I need to be "selected." If not, then my future is uncertain and tenuous at best. But how am I to outshine the Old Masters? I feel like a Kansas farm girl arriving by Greyhound to Hollywood, dreaming of becoming a starlet. While back home they tell me I am pretty, here are Marlene Dietrich, Olivia de Havilland, and Katherine Hepburn. Judy Garland is making a new movie, and I can't sing; so is Ginger Rogers, and I can't dance, not even a little shuffle. But so is Loretta Young, and we share the same sweetness, and they tell me Marie looks like Vivian Leigh when she was a girl.

I have to be optimistic. I have to look pretty. I have to curry the eye of someone to love and protect me. My master told Marie, "Young lady, you hold the beauty of a fresh bouquet ready to blossom." I must blossom. Madame Vallard, help me. I know you can't protect me. I overheard them whispering about you. They are suspicious of you. They don't trust you. The only French person in the Jeu de

Paume. A witness to their thievery. They say, "What is she writing in her booklet? It is all in French."

Madame, help me!

I need my master to fight for me. And across the hall I see a Caravaggio. *Caravaggio!* But instead of a drunken brawling Caravaggio drawing his sword and dueling with a foe, my master tends to broken sparrows and cuts off his own ear when his love is unanswered. And instead of painting blood—dripping severed heads like Caravaggio's *David with the Head of Goliath* or his *Medusa*—my master paints sunflowers and iris and starry nights. I miss him. Dead at the age of 37, same as Caravaggio—both under suspicious circumstances.

He is here! Hermann Goering.

The Jeu de Paume stiffens to attention. Not only the soldiers inside but the building itself seems to strengthen; columns become stouter. Rose Vallard seems impassive, but I sense anger inside her, a burning hatred. Officers salute, exhorting "*Heil Hitler!*", and escort him through the exhibition. He is gregarious, pompous, and portly. I heard soldiers talking about him, saying he was decorated in the Great War with the Blue Max, flying his Fokker alongside the Red Baron—von Richthofen. He has lost all aerodynamics but is in a jovial mood. A friendly round face. Clownish in his crème-colored, gold-embroidered Reichsmarshall uniform and jewel-encrusted cane. Some little girl is lucky to have him as a grandpa, I think.

Hands behind his back, he peers at paintings, some with a glint of true affection, others with a dismissive wrinkle of his nose and a wave of his hand. Across the hall I see another painting signed, *Vincent.* It is by my master, too, a bridge near my home outside of Arles. Spanning a canal, it is a fascinating contraption of pivoting great wooden beams, leveraging up and down or side to side, I cannot figure out which. It looks like a war machine Leonardo was so fond of designing—a massive catapult or a trebuchet. We nervously nod to each other. But my sibling is quickly dismissed, and I am left to worry.

Of course, Rembrandt and Vermeer are chosen first with the delight reserved for a man who has unearthed pirate treasure. But I am surprised at his glee to find a Cranach, a German painter from the 1500s, a dark religious work.

"For the Führer's museum in Linz," he pronounces, and his minions pounce, carefully removing it from the wall.

If Cranach is his passion, then I am for sure to burn.

Finally, he stands in front of Moi. Rose Vallard stands behind him, implacable, but I can tell she is nervous. Not for herself, but for me. She is brave enough and tall enough to look Goering in the eye and not blink. He stares at Moi. I stare at him. He stares at Moi. I stare at him. He makes me cringe, a creepy, sick feeling. He is not looking at the painting itself but leering at Marie. At sixteen, she is not yet a woman, still only a girl on the cusp of womanhood. Blossoming. His hand moves deep into his trousers.

"This one for me," is all he says.

I have been *selected!*

CHAPTER 1

May, 2002
Pill Hill
Oregon Health Sciences University
Portland, Oregon

"I can't do this," she said.

Giving her tassel a playful swipe, Professor Sussman encouraged, "You got this," and walked to the podium in a ruffle of black and purple satin, a roundish man looking like a specially-wrapped holiday pear from Harry & David. Julie watched him through a slit in the side curtain, and he gave her a little smile as he pulled the microphone down to his height. He surveyed the audience over the top of his glasses.

"I am bursting with pride," he said, beaming a huge grin that barely made it over the podium. "Ladies and gentlemen, faculty and students, it is my heartfelt honor to introduce to you the 2002 recipient of the Gold-Headed Cane Award.

"I read: *This award is given to the medical student by their peers and teachers in recognition of the compassionate devotion and effective service to the sick."*

People, I introduce to you, Julie Tolle." He held up the cane, a wooden stick with a golden metal head.

Julie heard the audience gasp and her classmates tossing their heads side to side in a tempest of tassels, searching for her. She imagined their whispers: *She won't show. Not after what happened. No way. She's a mess…*

Professor Malcomb Sussman escorted Julie to the microphone and continued, "I have known this young woman her entire life. Her father and I smoked smuggled Cuban cigars together in the old Obstetrics Unit the night she was born. Her father, my friend and your pediatrics professor, was a great man. His sudden passing this week leaves us all grieving. Before Jacob Tolle focused his intellect on researching childhood leukemia, that diagnosis was a death sentence. Imagine, my young doctors, being the bearer of that devastating news, and parents, imagine it is *your* child who is sick. Now, every day, his discoveries save lives. I will miss you forever, my old friend.

"He left us his most precious gift, an only child. After graduating from the University of Utah in Salt Lake City, she returned to our medical school and to the hospital she roamed as a little girl, tagging along on her father's Sunday morning rounds. A little mop of black hair, bedhead amongst long white coats." Professor Sussman stepped aside, lifting the microphone. "Julie, you're up."

She moved dizzily on unsteady legs amongst hesitant applause. When the professor tried to sit, her clammy hand clutched his, and she whispered, "Malcomb, stand up here with me. Please."

Eyes too reddened to harbor contacts, she donned her thick glasses.

"Thank you, Dr. Sussman," she croaked in a thin voice. "And thank all of you."

"We have a bond," she began. "A bond has formed between classmates as we became physicians. Not unlike the bonds I made while learning to rock climb in Utah." Her voice strengthened. "When changing leads on a big wall, you place your life in the hands of your partner, then he places his life in yours. Now, as sick patients' lives are being placed in *our* hands, we are like knots, cinching tight and holding firm. These bonds are sometimes tested, like when we lose a revered pediatrics professor." A long pause followed the mention of her dead father. The audience stirred. Parents held hands. Julie fought back tears.

Malcomb Sussman took her arm just as she regained composure. "It is a bond formed of the greatest joys: excising a cancer, setting a child's broken arm, delivering a newborn baby. On my father's Sunday morning rounds, he was fond of saying, 'No one cares how much you know, until they know how much you care.'

"Or during a life-saving emergency, 'Action conquers fear.'

"And… 'Forget about making a living—go make a difference.'

"I want to thank all of you who loved my father, and your kind generosity, and for this award." Holding the Gold-Headed Cane in her hand and bowing her head into her heaving shoulders, the microphone amplified her sniffles as she buried her head into Dr. Sussman's tender hug. Breaking free and with tear-stained cheeks, she spoke, "Let's go make a difference!"

Fleeing the auditorium well-wishers, not with the deft bob-and-weave of a boxer in the first rounds, but that of the punch-drunk fighter on wobbly legs with a puffy face and swollen eyes, Julie dodged the awkward combinations of "Congratulations! Sorry about your father," and "Sorry about your father. Congratulations!"

Marching across campus in her black gown and thick glasses, she looked away from classmates enveloped by family and passed the jumble of hospitals, research labs, clinics, and libraries, the Schools of Medicine, Dentistry, and Nursing all perched above the city—*Pill Hill.* She took no notice that Portland, the City of Roses, was blooming with azaleas seducing bees to their sweet nectar, while rhododendrons wore their garish blossoms in the way a fading burlesque queen dons her pink feather boa. She spied Malcomb Sussman hurrying behind her, sweaty in his black gown, and slowed her pace. At the edge of campus, where Douglas Firs anchor cliffs overgrown with fiddleback fern and English Ivy (an invasive species she and other volunteers—The Ivy League had attempted to eradicate), he plopped on the bench like an old crow.

Together they sat surveying the city below. A Canadian warship, arriving early for the Rose Festival, steamed up the Willamette River surging with spring runoff, and the Burnside Bridge was closing as the Morrison Bridge opened. The ship was green-grey in color and not the battleship gray of the US Navy. A deepening alpenglow radiated from distant Mount Hood, a mountain she had climbed three times with her father, a trip leader for the Mazamas Mountaineering Club.

"Thank you, Malcomb, you said such nice things."

He nodded and asked, "How are you?"

"Tired. And confused. I don't deserve any awards," she said, holding her diploma in one hand and the Gold-Headed Cane in the other. She thought, *Really? A cane? A mountaineering ice axe would be more useful.* Looking down at her sandals, she watched a honeybee entangled in wind-blown spider webbing. "I told myself, I'm *not* going to cry. Thought I was all cried out."

"You were splendid." He padded her hand. "I have some good news, but it's TOP-SECRET. No one is to know."

"Tell me. Tell me. I won't say a word," she said, zipping her lips.

"As the new Chief Editor of the *New England Journal of Medicine,* I'm shortlisted to be the next U.S. Surgeon General. I leave tomorrow for meetings in Washington."

"Oh wow! That is awesome. Happy for you. I'm leaving tomorrow, too. For France. For two weeks. Father wanted his ashes scattered in the Alps."

"I remember. But are you up for that? It could wait."

My father's ashes on my mantle for years? No thanks, she thought. *Hopefully, I'll get some sleep on the plane.* "I have an itinerary. I arrive in Paris and visit places my Dad took me to when I turned sixteen. Then a train to Saint-Rémy in Provence."

"That's where your dad was born."

"I want to find some family history. The family estate. Maybe cousins. An old friend of my grandmother's is still alive. I hope to visit with her. Then to Switzerland. To the Alps." The actual mechanics of traveling with her father's remains through airports and train stations, and up mountains, were daunting. *Tramping across Europe with Dad in my backpack? Maybe that was his plan after all?*

"Have some fun, too," he told her. "Julie, you are a young woman. Sow some wild oats. Kick up your heels. I hear Saint Tropez is nice. Come back tan with a smile on your face."

Those sentiments seemed as impossible as sprouting wings and flying.

"When I come back, I start my Internship at the University of Utah, but without a Saint Tropez tan. I'll work on the smile."

"Why Utah? Why not Harvard or Hopkins? Is this about a boy?"

Oh God, I hope not. "It's not about Kiki. We're just friends. He still writes me letters from crazy places like Tibet and the last one from the Bío Bío River in Chile. He's a great guy, but..." she searched for words, "he's always chasing some new adrenaline rush. I think he's still working on his Bachelor's degree—eight years now." She saw him, a flicker of memory, leading her up a cliff face, wind in his hair, arm muscles taut, calling, "Belay On!"

Lost in thought, they watched the Cascade Mountains forested with old-growth timber and a patchwork of clear-cuts darken from green to blue. Overhead, a chattering squirrel broke their silence.

"Your father truly loved the mountains," Malcomb said. "I did not always understand him. He had wounds too deep to fathom. But I know he loved you with all of his heart."

"Like I always do when I have a question, I called his phone yesterday. He didn't answer. I can't believe he's gone. I alternate from anger to heartbreak. I want to crawl into a hole. Stay in bed forever. I feel so alone. It's just me now."

Julie started crying. Malcomb put an arm around her.

"One step at a time."

"Step one: Stop crying," she said, wiping away tears and mascara and snot.

"This trip to Europe? Are you up for this?" Malcomb looked at her with the worry of a father sending his daughter off to college.

"I'm fine. I'm good. I got this." And to dissuade his concern, she said, "I'm Daddy's Girl!" and gave the Gold-Headed Cane a majorette's twirl, but muffed it, and it flopped on the ground.

"I'm always here for you. Any time. Any place," he said.

Watching city lights flicker on and elegant Mount Hood flipping from pink to purple, Julie pondered a gnawing question. Wind rustled cones atop fir trees. The honeybee freed itself and flew off.

"Malcomb, before you go, I have a question. I don't know how to pose this, so I'm just going to say it." She steeled herself with a big breath. "You know the Medical Examiner reports father died of an accidental insulin overdose and hit his head—a subdural hematoma. He had brittle diabetes, and that can happen. I've seen it. A patient forgets he already took his insulin, so they inadvertently take an additional dose. And their blood sugar plummets to zero. Confusion. And die in a diabetic coma. But Daddy was a careful man." She took another breath, "So my question is: do you think Father did this on purpose? Was this intentional? Suicide?"

Malcomb shook his head. "No way. Your father was a survivor. Even as a little boy in the ravages of a world at war, he survived. He came to America with nothing. *Nothing*. And he made miracles. Be proud. Find happiness. That's what he wants for you."

He left. She sat and asked herself, *Are you up for this?* Luckily, she had a response: *Action conquers fear.*

CHAPTER 2

May 2002
Portland, Oregon

With long screeches of Scotch Tape, Julie bound her father's MARANTZ stereo and his JBL speakers into their original boxes. Then sealed Nat King Cole, Henri Mancini, Ella Fitzgerald, Frank Sinatra with Count Basie at the Sands, and his precious beloved Louis Armstrong into a reinforced box. Wrapping two graduation photographs of her with her father, one from high school, the other from college, she realized she had no photos from yesterday's medical school ceremony.

What will my wedding photographs look like? Just me?

Remembering her sixteenth birthday and their trip to Paris, a little smile grew across her face. Climbing to the top of the Eiffel Tower. Strolling the Champs-Élysées in the evening. Picnicking along the Seine and shopping for the perfect Paris outfit along with a French perfume to replace her Tommy Girl.

A chill shuddered her—the Paris Catacombs with thousands and thousands of human skulls following her in the darkness with their haunting vacant stares.

My first sip of Champagne…

At a sidewalk bistro on the Rue Montorgueil, the waiter, pouring a glass of Champagne for her father, poured one for her too.

"I'm not eighteen," she said.

"I will not tell," said the waiter. "If you do not."

Her father told her, "Bubbles are good for the heart and soul."

Julie laughed to herself, recalling the bell tower at Notre Dame when her father, assuming the low crouching posture of the Hunchback and adopting a goofy accent, asked her, "Esmeralda, is that you?" Then started twirling her around and around.

Looking around her old home, sadness crept in as stacked books and her father's reading chair, smothered in plastic wrap, waited for an unknown future in the house that had opened its arms for her every day, good days and bad. Organized on the kitchen table were her plane ticket to Paris, train ticket to Provence, passport, euros, and asthma inhaler. Looking at the myrtle wood chest holding some of her father's remains, she said, "You're coming with me. Every step of the way."

May 2002
Museé d'Orsay
Paris, France

Examining the self-portrait of Vincent Van Gogh, she was at a loss to make the diagnosis.

Clearly, Vincent, you are not well.

Nicely dressed in a pale blue jacket and matching vest against a background of swirly blue brushstrokes, he was thin, emaciated, but not cachectic like a cancer patient. His face with sunken cheeks and temples accenting his sharp nose and high cheekbones, his pale greenish skin was framed with reddish thinning hair and a close-cropped red beard. He was evaluating himself, but not happy with what he saw; a man in the mirror worried about who he had become.

Julie studied his eyes: *No signs of jaundice or Graves' disease.*

But it was in his eyes she saw it. Not the weary eyes of the physically ill, but the wary eyes of the mentally ill. Eyes that were clear, bright, and processing the world with a disconcerting glint, making her wonder, *What is going on inside your head, Vincent? What are you thinking? What is your madness?*

Madness isn't a medical term, she thought, *and it's certainly not a diagnosis.* Any more than when her colleagues would toss out terms like, *basket case. Looney Tunes. Crackers. Bonkers. Not playing with a full deck. Both oars not in the water.*

A patient's face can be the face of their disease, and she had seen the expressionless 'masked faces' of Parkinson's and the wide-eyed bulging stare of Graves' disease, and the 'moon faces' of Cushing's disease.

Vincent, what is wrong with you? In your day, it was melancholy or hysteria or mania.

She thought about digging into her purse and shaking out a couple of her own Xanax and Zoloft and offering them up to him.

Turning around to the opposite wall, she saw Van Gogh's portrait of his doctor friend Paul Gachet, his head in his hand and a sprig of foxglove flower in a vase. She knew that foxglove, of the genus *Digitalis*, was used as an herbal medicine. The doctor looked forlorn, heartbroken even. Today, digitalis is formulated into Digoxin, a treatment for heart failure, and as a young researcher in heart disease, she knew all about how digitalis increases calcium in cardiac muscle, creating more forceful contractions.

Julie remembered a night in the Emergency Room caring for an elderly woman with "dig toxicity." She presented with a cardiac arrhythmia and visual hallucinations—a tipping of the color scale to yellows and halos around bright points of light.

Vincent, is Dr. Gachet treating you with foxglove? Are those hallucinations giving you Starry Nights?

In the gallery room just next door, Julie had examined Degas' painting *L'Absinthe,* displayed along his other masterpieces of sweeping ballerinas, which depicted a man and a woman in a brasserie, sitting apart, dejected, sodden, benumbed.

Vincent, your penchant for drinking absinthe is a problem, too—a toxin made from wormwood. The "Green Fairy" also messes with your head.

Leaning into the painting, squinting at the brushstrokes, then standing back and, with her hand to her chin, taking the whole portrait in, pondering his predicament, she said to herself, *the DSM IV, our trusty bible of psychiatric illness, has no category for you. A couple for me, but none for you. You are a "one off." An original. Entirely your own mischief.*

She said aloud, "I can see why my father loved you so much."

"Tragic," a young man said, sidling up next to her. "His last self-portrait." Turning his face to hers, he asked in accented English, "So you like Van Gogh?"

Boyishly handsome, a little disheveled with tousled hair, round glasses, a bulky, worn sweater, black Converse All Stars, and carrying a sketch pad, Julie figured he was a graduate student from the nearby École des Beaux-Arts. His choice of English was curious, but she realized her hoodie sweatshirt, low-rise baggy jeans, Nikes, and her ponytail pulled through a baseball hat gave her up as an American.

"I'm more of a Renoir girl," she replied.

"*Oui.* I can see that," he said, standing back and taking her in. "Dark hair, *bleu* eyes, rouge lips, a nice bosom. We hand you a parasol, and you are skipping down a summery hillside of red poppies in full bloom."

Julie blushed.

"Oh my. Mademoiselle, you are blushing. *Pardon moi,* did I say something to offend you?" Looking back at the portrait, the young Frenchman said, "Dead at the age of 37.

Imagine if he lived to 86 like Monet? Oh… but to burn so bright."

"Suicide," she whispered.

"*Non*," he whispered back. "Van Gogh did not shoot himself. Hooligans. Bullies."

A tour group crowded around them, all elbows, craning necks, and point-and-shoot cameras. The two of them were jostled together, their bodies smashing into each other, and they came face to face, giggling. Placing his hand around her waist, then taking her hand, he extricated her from the buzzing tourist hive. Exhaling with a *whew*, she was still at a loss for words, her jet-lagged brain unable to engage her tongue. *Should I ask him to coffee? His name? His school? What did Rose say to Jack Dawson when they first met?*

Dumfounded, embarrassed, she said nothing. *Really? You are going to say nothing? Talk to him. "Sow some wild oats." That's what Malcomb told me. Wild ones? Or just plain oats like Quaker oats? Is it sew like stitchery or is it sow like trying to grow something? I think it is sew, like running needle and thread, creating a string of popcorn or cranber-ries, a garland to decorate the Christmas tree. My brain is not working. I need coffee.*

Julie turned to ask him to coffee, but he was gone, walking away into the next gallery. Leaving, he turned, and their eyes met; they shared a smile, his a wry, knowing grin. She imag-ined him saying, "*au revoir*," meaning we will meet again, as opposed to "*adieu*," meaning goodbye, maybe forever.

Lunch in the elegant 1900s Belle Epoque museum restau-rant—white walls gilded with gold, tall sunny windows, and the ceiling painted with fanciful scenes—she smiled at the cherubs flitting about. Handsome waiters in formal white jackets served fancy food on silver platters. Glittering like diamond necklaces, sparkling chandeliers twinkled from the high ceilings. It seemed she had been miniaturized like a Lilliputian and dropped into the jewelry box of Marie Antoinette.

Her reverie was shattered by a plate of steak tartare passing under her nose, a mountainous pile of raw ground beef with a shallow crater holding an uncooked quail egg. Retching just like she did when her father took her here for her sixteenth birthday, she covered her mouth with a linen napkin. Ordering a Niçoise salad and a glass of Pouilly-Fuisse (because she liked pronouncing the name), she remembered what a friend had told her: *a girl should first visit Paris with her father, next with her lover, and finally with her husband.* Raising her glass to the empty chair across the table, she toasted, "To you, Dad." And she wondered how to get his ashes in her pack all the way to Switzerland. "You with me every step of the way."

Using one of her few French phrases, Julie asked the waiter for the check, "*L'addition, s'il vous plaît.*" She reached inside her purse for her wallet. It was gone. Gone!

Gone: all her money, credit card, her passport. *Gone!* Her mind toggled to where she could have lost it—somewhere in the museum? *Maybe it is in the lost and found?* Red-faced and panicked, she tried to explain to the waiter. He called for the maître d', who called the manager, who called museum security wearing a vest emblazoned with the dayglow green word *SECURITY*. Embarrassingly, they all stood over her table as other diners looked on. Questioning from security caused her mind to flash to the young, flirty Frenchman admiring Van Gogh and exclaim, "Oh, a pickpocket. I've been pickpocketed!"

Julie ran downstairs. Her father's ashes, sealed inside a wooden chest, were in her pack and checked into the coatroom.

Get to the U.S. Embassy. Stat.

Fishing inside her pilfered purse while the clerk waited impatiently, she could not find the claim token.

Gone too!

"It's a large daypack," she explained in English. "Dark red, a maroon, a burgundy."

"Which is it, madam? Each color is a different hue."

Gawd, only a clerk in an art museum…

He questioned, "A burnt crimson with black straps?"

"Oui, that's it!"

"A man just claimed it. It is no longer here. It is gone."

"Ohhh… Can I just look? Let me look."

Inside the coatroom, she searched but came up empty.

"It is gone, madam. *Disparaître.*"

Hiking fast, crossing a bridge on the Seine, and using a huge Egyptian obelisk planted in the Place de la Concorde like a navigational beacon, she made her way towards the United States Embassy. In the Place de la Concorde, she kept her eyes glued to the stone pavement. This is where the guillotine reigned during the French Revolution, and she checked for blood stains and imagined tripping over the severed heads of King Louis and Marie Antoinette rolling across the plaza.

The US Embassy, on a tree-lined street and flying a fashionable Stars and Stripes, was an unwelcoming sight. Concrete pillars were being installed as barricades, and two dark blue vans marked "GENDARMES" were parked in front. Armed US Marines in battle fatigues stood at the door, cradling machine guns.

Scanned and frisked, she crept inside.

———

"You lost your wallet, pack, *and* your passport, and you have been in Paris for less than 24 hours? You should be more careful, young lady."

"I didn't lose them. They were stolen. A pickpocket."

The embassy staffer rolled her eyes and brought out an official paper form and a pen, then logged into her computer, the monitor screen reflecting off her stylish glasses.

"Emergency passports require due diligence. What is your birthdate and Social Security number?" Julie answered, and the staffer exclaimed, "Ah! Here is your old passport and profile."

Profile? They have a profile on me?

"Since the terrorist attacks, the Justice Department and State Department have been ordered to share information. Hence, we have criminal records to consider."

The prim middle-aged American staffer who had successfully adopted Paris fashion, with a designer dark blue jacket, an expensive white blouse, modest white gold jewelry, short brown hair, and minimal, but no doubt expensive cosmetics, looked at the old passport photo and back and forth to Julie, straining to reconcile them. Jet-lagged and sweaty, Julie thought, *I must look like shit.* Tucking wayward strands of hair beneath her baseball hat and behind her ears, Julie straightened, trying to look more proper.

"You were just a teenager back then," the staffer said. Using the paper checklist, she asked, "What is the nature of your visit? Business? Tourism? Educational? Looks like you have been in college."

"I just graduated from medical school." And added, "I'm here to scatter my father's ashes. They are in my pack." Julie covered her face with her hands.

"Here? In Paris! Do the authorities know you are traveling with human remains?"

"Nobody has asked except for you. He wants his ashes scattered in the Swiss Alps."

"Father's full name?"

"Dr. Jacob Tolle."

The woman rattled her keyboard. "Oh yes. Here he is. You share a strong family resemblance." Julie could see his passport photo reflecting off the woman's spectacles. *We do look alike. He looks so distinguished; I remember that paisley tie. Before he left for work at the hospital, I would straighten his tie, button up a missed collar button, and tell him if he still had shave cream in his ear.* "He passed away just last week," the woman read. "Oh, dear! A drug overdose."

"An insulin overdose."

"Intentional?"

"We don't think so."

"Okay. Let's get back to you." With her impatience and smugness replaced with worry and concern, the staffer said, "We are swamped with counter-terrorism. Since the terrorist attacks. I am required to ask: any undocumented travel to Afghanistan, Iran, Iraq, Turkey, Lebanon, Syria, Somalia?"

"Nope."

"Any felonies or misdemeanors?"

"Nope."

The staffer squinting at Julie's profile said, "Possession of marijuana, indecent exposure, nude sunbathing."

"That's high school." Julie grimaced.

"Medical conditions."

Frustrated, Julie wanted to rattle off: scabies, ringworm, bubonic plague, cholera. But thought the better of it. "I'm healthy."

The woman pushed her glasses up on her nose, focusing on her screen, and recited: "Anxious depression. Asthma. Heart palpitations."

Oh shit! They have my medical records, too? Those are supposed to be private.

"Look, can't you just issue me an emergency passport? Then I'll be on my way to Provence and on to Switzerland. My train leaves tomorrow. I *hate* Paris."

"No. You don't *hate* Paris. All girls *love* Paris. Paris is like a bad boy boyfriend, irresistible." She added, "An emergency passport requires government-issued ID, like a driver's license, which I assume you no longer have. A birth certificate, which I know you probably don't travel with, a

2-inch by 2-inch photo, one hundred twenty-five dollars, and four to five working days. Even then, most countries don't accept them. Certainly not the Swiss."

Slumping into the chair, she wanted to cry or scream or curse or drop kick the computer, but unable to land on the appropriate emotion, all she said was, "Thank you. *Merci.*"

"Look, let me help you," said the staffer like a high school counselor trying to get a kid into college. "Where are you staying?"

"The Hotel Minerva. My carry-on luggage is there."

"Oh, Le Quartier Latin. We have reports of a bedbug infestation in the Latin Quarter." Slipping on her black pumps, which she had kicked off under her desk, she said, "Give me a few minutes. Wait here."

Half an hour later, she came back, scooted in her chair, and said, "After 9/11, this place is crazy. All our Embassies are on 'ORANGE High Alert'. These are extraordinary times, and my actions on your behalf are unprecedented. This is what I can do for you." She gave Julie an envelope of five crisp $100 bills. "You may feel like a vagrant landing in small-town USA and the Travelers Aid Society kicking you down the road. But take it. Your tax dollars at work."

"Thank you."

"And this letter."

On State Department letterhead and addressed "To whom it may concern," a letter announced her United States citizenship and all rights entitled. And granted free travel through the European Union and back to the United States. And stated a few words about her lost passport and some legalese. It was signed, *Howard H. Leach, US Ambassador.*

"A letter from the Ambassador?"

"Yes, he is a wonderful man. Overwhelmed, of course. Our first ambassador to France was Benjamin Franklin, and the second was Thomas Jefferson. Ambassador Leach is no genius statesman, but he has a heart of gold. This is just a letter of introduction. It carries no legal weight, but it might help in a pinch. I'm going to start the process for an emergency passport. Bring in a photo. But right now, find the nearest police station and report the theft. It won't do any good, but at least there is a record. Also, if you need a place to stay, my husband and I live on the Rue Monceau, not far from here."

They both rose, and the woman extended her hand and gave a heartier handshake than she was expecting.

"I'll expedite your passport. Check in at the US Consulate in Geneva on your way home. And Julie, sorry about your father. Congratulations on medical school."

Exiting the US Embassy, past the Marines, barricades, and gendarmes, and with no emergency passport, Julie walked across the street to Jardins des Champs-Elysées and sat on a park bench along a path named for writer Marcel Proust. Forced to study Proust in her World Literature class, she knew the influential author suffered from asthma as she did, and his father was a physician, too; one of the world's first epidemiologists, an expert on cholera. His mother, like her own grandmother, was from a wealthy Jewish family.

His physician father, believing masturbation caused homosexuality, sent 16-year-old Marcel to a Paris brothel with ten francs in his pocket, where he nervously fumbled his virginity.

Onto the park bench, she emptied the remaining contents of her purse. Overboard and dumped into a life raft, she took inventory of her provisions: *Let's see what we got.* Cherry Lip Smacker SPF 15, Wrigley's Spearmint, eye-glasses, a tampon, pill bottles, asthma inhaler, comb, hairbrush, dental floss, contact solution, and an iPod with new songs from Alicia Keys. She dug deeper to find her cellphone. *Where's my phone?* Clawing into the grunge at the bottom of her purse, she exclaimed, *Oh... my phone's gone, too!* Her body hit a thud, and she let out a long groan, bending over at the waist, exhaling the last molecule of air into the effort with a wheeze. *Damn...*

Studying her tourist map, she could only find useless locales like Gucci, Cartier, Longines, Chanel, Rolex, Maxims, and Christian Louboutin, and landmarks like the Arc de Triomphe and the Opera House, but no police station. *Great, bag the police, I will go shopping instead; a dress and heels with shiny red soles to wear at the opera. Wonder if the Phantom will greet me?*

Winded, walking to the Metro Station Concorde and catching her reflection in a boutique window, she did not recognize herself. In this city of high fashion, she felt like a carp out of water gulping for air. She crossed the street.

There he is! Oh my god!

Smoking a cigarette, he was standing on the first corner

of the Rue de Rivoli underneath a statue of a lion with a bouffant mane ready to pounce.

He is wearing my backpack.

Approaching him with caution and with thoughts of: *Swipe it back? Confront him? Call the police?* Their eyes met. Behind round glasses, his stare grew wide with surprise and recognition, freezing her in her tracks. Flicking his cigarette in her direction, he dove into the entrance of Metro Concorde.

Looking into the subway entrance with escalators descending into an underground abyss, she spied him wearing her pack, dodging people like a bat twisting into a dark cave.

Julie flew down after him, hurtling herself into the depths of Paris.

CHAPTER 3

May 2002
Metro Station Concorde
Paris, France

> *The apparition of these faces in a crowd;*
> *Petals on a wet black bough.*
>
> In a station of the Metro
>
> Ezra Pound 1913

Hurdling the subway turnstile, then bounding down the long flight of stairs to Line 8 Lavender, Julie stopped, looking both ways. He was gone.

Running deeper down to Line 1 Yellow, she knocked a woman to the stairs, "*Pardon,*" she offered. She stopped, again looking both ways. He was gone.

Down to the bottom of the Metro, where the air intensified, a warm viscous brew of oil and electricity, of people and machines, odors both felt and smelled—Line 12

Green. Here, the Metro was surprisingly clean with shiny white tiles encasing the tunnel, each white tile with a blue letter—a massive circular French crossword puzzle, a huge tubular game of Scrabble. Julie looked at the faces ready to board the train pulling up with a slowing *clickety clack* and a whining screech to a stop. The doors opened, disgorging Parisians and tourists into the 1st Arrondissement. Praying for a glimpse of the thief, hoping to see a dark red pack or Converse All Stars, she watched people up and down the platform getting on the Metro.

There he is! Backpack on his shoulder.

As he got in the car just ahead, she jumped on board as well. But as they both stepped on, their eyes met, less than a glimpse. But this time, his stare did not scare her.

Action conquers fear.

Just before the doors slammed shut, he jumped out of the train back onto the platform. Julie jumped too, the closing doors smashing her hips, twirling her into a stumbling pirouette. Now the platform was empty. They were alone. Each facing the other.

"Give me my backpack," she said, "It's mine!"

Taking steps forward, he raised his chin, trying to look tough. Taking out his switchblade, flicking it open with a click, he brandished it at his side.

Julie stood taller.

A flock of office workers filtered in between them, clutching briefcases and newspapers. The thief backpedaled, closed his knife, turned, and ran into the dark subway tunnel. Julie followed, running along the narrow walkway, tiptoeing down the sidelines like a wide receiver trying to stay in bounds, and skidded to a stop at a sign depicting a stick figure being electrocuted by a lightning bolt and the word "*MORT!*" At first, she did not know what that word meant, but then realized it was the root word for mortician, morgue, and mortuary. Ahead, scampering into blackness, she saw him looking like a big shiny rat. The tunnel began shaking with a growing rumble and a fast metallic clacking. Before she saw it, she could feel it and hear it—a train coming! A windy roar flattened her against the grimy wet tunnel, and she sucked in, trying to make herself skinny. Like an old Hitchcock movie that had been colorized from the original black and white, she watched frame after frame of passengers flash by.

After the train passed, the tunnel was hollow and empty except for an incessant buzz and fumes that stung her nose and windpipe. He was gone. *Gone!*

Trudging up out of the Metro, following lighted yellow signs with black lettering saying SORTIE, her oily skin sweaty with a dull sooty sheen, shoulders slumped and wheezing at the end of expiration, she raised her eyes to the opaque people descending the escalators. One couple was different, glowing as the young man pulled his girl's scarf away, nibbling and kissing her neck, giving the girl shivers and giggles. She wondered, *Why am I doing this trip alone? By myself?*

Back on the Rue de Rivoli, the sun disappeared behind late afternoon clouds, and the same lion stood on the corner, his curly mane styled in a bouffant fashioned for King Louis and not a wild beast. Instead of pouncing, his eyes focused forward, and a paw planted; he was stalking—the timeless act of predator for prey, and Julie looked around, seeing nothing but Parisians to prey upon.

At the top of a stairway, Julie found herself in front of a magnificent building of creamy limestone, long and stout with an entrance of Ionic columns and modern glass doors, a museum: the Jeu de Paume.

Sitting on the steps of the Jeu de Paume, she took two hits of her asthma inhaler. A poster announcing a new exhibition of photographs by the German artist Leni Riefenstahl had been defaced by a swastika. Pulling her hood over her head and her knees to her chest, she rocked back and forth, thinking about her father. *What will happen to his remains? Will the guy chuck them in the gutter? Pitch them into a back-alley dumpster?*

Her favorite bedtime stories were not of Winnie the Pooh but the stories her father told her of his own boyhood growing up. *He* was her hero, not Christopher Robin and not Laura from *Little House on the Prairie,* and she would beg him for one more boyhood story way past her bedtime. As a boy, the family traveled to the Swiss Alps for vacation, and with a young Swiss mountain guide, they climbed the Lagginhorn. He told of how his big sister, Eloisa, home from boarding school in England, fell in love with the climbing guide, and Julie would press her father on more details of that crush, and he would oblige with stories she knew he was making up. That trip began his love affair with mountains and climbing, and he said, *"I'm going to be a mountaineer when I grow up."*

At the end of that summer in the Alps—1939—the Swiss Police arrested the family and deported them back to France. *That was the first time I found out being Jewish was being different and that it was a bad thing.*

One summer, when she was home from college, they hiked from Mazama Lodge up the Zigzag River gushing with snowmelt from Mount Hood. And he told Julie, when he dies, he wanted to be cremated and, "Cast me to the sky off the top of the Lagginhorn," and, pointing to clouds racing across the mountains, exclaiming, "There is our family's burial plot."

A gutter.

A dumpster.

Wanting to curl into a little ball like a fetus in the womb seen on ultrasound sucking its thumb, she continued rocking back and forth as her sadness could no longer be moored amongst the waves. No reason to hide it. No reason to put on a brave face. No reason to be gracious. No reason to "buck up." No reason not to let her heart break into a thousand pieces, shatter, and tumble down the steps of the Jeu de Paume. *I want to crawl into my "dark place,"* she wished, *my warm blanket where the clutches of depression cradle and comfort.*

Starting with a singular tear rolling down her hot cheek, a tiny sob, a sniffle, tears filled her eyes. But before a flood of tears burst forth, she looked up with one eye, a watery peek.

Oh my god. He's here!

Strutting past her, wearing her backpack, she blinked away tears. Not an apparition. He sat on a secluded park bench, her backpack at his side, oblivious. Hidden, Julie watched him, adrenaline flowing instead of tears.

From underneath his bulky sweater, he brought out a baguette sandwich, wiping mustard from his mouth. From her backpack, he extricated the myrtle wood box, and his eyes lit up. Glossy, honey-colored wood caught sunlight and reflected beams from tiny swirling burls. Crafted from a myrtle tree grown on the Oregon Coast, the chest was sealed and locked.

Julie felt the key deep in the pocket of her jeans.

He examined it, turning over and around, his eyes curious and gleaming, and then shook it like a little kid on Christmas morning.

He flicked open his knife.

Julie rose and crept closer, careful to keep out of sight, her muscles taut, flexing, firing on fast-twitch. Stalking. A huntress.

He twisted the tip of his switchblade into the lock.

Julie could hear the knife grinding metal to metal.

"*Putain!*" he cursed.

She crept closer.

Stabbing the knife in between the chest and its lid, he began prying it open. Wrenching his wrist one way, then the other.

The lid was ready to pop. Ashes about to spill.

Julie pounced.

CHAPTER 4

August 1942

Jeu de Paume Museum

Paris, France

Hanging on the museum wall, Rose is relieved for Moi, I can tell. And tonight the Jeu de Paume is quiet. No deliveries tonight. The light is dim. Soldiers are left to their cigarettes and gossip. I know about them, you see, I hear about the ways of the world. Dinner conversations, fine music on our gramophone, and our Zenith radio with programs and news from around the world. Lately, it has been surreptitious listening to the BBC, late at night, with Paul and Clara covered in candlelight. I've heard Chamberlain, Churchill, de Gaulle, and the rants of Adolf Hitler. I hear all the news, the horrible news.

Now I am left with the memory of what soldiers did to my family. Thoughts that are inescapable, a nightmare spinning in my head, a carousel of horror starting with:

BANG!

BANG!

BANG!

BANG!

Unrelenting pounding hammering our front door.

Jacob ran to see what was happening, but his mother, Clara, clotheslined him with a forearm across his neck. Sister Eloisa locked herself in her bedroom. Father turned up the gramophone, the music reverberating the wall I occupy; a solo horn is blaring, and the raspy voice of Louis Armstrong is singing, *"This song is over… but the melody lingers on…"* Moi's favorite is *"I'm in the Mood for Love."* That is the song that Clara and Paul always dance to.

"Open the door! Open up! Vichy Police!"

Wrestling Jacob into last winter's coat, mother stuffed his pockets with money and her jewelry and, kneeling to his face, told him to run. "Run to Madame Demolins!" Her friend and our neighbor. She gave him a look only a mother losing a son could give. A look of, *Will I ever see you again?* A look to take him in, *Maybe for the last time?* Pushed out the backdoor, he looked over his shoulder as policemen crashed in the front door, flooding our living room with dark green uniforms and guns.

"Run, Jacob! Run!" she shouted.

But I know Jacob. He is an eight-year-old boy. And he did not go to Madame Demolins; he hid in his fort. On the edge of the estate where a tangle of ancient olive trees planted by Romans cast deep shade, he has a cavern of fruit crates, boxes, and slats of board.

Watching Clara and Paul pushed into the back of a black sedan, I felt topsy-turvy, like someone had hung me upside down. Next, the soldier-police came, the ones with slate gray uniforms. Stealing everything: our gramophone (but not Louis Armstrong), furniture, silver tea set, and candlesticks, were hauled into a truck. One soldier even carts away Montrose, our calico cat, and takes her for himself.

With the house empty, only a single house fly buzzing in an endless hexagonal pattern in a beam of sunlit dust, and the fading aroma of a chicken dinner, Jacob crept back into the house, careful not to step on broken glass and dishes. With his pistol! He was trembling, his heavy coat over freshly-peed pants. I know what he is looking for, he is looking for his "Treasure Chest"—all of his valuables in a big cigar box. Things I observe him playing with when no one is around: a pocket watch that does not keep time, a tiger's eye marble, a trilobite from the Paleozoic, a widow's mite from the Bible, a medal from the Great War, and his most recent addition—fool's gold and a quartz crystal from the Lagginhorn in the Alps. But also inside is a family portrait taken by a photographer with a Leica camera. The photo shows the family posed: mother, father, Eloisa, and little Jacob, all in their finest. Jacob is wearing a suit jacket, tie, and shorts. And Moi is in the background; indeed, I am a member of this little family.

We hear a sound. Someone is here. We listen... a cry? From his sister's room? But it does not sound like Eloisa. Who? What? Jacob slinks to her bedroom like Montrose and presses his ear to listen.

The door flies open. A Soldier! An Officer! Big with tall black boots, lightning bolts on his collar, sweat beaded across his forehead, zipping up his pants, cinching his belt, Luger dangling. We see Eloisa naked on her bed, crying, her face twisted in terror, blood streaking between her legs.

The officer bent down, looking Jacob in the eye, fixing him with a glare.

"BOO!"

Jacob flattened himself against the wall, dropping the pistol and cowering underneath Moi. He shook and cringed and closed his eyes in a tight scrunch, hearing boot steps coming closer. Jacob, opening his eyes, came face to face with the officer's holstered Luger, smelling of leather and freshly-spent gunpowder. I was face-to-face, eye-to-eye with evil itself. An incarnation of Satan admiring me.

He ripped me off the wall.

"Run, Jacob! Run!" Eloisa screamed.

* * *

Selected!

Rose comes to me again. I am special to her. In the dim light, she is jotting in her little notebook. She jumps when two officers come up behind her and say, "Madame Vallard. What are you doing?"

"A notation." And she tries to put the notebook away, but they snatch it from her hand.

"Let us see." They flip through pages. "It's in French! Is this a record? A ledger?"

"*Non,*" she lies. "Only a little note to myself." She speaks to them in French, but, unknown to them, is fluent in German too. I heard her speak German to a truck driver, inquiring where a painting came from and where it was going. The Mousy One is sneaky and clever and listens to all their conversations. They do not suspect you. Or do they?

"Madame Vallard, there are *only* German records of transactions at the Jeu de Paume. Repercussions are swift."

"*Oui*, Monsieur."

Watching her walk away, I heard the SS Officer confide, "Don't be fooled by our dowdy volunteer curator. She knows too much. She knows and is recording what we are doing. But we're not criminals, we are conquerors. She must be silenced. Perhaps she needs a vacation? A stay at La Santé Prison."

I want to warn her. But how?

The next day I am crated haphazardly with open slats and they haul me off to Gare de l'Est, the Paris train station where the previous generation of young Frenchmen were sent east during the Great War to fight in muddy vermin-infested trenches, dying in great battles of machine gun fire, howitzers, and poison gas, surviving only to be cut down by the Spanish Flu. There is another painting already here greeting us, a huge mural by an American artist whose son, fighting for the American Expeditionary Force, was killed in 1918. It depicts the Gare de l'Est and young men leaving for war. One soldier stands with his wife, cradling their newborn baby. Another is on bent knee, saying goodbye to his two young sons. I want to believe these soldiers survive the Great War, return home to raise their children, and are now fighting with *La Résistance.* But I am a dreamer, you know.

I am packed into a boxcar, tossed on top of furniture, silver, and art. Boxcar after boxcar, we are off, leaving the station with the lurch of a metal behemoth. My view is a window slit. I have never been on a train before, and this would be novel fun except I do not know my destination. Where am I going? Maybe to Goering's own estate, Carinhall. Also, I have heard rumors of the planned Führer's Museum in Austria for all the favorites. Also, storage in Mad King Ludwig's fairytale castle in Bavaria. Nice places for Moi. But there are also stories of hidden storage in underground salt mines. I shudder at the thought. I am born of Provençal sun and flowers. I will shrivel and die in a cave. I will make myself look pretty. I will do what I need to survive. I must.

On the outskirts of Paris, we are stopped on the tracks. It is midday, and the sun heats our boxcar like an oven. I can melt, I think. An oily, dripping multihued puddle, like wax from burning candles. How long will we stay here? It is a stifling death sentence.

Another train is ahead of us, stopped on the tracks, and is in our way.

Shouted orders and the tug of a locomotive brought us alongside the other train. I cannot believe what I am seeing through my window. The cattle cars are crammed full of people! They are silent. The narrow slits are barred. Thin arms and hands protrude to catch a non-existent breeze. I see faces too. Pressing to the slits for a chance at a breath. The sweaty faces look exhausted and terrified at the same time. Our train is escorted, passing them as they are condemned to sit and roast. We are more precious. A slow, horrifying tour—cattle car, after cattle car, after cattle car, after cattle car…

Through one slit, I see a mat of sweat-drenched black hair covering a woman's face. She wipes her hair away and takes a gulp of dirty air.

I see her. An image. A hallucination? An illusion? Blue eyes wrung of life, instilled with terror, but with a glint I recognize.

It is only a passing glimpse. I know it is her.

I see Marie!

I shout, *"Marie!"*

CHAPTER 5

May 2002
Jeu de Paume Museum
Paris, France

Julie body slammed him.

Knocked to the ground, the Frenchman yelled, "*Jésus!*"

She kicked at him. "Give me my chest! It's mine. Give it to me!"

Rising to his feet, he used the chest to fend off her kicks. Julie lunged at him, her fists flying with punches that did no harm, like an angry grandmother spanking an overgrown teenage boy. Julie clawed him and tugged his sweater up over his head and off one arm. Backing off, they squared themselves. Both the same height. Looking into his eyes, she saw vulnerability, not the mean-eyed glare of a hardened street criminal.

Up his pale left arm, a string of needle tracks tattooed up both the basilic and cephalic veins.

A heroin addict.

Embarrassed, he pulled his sweater down over his puncture wounds, some fresh, one purulent oozing with pus.

"My Renoir Girl. Best you take your parasol and skip away. Keep skipping and never stop."

"I'm an American Girl, and if I had my lacrosse stick, I would crack your head wide open." Julie had an idea. "How about a deal? You give me my pack, and we go get you help. Fix up your arm. And…"

"My Renoir Girl is a Good Samaritan? My lucky day. Florence Nightingale in the flesh."

"I know first aid."

Torquing his knife, still wedged in the myrtle wood chest, he could not free it.

"*Putain!*" It was stuck. He spat on her. Yelled, "*Garce*—Bitch," and ran with the chest tucked under his arm like a loaf of bread.

Wiping his spit from her face, she chased him; she did not call out "Stop!" or scream, "Thief!" or yell, "Police!" Instead, she ran fast, steeling herself that when she caught him, she would scratch his eyes out, bite him, kick him in the balls, take him down. *Give back my father!*

She was faster than him.

Sprinting across the wide bridge that spanned the Seine, she was closing in on him. To the right rose the Eiffel Tower and ahead the Assemblée Nationale flying the Tricolour. Beneath them, the Seine flowed a lazy green. But she saw only the nape of his sweaty neck as she grabbed for his collar.

Looking over his shoulder, he snarled.

She grabbed and missed.

Clawing again, her nails shredding his neck, she latched onto his sweater collar.

Knowing he was nabbed, he began thrashing, cussing. Julie tackled him, unleashing a flurry of kicks and punches. She bit his face, tasting his blood. Jabbed her thumb into his eye.

The thief struggled to his feet and screamed, "Fook you!"

He gathered the chest with both hands over his head and heaved it over the side of the bridge. Julie watched it fly in a slow-motion trajectory. As she released her grip, the thief twisted free and ran away, cursing her.

Landing with a splash and bobbing to the surface, Julie watched the chest float downstream.

Jumping to the top railing, Julie took a breath and dove in.

Cold water flooded all her senses, the river tasting of dishwater with notes of diesel fuel and a salty finish of brackish sea. Swimming hard, she captured the box, clutching it to her chest and floated toes-and-nose downstream like she was schooled by her friend and raft guide Kiki when they ran whitewater. *If this were the Rhone River, I could float all the way to Provence.*

With a side stroke swim to a houseboat moored on the Left Bank, she clambered aboard, dripping wet with a soggy purse and her father's ashes. A Keeshond stood barking at her, and she held out her hand.

"Come here, sweet pup."

CHAPTER 6

May 2002

Provence, France

...I always think that what we need is sunshine and fine weather and blue air as the most dependable remedy.

29 September 1888

Vincent Van Gogh, letter to his brother Theo

For four hours on the slow rocking, fast TGV train leaving from majestic Gare Lyon, Julie slept; her brain arousing with a groan as the train slowed to her stop in Arles.

What time is it? Three AM my time?

Inside, the train station was old, worn, and more tired than she was, and she looked for the LA POSTE. It was here that Van Gogh forged a friendship with the postmaster, sending and receiving canvases and letters from his brother Theo. His portrait, *The Postman,* Julie had seen in Boston's

Museum of Fine Arts on a trip with her father to Harvard Medical School. It displays a proud man in a blue uniform with gold buttons, high rosy cheeks, blue eyes, topped with a cap—POSTES, his golden curly beard catching rays of afternoon sun.

She stood in line at AVIS. Reserved was a compact Citroën.

Wait! What am I doing? I don't have ID. No license. No credit card. Oh no…

Tugging her carry-on, pack, and purse down the Avenue de Stalingrad, she found VELO—a bike shop.

Sneezing as she entered with a full-on attack of itchy eyes, snotty nose, and a fresh stream of clear mucous, her body stopped everything, seized with a building… building… wait for it… "Ahhh Chooo!"

"*Pardon,*" she said, "Hay fever. Allergies."

"*Mon Dieu,*" said the salesman. "Lucky you are not here in autumn when American ragweed fills the air. It is awful!"

Gleaming new bikes, finely crafted art by Peugeot, Cycles Mercier, Renault, Gitane, positioned in rows, seemingly called, "Pick me! Pick me!"

"Rental bike?"

"*Oui.*" And he pointed to a row of forlorn orphan bicycles.

Julie chose a veteran Gitane girl's ten-speed, a commuter bike with fenders and a wide cushioned seat. Not built with carbon fiber or ultralight aluminum alloy, her bike, this tank, was manufactured of heavy metal. Over the rear tire was a rack for strapping her carry-on. She promised to return the bike to their shop in St Remy, bade, "*Adieu,*" and was off.

First stop, the Roman Amphitheatre of Arles.

Huge, quarried blocks of limestone fit together in two tiers of Roman arches in 90 AD to seat 20,000 spectators for gladiatorial games, chariot races, and wild animal hunts. Julie spied a poster: *FERIA de Pâques* for an upcoming bullfight.

They still do that? Rituals to slowly kill animals for fun?

At the end of the pageantry, the matador was often given a *trophée*—the severed ear of the murdered bull and, if amorous, would gift it to a lady in the stands.

How thoughtful.

In the center of the amphitheater, she bent down and grabbed a fistful of dirt and let it run through her fingers–ensured. *dust. Blood.*

Like Russell Crowe in *Gladiator,* she raised her hands to the stands and called, "Are you *not* entertained!"

Peddling out of town, a sign reported: Saint-Rémy-de-Provence 24 km.

Fifteen miles.

After five miles on the hot highway, her legs were aching, and she was sweating everywhere. Her bike was, as her dad would say, "A rattle trap bucket of bolts." Julie nicknamed it *Iron Maiden* after the British heavy metal band.

Closer to St Remy, the Provençal sun was low in the sky, illuminating farms and mountains with a golden glow and casting shadows of darkening blue and green. A sunflower had her face raised to the light, a special light warm and yellow, rounding off the hard edges of nature. A lantern light, shining beams from inside out, attracting artists like moths to a candle flame:

Vincent Van Gogh and his invitation to Paul Gauguin

Monet

Matisse

Cezanne

Chagall

Picasso.

Coasting downhill towards St Remy, breeze in her face, sun on her back, the air of Provence bathed her, a lotion of lavender and vineyards. Shedding bustling Paris and the misty Great Pacific Northwest, Provence showered her with ancestral fragrances. A welcome home.

Invigorated, she sped into Saint-Remy as streetlights flickered on and townspeople gathered at bistros and brasseries to smoke and drink and talk. She found a cheap hotel, showered, and went to bed.

From the patisserie next to her one-star hotel in downtown Saint-Rémy, aromas of fresh pastries and roasted coffees filled Julie's nostrils. Another sleepless night had left each neuron in her brain pleading for caffeine. Inhaling as she entered, wearing her bike shorts, cycling jersey, Nike shoes, and French messenger bag, she ordered from the man behind the counter.

"*Bonjour*. I will have a vanilla latte, *merci*, please."

"*Anglais non.*"

Pointing to the menu, she said, "Va… nil… la… lat… tee."

With practiced machinations upon the espresso equipment, he coaxed it to ooze black coffee, steam, and foam, and placed the cup on the countertop, folding his arms across his chest, trying to look regal like he had just completed a miracle performance, perhaps a violin concerto. But to Julie, he looked more like a street performer, unshaven, with thin, hairy forearms, and poor dentition, standing in a stained apron.

"Also *merci*, please, I would like a croissant."

He corrected her pronunciation, "Croissant."

"Croissant," she tried in earnest.

"Non, non, non, croissant, qua, qua, quasaunt. Croissant!" he implored, gesturing to his lips. As other diners looked over the tops of their newspapers, watching her receive this French tutorial, warm embarrassment rose in her cheeks.

With concentration, coordinating her anatomy—tongue, lips, uvula, nasal turbinates, tonsils, adenoids, and larynx, all in vibration, she resonated, "Croissant."

"Perfecto!" he said, raising his arms and giving her a large tooth-missing smile.

She had found no Toledanos in the local phonebook, so she focused her efforts on finding Madame Demolins, an old friend of her grandmother living in a nearby town. Tracing the route on her Michelin map with a yellow marker in one hand and latte and croissant in the other, over a mountain pass to the town of Maussane les Alpilles, she wondered what exactly she would ask the old woman. *Maybe I should write down questions? French interpreter? She will be in her 90s. Maybe she has Alzheimer's and remembers nothing?*

Straddling *Iron Maiden* and strapping on her helmet, she waved a cutesy goodbye to the waiter, he saluted in response and she peddled away wishing she was on her own carbon fiber Trek, a bike similar to the one Lance Armstong had ridden to dominate the Tour de France the last three years (all while sporting only one sterile gonad hanging from his chemotherapy-treated and recently-rumored blood-doped body). On biking trips to Napa and the Willamette Valley close to home, she would visit wineries like Stag's Leap and Ponzi Vineyards, but those tastings were definitely not performance-enhancing. She'd spied multiple wineries on her Michelin map designated by a small cluster of grapes.

Riding south out of town on Rue Pasteur toward the low mountains of the Chaine des Alpilles, she came to the Saint-Paul Asylum. A surprise. This was where Van Gogh had been hospitalized. After Marc Chagall, Vincent Van Gogh was her father's favorite painter. Tall trees lined a lane through idyllic grounds of flowers and big shade trees surrounding an old building with a chapel spire. The asylum beckoned.

This place is beautiful. Something is in there I need to see. Something is in there I need to know.

On the self-guided tour, she learned that this 9th-century monastery had been converted to an asylum by Franciscan monks, and Van Gogh admitted himself there in the spring of 1889 after townspeople of nearby Arles, fed up with his bizarre antics, signed a petition and gave it to the town's mayor.

Inside, the stone building was cool and dark with low arched ceilings, sparse and barren, giving her a haunted feeling. Up one flight of cramped stairs, she came to the room Van Gogh had occupied. A small bed, a chair, and a desk, seemingly waiting for him to return after a day painting in the gardens and fields. Looking out his small window, the courtyard was blooming, and Julie's mind filled with images of irises and sunflowers and red poppies.

That reverie was shattered reading the tour pamphlet "...of the 19th-century care of idiots, the deranged, deviants and hysterics, notable practitioner Brachet writes, "flogging, nettle rash, pinching-out, vesicatories will often be useful. The good effect of hair pulling and tearing, particularly from the temple, can be retained." Cubi, another practitioner, proposes the *Cephalic Corset,* its application to "improve the encephalon shape and action."

Standing over a metal bathtub with a locked wooden hatch, a hole for the trapped head to protrude, she read from the *Notice L' L'Establissant Hydrotherapique 1887,* "The surprise bath is effective for the mania. The strong unexpected sensation of cold water flooding the head disconcerts the insane and distracts him from his predominant thoughts."

Wondering which treatments they tortured Vincent with, she shuddered and recalled the last visit she had with her therapist.

"Julie, you are grieving," she said. "Probably in the denial and anger stages."

"I know all about Elizabeth Kübler-Ross and her 'stages'. I'm fine."

"On the heels of those stages is depression."

"Forget it. No way. I'm *not* starting back on Zoloft and Xanax. All I need is the sunshine of Provence and the fresh air of the Swiss Alps."

But she was feeling herself sliding, a sideways dance around the dark hole, skirting an open grave with crumbling edges, pulling at her, waiting for her, whispering to her, "Careful. Don't slip. Don't fall."

CHAPTER 7

2 June 1889
Saint-Paul de Mausole Asylum
Saint-Rémy, France

"Careful, steady monsieur, it is wet and slippery," said the attendant helping him stand.

Frail, weakened, taking only thin soups over the last four days as his throat was still sore and swollen after ingesting paints and paraffin, he stepped into the tin metal tub. His red beard mottled, skin pale and dry as parchment stretched loosely over his thin and naked frame. A fresh episode of madness had seized him with anxiety and panic, morphing into loneliness and melancholy. His words were incoherent. He did not recognize his doctors. The other patients frightened him.

He could not paint.

Hopeless, he had fought so hard to reclaim his sanity by painting again. First, tentative sketches with pencil on wove paper. Then onto self-portraits, not of his image but of his empty chair, one with his pipe and tobacco, the other with books and a lit candle.

Clawing to emerge from his tunnel of madness, he painted *Entrance to a Quarry*. But it was a dark, jagged abstraction of an open wound scarring the earth, and it saddened him.

Fighting for his sanity, he was losing. He was losing his mind, again. Downcast, demoralized, defeated, resigned to his nadir, he sat in the metal tub as the wooden hatch was lowered and latched. Only his head protruding, he waited…

God, please give me one day. A sunny day. A canvas. My paints.

Ice cold, the douche started without warning–a flood of water spilling over his bare head from on high. Shaking in stoic silence, the pour seemingly lasted forever.

Done, Vincent was swaddled in blankets and left in his chair, alone.

8 June 1889

Monastère Saint-Paul de Mausole

Dear Theo,

Your gift of paints has arrived and is most timely, as my supply is exhausted.

I have befriended a local family near the Hospital and plan to undertake a large portrait of their young daughter, Marie. The Toledanos are a Jewish family with features reminiscent of

Rembrandt's Jews of Amsterdam City. They are most kind while I paint in their olive groves, bringing me refreshments and admiring my work.

The girl will make an interesting model. My previous models have never radiated this kind of beauty, the loveliness found in springtime—a girl on the cusp of womanhood. She brightens my day with her innocent cheerfulness, chasing away the melancholy that settles into the recesses of my mind.

The summer sun wilts me, and the cicadas create such a noise that at times I wish I were a studio painter. But the natural world is my only connection with the sane world and my truest inspiration comes from subjects found only under an open sky.

If you truly love nature, you will find beauty everywhere.

Give word to Gaugin that I am well and painting again. Thank you for the paints and give Jo and little Vincent my best wishes.

A good handshake,

Vincent

June 1889
Toledano Estate
Saint-Remy-De-Provence

Is this lovemaking? I am innocent of the desires of the flesh, but my blank canvas is having love painted upon it. A man's passion is pouring out of him and all over Moi. It feels good. Caresses of his brush. Some strokes light as a feather. Others strong, impulsive. My master is daubing me with paint. Stroking me with swirls. Thick pigments of his bright palette. He looks at me with such intensity—a lover's gaze. I blush. My warm canvas is starting to glow as this day, this moment, this garden, this beautiful girl is recorded in all its magic.

They speak. I listen:

"Did that hurt?" the girl asks, pointing to her own ear.

"There are pains much worse than physical pain," he says without peering around his easel.

"What did you do with it after you cut it off?"

"I gave it to a friend. A girlfriend."

"Did she like it?" She winces.

"Not much."

Standing on one foot, then the other, dressed in white lace with a wooden wheelbarrow overflowing with flowers, she told him, "My boyfriend will give me red roses and maybe a talking parrot. And we will ride in a hot air balloon. And he will write songs about us. And—"

"Marie, ssshhh. Ssshhh!" The painter scolds with a finger to his lips.

Cicadas with their relentless clicking chatter already unnerved him. The afternoon sun roasting all of us makes my master impatient. He sweats. She fidgets. I revel. I am being born.

Her silence lasts only a moment.

"What is Paris like? Papa said he will take me there next year when I turn seventeen. He says all girls should first go to Paris with their fathers."

"Ah, but there is only one Paris. Both soft as a petal and hard as stone. Both pure poetry and a desperate scream."

I see it in his eyes. Love. A tender heart full of love never given to another. Enchanted. I am in love with my master. Probably forever. My first experience with a man is love, and I wonder if all men are like this.

"Vincent, you won't make my face green in your painting, will you? Sometimes your colors are more than just colors."

"What colors are you?"

"My eyes are blue. My cheeks are pink. My hair is black."

"Your hair is not only black. It is like a raven's feather falling from the sky. Floating in sunlight, catching blues and reds and purples. You are like a raven's feather. And like that hummingbird. Oh… If I could paint a hummingbird…"

"Vincent, why do you live at the 'Crazy Hospital'?"

"Sometimes I get sick."

"Are you contagious?"

"Sometimes the world makes no sense to me, and vice versa. It is better for me. I can paint. Like today with you here in the garden, the sun warming my back and lighting up your face. It is a God-given day."

"Vincent, is your God and my God the same? People say my God is different. They make fun of me at school. They call me names."

"We are all of the same God. We are all His children."

"But I worry God does not love me because of what people say."

Peering around his easel, looking into Marie's eyes, and pointing to his absent ear, he says, "Do not hear those people."

"Marie!" Her Papa is calling.

12 June 1889

Monastère Saint-Paul de Mausole

Dear Theo,

I have put your recent shipment of paints to excellent use. It has truly taken all my skills, all of my energies, physically and emotionally, and although I am spent, I am delighted with the result.

The portrait is of a young Jewess in her estate garden. Rising in the background are olive groves and the Chaîne des Alpilles. In the past, I have painted with respect to Millet, that which is being sewn or harvested; this painting celebrates and captures what is full and blooming.

The girl is in a white sundress, black hair cascading across her shoulders. I completed the painting and the girl herself in my hospital room, having no fear I could conjure her image later. I could paint her now or in one hundred years—that is how indelible her beauty is imprinted upon me.

Today, I gave the painting to her father; it is the appropriate gesture to repay their kindness to me while I recover.

My recovery is slower than expected, but painting settles me and keeps dark thoughts at bay.

If I am worth anything later, I am worth something now, for wheat is wheat, even if people think it is only grass in the beginning.

A hardy handshake,

Vincent

CHAPTER 8

On her rental bike, Julie toggled through the gears and got up to cruising speed when she slammed on the brakes. A dark blue Peugeot sedan pulled out of a gated driveway onto the road right in front of her without looking, then sped away. A gatekeeper saw her, gave her a little, *I'm sorry, what to do* shrug, and closed the gate. When they closed with a *clang,* the gate doors came together with a wrought iron image of a large honeybee. *A honeybee!* Her bike fell to the asphalt, and she stood, stunned. Just like her father had described, the entrance to the Toledano estate: "a tall yellow stone fence and the Honey Bee Gate." *This is his home! The family estate.*

Julie talked to the gatekeeper and found out that the estate is owned by a man named Depue. A businessman and senator living in Paris, and his family has lived there for sixty years, since the war. When she asked to tour the home and gardens, he replied, "*Non,*" and pointed to security cameras and two Doberman Pinschers sitting in the sun, ears forward and watching her.

Biking up the hills above Saint-Rémy, on her way to find Madame Demolins, she stopped at Glanum, an ancient Roman ruin from the fourth century BC with a triumphal arch and a sacred healing spring. A stone stairway, the remains of a temple dedicated to Glanus, the Celtic goddess of health, descended to a deep, clear pool, flecks of bright green algae floating on the surface. Cupping her hands with cool water, she held them to her lips and thought of the lectures she attended on waterborne illnesses. Oregon, home to a healthy population of beaver, the animal host for Giardia, demanded the use of a water filter or a week of Flagyl. *Drink from a Celtic Goddess? What if I time-travel from just a taste? A maiden for a Centurion? A Celtic warrior Princess?* She took the tiniest of sips and closed her eyes. When Julie opened her eyes, she was wearing sandals, a tunic, and gold bracelets, her hair in elaborate braids.

Looking at her reflection in the pool. It was *not* her reflection. A shocking resemblance—she was younger, her hair in long black tresses cascading over her shoulders, eyes bluer, face fuller. A girl on the cusp of womanhood. She touched the watery image, and it vanished. Now just sweaty bangs, a ponytail, and a baseball hat.

Cresting the Chaine des Alpilles—*The Little Alps*—hot, panting and wheezing, she alternated gulps from her water bottle and hits off her asthma inhaler. Hunched over *Iron Maiden,* sides heaving and heart pounding, she looked north and could see Mount Ventoux, a stage of next month's Tour de France 2002 and thought not of Lance Armstrong, but of the great English cyclist Tommy Simpson dying on the mountain during that leg of the Tour in 1967, still clipped into his pedals, stimulants coursing through his veins. She imagined his amphetamine-fueled heart racing out of control, beating *faster, faster, faster,* then suddenly saying, *"no more!"* seizing up, quitting—a quivering mess in the middle of his chest.

To the south, the view was hazy as fog lifting from the Mediterranean obscured her hope of seeing Marseille.

A speedy descent flying past lavender fields and vineyards, she came to Maussane les Alpilles, where Madame Demolins, her grandmother's best friend, was living. She found a cafe and, still stung by this morning's French lesson, she ordered an Italian dish, pasta alla carbonara, and a carafe of Pinot Grigio.

Apparently a local celebrity because of her piano school, her waiter knew exactly where the old woman lived, "Madame studied in Vienna!" Julie found her small house on Rue du Sale. She was living with a nurse—a stern woman unhappy with a surprise visit from an American. When the old woman was wheeled into the living room, Julie approached with caution. Madame was propped up with white pillows and covered with a white flannel blanket: her bright white hair coiffed, her skin translucent with purplish veins spidering across her expressionless face. Her face was still smooth and shiny white like the porcelain figurines that were perched on every shelf, everywhere. Sitting in her wheelchair, the woman's head bobbed, and Julie detected a pill-rolling tremor of her hand that she recognized as the advanced stages of Parkinson's disease. A baby grand Steinway stood in the corner with Debussy sheet music adorning it.

The ancient woman motioned for Julie to come forward, and she smelled of urine and lavender. Tracing Julie's face with a palsied hand, she cried out, "Marie! Marie!"

"*Non. Non.* I am not Marie. I am her great-granddaughter. My name is Julie. Julie Tolle. Shortened from Toledano," she said as the nurse translated into the old woman's ear.

"Marie! Marie!" she kept calling.

Julie explained that Marie was her great-grandmother. The translation did not register in her face but flickered in her eyes, darting, wary eyes that Julie could tell had seen too much pain. Like the eyes of a woman who had seen hard-hitting fists, perhaps from a husband. The old woman did remember Clara, her best friend. When Julie mentioned her father, Jacob, the elderly woman's arms flailed and she wailed, "Jacob! Jacob! *Mon petit* Jacob."

Madame!" said her nurse, restraining her, pulling her rigid arms out of the air and down her lap. "*Arrête*! Enough! You are upsetting Madame. You must go. Now!"

"But *merci*, please, I have more questions. I came here just to see her," Julie pleaded.

"*Non.* No questions. This is not a good day for Madame. She has no memory! It is all gone. No answers for you. Go. Go away!" the nurse yelled in Julie's face, then gave her a shove in the back.

Julie recalled that recent research into dementia had

found that music from a patient's past was therapeutic. Music from one's own life. Songs from a school dance. Tunes on the car radio. First album. First concert. First date. First love. Songs lingering in your brain, linked by a synaptic network of neurons to fading memories difficult to access without a musical note, lyric, or riff of a guitar. Indeed, Julie remembered singing at a nursing home as a high schooler and how the old people's faces would light up, and their eyes would sparkle, sometimes even dance a little off-balance arthritic jig. *Joshua Tree* by U2—her first album. Bon Jovi—her first concert; dressed up in a lacy camisole her father never knew about.

"May I?" Julie pointed to the Steinway.

Madame Demolins nodded a perceptible "Yes," amongst the other tremors of her bobbing head.

Julie had not played a piano since 10th grade and sat on the bench staring at the keys. Her father made her take piano lessons, "I had to take them, so you do too." She knew her Aunt Eloisa was Madame Demolins' favorite pupil, a protégé, and in a surprise shuffle, Madame scooted next to her. Julie's repertoire of music, never extensive and now severely pruned, began to circulate like an old Motorola juke box, its arm traveling back and forth across a line of 45s. It hovered over *Blackbird* by The Beatles but landed on the simplest of Beethoven's melodies, one she had practiced a thousand times for a recital.

Just before she began to play, Madame Demolins straightened Julie's posture—a nudge in the small of her back, a tug on her shoulders correcting her Quasimodo hunch over the keyboard. Blunt and club-like, her fingers began to play with keystrokes that bludgeoned Beethoven's simple, most recognizable melody; butchered, albeit well-meaning.

"*Halte!*" cried Madame.

With her own skeletal, palsied hands, she uncrimped Julie's fingers and curled her hands into a position that virtuosos use to strike any key with every kind of nuance.

Beethoven's *Für Elise* came to life, filling the room with its magic. Transportive. Genuine. Madame Demolins closed her eyes and put her hand on Julie's lap. When the last note furled away, Madame whispered, "For Eloisa."

And Julie whispered, "For Jacob, too."

"*Oui.* For my Jacob, too."

The nurse pulled Julie up off the bench. "Now you go."

"*Halte!*" called the old woman and motioned for her nurse's ear, giving her an order in an inaudible whisper. The nurse brought her a cookbook and, with arthritic fingers, she plucked from the pages a yellowed, stained piece of paper; a recipe: *Poulet á l'Estragon—Marie Toledano.*

"*Un moment, s'il vous plaît,*" Madame said, holding up one finger. She had her nurse wheel her into her bedroom and came out quickly with a velvet pouch. The pouch was deep purple, embroidered with a gold *COURVOISIER VSOP.* Julie knew it was a special kind of French Brandy. The gold drawstring was tied tightly in a knot.

"For you," the old woman said in English. "From your grandma, Clara."

"Now you go," demanded the nurse.

Biking a different way back to Saint-Rémy, Julie felt

deflated. Hoping for a nice tea with her grandmother Clara's best friend, sharing stories and photographs, she had only gained a bottle of booze and a hand-scrawled recipe for stewed chicken, *in French!* But in her mind, an image began to grow; her grandparents, her father Jacob, and aunt Eloisa around the dining room table. It is Saturday, the Jewish Sabbath, and challah is baking; her grandmother is pulling the top off the cassoulet, and aromas fill the home. Lost in these thoughts, she became confused at an intersection of country roads. *Which way to go?* And standing on the side of the road, sweat running between her breasts, bangs plastered to her forehead, she squinted in the hot sun at her Michelin map—*Michelin Carte Routiere et Touristique.* Looking from her map to her surroundings, she identified no landmarks and no road signs. On one corner, she saw a small cemetery surrounded by tall cypress trees and a lone figure tending graves.

"Excuse me, please. Excuse me, please," she called while walking into the cemetery. "I am lost." Pointing to the map, she asked, "Can you help me, *merci,* please?"

Clutching his back and straightening slowly, a thin elderly man met her with suspicion, and Julie, using an engaging smile and disarming, pleaful gleam, failed to wipe away his scorn.

"*Oui, mademoiselle,* how may I help you?"

"I am lost." She gave him the map, which he scrutinized at various focal lengths, a bead of sweat dripping from the tip of his pointy nose onto the map.

He dismissed her. "You are lost. You are off the map."

Julie stood with hands open and an expectant, pleading look.

"Where do you want to go?" he finally said.

"Saint-Rémy."

"It is that way. Twenty kilometers," he pointed, then bent over to right a fallen headstone.

"*Merci beaucoup*," she said, helping him right the marker. The inscription was in Hebrew. Looking around, she saw other freshly uprooted graves. Those still standing bore Hebrew inscriptions spray-painted with black swastikas.

"*Les petits voyous*—vandals," he said to her puzzled expression.

She helped him straighten tombstones, but the swastikas remained despite vicious scouring. Resting in the shade of a cypress tree, he told her he was a retired librarian from the University in Aix, widowed, with a granddaughter about her same age studying journalism in Paris. Julie envisioned him in a big library answering a hundred questions a day: how to look up a book, where to find an author, good references for this and that. She decided to pose her own.

"Did you know the Toledano family?"

"*Non*." And he fell silent, looking at his dainty hands more used to shuffling a card catalogue than shoveling graves. "I know *of* them."

"They were my grandparents."

"They lived close by. They were wealthy." He took her measure, a quick study for a man skilled in helping clueless students. "What do you know about Jewish history?" and added, "Miss Toledano."

"I was a science major. My father was not religious. I went to a Bar Mitzvah once."

"I see. Sit. Let me tell you."

His history did not start with Abraham or Moses or Jews fleeing the Pharaoh of Egypt as she expected, but with Jews fleeing Spain in 1492, and she was initially relieved it would be an abbreviated history. It was not.

He rolled out a story starting in Spain at a time when Jews, Christians, and Muslims lived together as neighbors, trading with one another, in peace and prosperity. That coexistence was crumbling with the Black Death, followed by the Spanish Inquisition, when Jews were forced to convert to Catholicism or burn at the stake. His story included people: the Moors defeating King Rodigio and capturing Toledo. El Cid, Maimonides, and even Christopher Columbus.

"King Ferdinand and Queen Isabella expelled all Jews by decree in 1492. A few hopped ship on the Nina, the Pinta, or Santa Maria, all others joining various rivers of exile to Turkey, Greece, Amsterdam, and some here to France."

The Black Death—Bubonic Plague—she knew all about: the bacteria *Yersinia pestis*, its life cycle of fleas and rodents and people, symptoms and physical findings, and treatment. But it was the mention of Maimonides that grabbed her.

I have just graduated from medical school, and I should be able to recite the Hippocratic oath, but it is Maimonides' Prayer for the Physician that I remember hanging on the wall of my father's office:

'Exalted God, before I begin the holy work of healing the creations of your hands, I place my entreaty before the throne of your glory that you grant the strength of spirit and fortitude to faithfully execute my work. Let not the desire for wealth or benefit blind me from seeing the truth. Deem me worthy of seeing in the sufferer who seeks my advice—a person—neither rich nor poor. Friend or foe, good man or bad, of a man in distress—show me only the man.'

"Your family, the Toledano family, are Sephardic Jews originally from Toledo and left in exile before they were burned," he said. "I knew *of* them. All are gone now. The French gave up their country to the Nazis. Neighbor gave up neighbor to the Gestapo. Synagogues are museums. Cemeteries left to vandals."

Julie's knowledge of her family and her father's escape from the Nazis, then his journey to America, were all from bedtime stories—her favorites. His stories, she knew, included "some stretchers," as Huck Finn would say. Those stories morphed as she grew older and, able to understand the harsh realities, from fairytales to disturbing images. They intertwined with her dreams, some fanciful, some nightmarish. A puzzle with missing pieces that her father did not have, pieces left to Julie's imagination. And Madame Demolins, lost in her dementia, was more disturbing than helpful.

Time and place to ask the hard questions, she thought.

"Monsieur, I am close to where my family lived. I can feel them close by." She waved her hand to the sky. "I have a question and fear the answer. My grandparents were arrested and sent to Drancy. My father said it was a stadium in Paris for bike racing and turned into an encampment. What do you know about Drancy?"

"Drancy was a hellhole!" He stopped talking. Julie gave him that expectant, pleaful look, and he continued in a soft voice, "A stadium on the north flank of Paris, the Velodrome d'Hiver was crammed full of rounded up Jews. Eight thousand people, probably more, were herded into that horror. Stripped of possessions, scant food, scant water, no toilets, stifling hot or freezing cold. Babies crying alone by themselves. Toddlers wandering alone by themselves. Conditions actually improved when the Nazis took over from the French Police. But then the deportations began, *'To build an Agricultural Colony in the East'*. The trains leaving from Drancy?" He looked into her eyes. "Went straight to Auschwitz."

Both fell silent.

"I am so sorry," he said, taking her hand. "I hope you find what you are looking for. Your way is that way." He pointed to the road climbing into the hills.

Pedaling away, she looked over her shoulder to see the old man saying a prayer after her that did nothing to stem the sick feeling that grew inside her or the deadening weakness encasing her legs. Riding the clunky Gitane, her butt ached, her eyes stung with sweat, the derailleur grinding the bike chain made a sound that hurt her teeth, and she kept swerving into roadside gravel.

Pop! Hisssssss.

Her front tire flattened to the bare metal rim, and the bike slammed her hard to the pavement, sprawling her onto hot asphalt that smacked her head and tore her flesh. Stunned, she sat on the roadside, then collected enough of herself to limp and drag the bike to a shade tree. Palpating her long bones like assessing a Trauma One patient for a fracture and, with slow windmill movements of her joints, checking her range of motion, she diagnosed only a nasty "road rash," the length of her right arm bloody, raw, and studded with gravel.

In the shade, she wished Kiki, an able bike mechanic, were there. Julie detached the front tire, pulled off the inner tube, found the leak, cleaned it, patched it, but used too much glue. Waiting for the repair to dry, she lay back, her head on the pack like a pillow. The carafe of Pinot Grigio had faded. More than exhausted, she was sleepy. Since her father's death, she could not fall asleep and would listen to late-night radio. Jet-lagged, her circadian rhythms were out of whack: when she was awake, France was sleeping; when she was sleepy, France was awake. Tumbling past all stages of sleep into the deepest region of sleep where brain waves follow a slow rhythmic cadence, she slept as the Provençal sun left the sky, the evening star appeared, a pair of bats quilting the warm night with erratic zig-zagging. Beyond deep sleep, Julie fell into a place where sleep and dreams and memory fuse—a mélange coalescing into a chimera both real and fantasy, both enchanting and nightmarish. Memories of her father's bedtime stories about escaping the Nazis and coming to America, but those were stories told when she was a little girl, falling in and out of sleep, colored by her own dreaming.

Most disturbing were her other memories; she called them "The Echoes." They were rare but recurrent. And she told no one, like a schizophrenic afraid to confess they are hearing voices. Memories *not of her own* but of her family's past. Events. Sights. Sounds. Images. Always troubling, always vivid, a family trove of misfortune and danger inherited on a wisp of a chromosome, now a cluster of her own neurons, sequestered, hidden, only accessible when triggered. And not of her own volition, more like the onset of a grand mal seizure—provoked by a stimulus, like being lost on a deserted country road near her ancestral home.

Much more than just a dream. A story, a bedtime story. But not with her father's usual, "Once upon a time…"

This one started with a knock on the door…

CHAPTER 9

August 1942
Provence, France

BANG!
BANG!
BANG!
BANG!

Mommy strangled me, stuffed me in my winter coat, then crammed my pockets full of money and her diamonds, and as she pushed me out the door, the police came crashing inside our house. A lot of them. She screamed at me to run. "Run, Jacob!" I was a fast runner. But instead of going to Madame Demolins', Eloisa's and my piano teacher, I hid in my fortress. My fortress has a hidden passage under big fruit crates. I was so scared. I waited until everyone was gone, and then waited some more, and then some more. Hot and hard to breathe, but I would not take off my coat. I could peek out towards the house, and it was abandoned, quiet. I needed to find Montrose, our cat, who, at night when we were asleep, Papa said could fly, and my treasure chest.

The back door was left open, I had my rusty pistol with no bullets, and I tiptoed across broken dishes and glass on the kitchen floor. *Mother will be so mad at all this mess.* My treasure chest was in the pantry, and I grabbed it. Then I heard a sound, like a cry, and it wasn't Montrose meowing. It was Eloisa. I went to her bedroom and listened.

The door opened, and a Monster came out!

The Monster was dark and sweating, eyes bulging and blood-red, like he had just arrived from hell—a devil. He smelled like a pig. And he smelled like gunpowder. And he pushed me against the wall. He stole our painting. And Eloisa screamed at me, "Run!"

I ran fast, in my winter coat and holding my chest like a rugby ball, across dry fields and not along the road, and I didn't stop until I reached Madame Demolins' house. She was standing in her doorway and jerked me inside, and I cried, wrapped in her arms. She told me my mother and father had been arrested and were at the police station. She asked me where Eloisa was. And I told her about the Monster in her bedroom.

She hid me. Mostly in the cellar, and it was cold and dark and smelled of onions, dirt, and the meat hanging in the corner, of dried blood. My days and nights ran together, and I wiped a river of tears and snot on my coat sleeve. I kept waiting for Papa to come and get me. But he never did. During the daytime, Madame Demolins played her piano, the same one Eloisa and I would play during our lessons, and Eloisa was her star pupil at recitals, but I hated to practice and was horrible at it. She mostly played sad songs that sometimes would make me cry.

At night, angry words filtered down into the cellar, and I heard her fight with her husband. The man would stomp his boots, rattling the floorboards, shouting, "Jew Boy!" and "Give him to the police!" In the darkest, coldest part of the night, I would hear the scurrying of rats, and I know what all boys know: *Rats love to bite children and give them hydrophobia rabies that make you froth at the mouth and die in convulsions.* I slept at the top of the stairs, wrapped in old quilts.

One song Madame played was not sad, *Clair de Lune,* and that music would take me to the sunny mountains. I was high in the Alps. An alpine blackbird. Floating along cliffs, twisting in afternoon updrafts, flying in the sun where snow is always clinging on mountains too high to climb.

Oh… If only I had wings. If I could fly? Then… Then…

One night, they were fighting, and it was worse. I could feel the anger. Shouting, yelling, ending abruptly with a loud *SMACK!*

Later, in the middle of the night, Madame opened the cellar door, and I fell out into the kitchen. Her face was swollen with purplish bruises, and she snatched me up, quilts and all, and carried me outside. It was warm outside; the moon was full, and I heard a horse and smelled fresh manure. A big man, his cigarette glowing, got down off his wagon, and I was passed into his arms, and he tucked me into his foul armpit, climbed back into the wagon, and set me on the bench seat like a sack of potatoes.

"What have we here, Madame?"

"A boy. A good Christian Boy."

"Where are his parents, Madame?"

"The police have them."

"Why? Are they arrested? Are they…?"

She cut him off, "I don't know *why*, Monsieur. But you must take him with you. To Marseille. To the YMCA."

"What is his name?"

"Jacob Toledano, er, I mean Tolle. Jacob Tolle—a good Christian boy."

"Madame, I haul fruits and hay and wine, whatever the farmers have for me. A load of melons is no trouble. But a boy... This boy? In these times?"

"Take this money. For a safe trip. To the YMCA. I have more."

She ran back into the house and returned with a ham, a fresh loaf of bread, jam, and brought me my treasure box, tucking it under the blankets into my hands.

"*Adieu*, Jacob. You be a good boy," she said and waved to me with one hand, the other hand covering her mouth, a fearful expression of, *Oh my God! What have I just done?*

The endless, slow clatter-clomp of hoofbeats lulled me to sleep, and the man pulled a tarpaulin over me. When the hoofbeats stopped, I woke up. The sun had not yet risen and I woke up bleary and my eyes would not focus; the sandman had visited me, leaving a crust on my eyelids and when I rubbed it all away I was in a nightmare. Hanging from a tree, three men twisted, their hands tied behind them, necks stretched, feet tied together, toes almost touching the ground. Almost. One was a teenage boy with a fresh face.

"Partisans, Jacob. *La Résistance*," said the big Frenchman as he took off his hat and stared at them. The man in the middle twirled one way, then the other, a note pinned to his chest, *FINNE LEGARE*—End of the Line.

"Come here," said the Frenchman, hoisting me to his massive shoulders, and I felt like Mowgli riding an elephant. Giving me his knife as big as a sword, we walked to the tree branch, and I was face-to-face with each of them. "Cut them down!"

I was ready to use all my strength to saw through the thick rope, but with just a touch of the sharp knife, the first one fell to the ground with a *CRACK,* like a board snapping in two. The next one landed with a thudding *WHUMPF.*

The third one, the boy, looked like a friend of Eloisa's; he had blood trickling from his mouth, and his purplish tongue extruded from a corner, clear snot running from both nostrils, and his bulging eyes, not yet a cloudy, lifeless glaze, but still shedding tears. With a slash, I cut him down, and he hit the ground with a moan like for his momma. When the big Frenchman stuck two fingers to the boy's neck and an ear to his face he shook his head and said, "*Mort,*" and he cut the rope from each of them and laid them to rest under the tree trunk, hands folded across their chests, and used his fat, dirty thumb to close their eyes. On the tree, with his big knife, he blazed the Cross of Lorraine.

All day we traveled in the hot sun. I had never been to Marseille; I knew it was a big city with people from everywhere, even Africa. I didn't know why I should go to the

YMCA and I envisioned it was synagogue like a fairytale castle or a special school, and Eloisa was in a girls' boarding school in England, maybe this one was for boys and I could play on a soccer team or cricket or rugby and study geology. I wanted to ask, but the man only spoke to his horse, the biggest horse I had ever seen. They were a matched pair, both hulking, black manes tossing at flies as the wagon creaked and moaned with casks of wine.

At a grassy Aerodrome, he stopped to watch a Stuka dive bomber landing in the setting sun, dropping from the sky like an angry hornet, and he stood up, shaking his fist, yelling, "God damn you all to Hell!" The horse shook in his harness and threw his massive head.

We camped at the end of a dirt road, along a stream with good grass. Released, free of his halter, collar, backband, and britchen strap, the sweat-drenched horse rolled onto his back in the tall grass, his huge, furry hooves thrashing in mid-air. The big Frenchman had me feed the horse oats soaked in molasses, and I came away a slobbered mess.

Around the campfire, I ate bread smeared with orange marmalade while the man holding the ham in one hand and carving off thick slices of ham with the other, slurped meat into his mouth with one slick motion. And he drank red wine from a jug that dribbled down his bearded chin, over his Adam's apple, and down his unshaven throat. I didn't know you could drink wine like that; my mother and father would sip wine from sparkling glasses with long stems. He filled a tin cup with wine and gave it to me.

"Drink up! Good for a boy."

"Sir?"

"My name is not 'sir'. I am Jean Cardinale! Champion wrestler and lover to many beautiful women. Ugly ones too! Proud Papa to 'King'—a Boulonnais, the strongest horse in all of France and sire to many fine foals."

Twirling around the campfire, jug in hand, he sang naughty songs about women and began a folk dance, boots kicking up sparks. At the end of his dance, he bent over, hands on knees, catching his breath, and gave me a sideways, sinister look. I moved away from him. Some men, I have heard, take young boys and use them for their own. Make them do bad things. He grabbed at me, and I spun away. Then hooked my coat collar and lifted me into the air.

"Sing, boy. Sing!"

In a rumbling bellow, he sang the words to *La Marseillaise*, our national anthem.

"Sing, Jacob! Sing!"

I joined in:

> *'Let's go, children of the fatherland.*
> *The day of glory has arrived!*
> *Against us, tyranny's*
> *Bloody flag is raised*
> *Grab your weapons, citizens!*
> *Let us march! Let us march!'*

We sang louder and louder as if we were trying to raise an army, and after we were done, Jean Cardinale kicked dirt on the fire, stuck the ham-smeared knife into his belt, and said, "Come with me."

We snuck back up the road, keeping to the dark where moonlight could not find us, and I worried he would slit my throat or slice me up the middle like a trout and I thought about running into the woods. But just then, we were back at the Aerodrome. At the end of the landing strip, we sat in a ditch with bullfrogs croaking, and we watched the lantern-lit barracks and a squadron of Stukas sitting in the moonlight, poised, bent wings ready to fly.

"*Bâtardes*," he kept mumbling, and when we heard dogs barking, "*Merde!*"

"Jacob, take this," he said, opening an Opinel pocket knife and putting it in my hand. I jabbed with it, poked, and slashed. "*Non.* Not that way. That is for fighting a man." Turning the knife around in my palm, he told me, "Grip it. Stab like this. This is for fighting a dog. Cover your throat and stab. Fight like hell!" he said, crouching low, the crook of one arm protecting his neck, the other stabbing downward, baring his teeth and growling.

"The Luftwaffe will not fly tomorrow." And he was off, a bear and his moonshadow galloping towards the Stukas.

I hid in the ditch, waiting, scared, imagining both of us hanging from a tree, jerking and twisting, trying to breathe through necks stretched by coarse rope, toes almost touching the ground. Almost.

Dogs started barking, and Jean Cardinale came busting out of the dark.

"Run, boy. Run!"

I ran fast but not for long, and the big Frenchman circled back, snatching me up over his shoulder and running like

King would if not harnessed to a wagon.

The next morning, he pointed to the empty sky, quiet and blue, and said, "See any planes, boy? *Viva la France!*"

All day, Monsieur Cardinale took tugs on his jug and taught me how to drive the wagon, and when he fell asleep, I was on my own, standing straight, gripping the reins in my fists. *I am driving the strongest horse in all of France!* But King, ignoring all my commands to "Whoa!" or "*Halte!*" and every pull on his reins, went at his own pace, a powerful plodding. King stopped at a barricade and snorted.

Jean Cardinale woke up and whispered a curse, "*Boche,*" as three German soldiers approached us. He said, "*Messieurs, vas-tu?*"

"*Papiers,*" said the soldier.

One soldier looped behind the wagon. Another, grinding out his cigarette with his boot heel, came to look at me. Squinting in my face with cold, mean eyes, he took my chin, turning my face one way then another. I could see his mind turning over, puzzled.

"*Juden?*" the soldier said, looking to his comrades and back and forth at me. Suddenly, like I was a poisonous snake, he jumped back, pointing his Mauser at my head, and announced, "*Juden!*" I almost passed out. I almost peed my pants.

Jean Cardinale stood up putting the muzzle of the rifle to his own belly and said, "He is my nephew. We are both Jews. Proud sons of Abraham and Moses. Fresh from Jerusalem with sacramental wine for synagogues around the world. See, the Rabbi has had his way with me!" he said, pulling his pants down to his ankles and unfurling his fat, uncircumcised penis. The German soldiers, laughing, gave him his papers back and motioned us through the checkpoint, but not before hoisting a cask of wine as "*maut*—toll."

Like gold cast by Poseidon onto the shore, Marseille shimmered yellow. And I had studied Greek Mythology, so I knew this, and I also knew that Hades was always close by. My first visit to a big city, and it is Marseille, *and* the Mediterranean Sea. Mesmerizing. Busy with people, some wearing fedoras, berets, fez, hajibs, sailor's caps, turbans. I saw no yarmulkes. Buildings, ancient and stout. Driving our wagon to the docks of Vieux Port, a small harbor packed with boats, the place seemed timeless— fishermen unloading their catch, repairing nets, longshoremen loading and unloading ships, merchants, markets. The streets were alive. The docks smelled of fish and rotting seaweed, creosote, and diesel. I pinched my nose, more used to vineyards and olive groves, and lavender.

"Used by the Pharos, sailors from ancient Egypt, and Greeks, and Romans, and now…" the Big Frenchman said as we watched a German patrol boat flying a swastika cruising the harbor, "by *bâtardes!*"

Monsieur Cardinale offloaded the casks of wine at a dockside warehouse. "Like the Romans." Wrapping his muscled arms around each one, hugging it to his chest, lifting it from the wagon, his red face dripping with sweat, neck veins popping, and rolling the barrels across the floor, stacked to be "bottled and shipped to America."

At a bustling dockside cafe, he ladled soup from a

steaming tureen. "*Bouillabaisse*—this is Marseille! Many different fishes all stewing together, never the same and always ready to boil over."

At night, we walked the narrow streets and, passing the colonnade of the magnificent white building like a palace built for Zeus, I asked, "Is this the YMCA?"

And Monsieur Cardinale fell down, laughing at me, saying, "Only if you can sing like Enrico Caruso! This is the Opera House, silly."

At a row of storefronts with red lights in their windows, Jean Cardinale stopped to talk with women laughing and friendly, and he took my hand and we went inside.

"I need a bath," he told me and walked deeper into the house hand in hand with a woman dressed in stockings. I sat alone in the parlor on a blue velvet sofa, and the place smelled of cigars and perfume, and in one corner was a white marble statue of a nude woman clutching a fallen robe, and on the wall a painting of a woman with her breasts exposed and thighs open, looking at me. I stared at my shoes.

"He's adorable!" said one of the two women.

"Look at that cute face," said the other as they sat on each side of me. "What's your name, handsome?"

"Jacob Julien Toledano."

"Master Jacob, we have something for you." The women took my face in their hands and pressed me to their powdered, perfumed cleavage and covered me in kisses all over my face *and* on my lips. Giggling, they left me, and I wiped their slobber off with the back of my hand.

It took forever for Jean Cardinale to return. He was clean

and smelled like a girl and he was aghast when he saw me covered in red lipstick. "*Mon petite—My little man. You are a Casanova!*"

Back on the street, three men in dark uniforms were walking towards us, and they were wearing tall black boots, peaked hats, lightning bolts on their collars, and pistols in shiny black holsters. *Monsters!* I hid behind Monsieur Cardinale, clutching his tree-trunk-sized leg, and we stepped off the sidewalk into the gutter to let them pass. One of them looked me in the eye, and I shuddered. Walking the Quai du Port, boats in their moorings in the inky black water, got me thinking about becoming a sailor and seeing Gibraltar, Malta, Corsica, and Delos, birthplace of Apollo and Artemis, but when a black Citroën sedan crept up behind us and slowed down, Jean Cardinale took my hand and we dodged into a tight alleyway and followed it to the warehouse where King was in a stall. That night, I slept on hay covered in my quilts with dreams of being a sailor, but I was in a storm at sea like Ulysses, shipwrecked off of Crete.

In the morning, we kept to back alleys, walking quickly, and Monsieur Cardinale kept looking over his shoulder and stopping and shuffling into doorways; at the end of the street was a sign: YMCA. But it was just an ordinary building, bikes out front. *This is the wrong place! This can't be for me.*

Inside, they told us they could not help us—"*C'est impossible.*" and told us of a place for "*des réfugiés*" on the Rue Grignan and added, "Be careful, *Monsieur*, it is being watched. Police are everywhere."

On an even more circuitous route, I asked, "What's a refugee?"

"A refugee is a person who is forced to leave their home. Sometimes hide. Sometimes run. Always be smart. Stay proud. Most important…" he stopped, got on one knee and looked me in the eye, "Jacob, you must be brave, very brave. Understand?"

I nodded.

On the Rue Grignan, Jean Cardinale stopped and smoked a Gauloise, waiting, watching a storefront office. I saw a small flag flying above its doorway with red stripes on it and stars, too.

"Let's go."

"I don't wanna go." I grabbed his leg. "I want to stay with you! I can help. I can drive King and take care of him. I'm strong. Don't make me. Please! Don't make me…"

The sign said, *'Centre Américain de Secours'*. I was brought into a small office, and the secretary said, "Monsieur Fry, you have a visitor." Monsieur Cardinale filled the doorway behind me.

"Oh, what have we here?" asked Varian Fry over his fashionable glasses. He was wearing a suit and bowtie, and a full mop of hair on top of his tall forehead, which was wrinkling in puzzlement. "Are you alright, young man? Your face is blotchy red. Is it a pox?"

"Kisses, sir," I answered, and I looked down in embarrassment.

Monsieur Fry looked to the Big Frenchman for an explanation, and he answered with just a shrug of his massive shoulders.

"What is your name?"

"Jacob Julien Toledano."

"And your business. Why are you here? How can I help you?"

I stood, silently looking at my shoes.

"Where are your parents, Jacob? Your mother and your father?"

I didn't answer. I didn't know where they were.

Monsieur Fry looked to Monsieur Cardinale, and he stood silently like a statue filling the doorway.

"The police took them," I finally said.

"Your parents, do they know you are here? Are they coming to get you?"

I looked behind me and saw the big Frenchman shake his head, an almost imperceptible "*No.*"

I could tell Monsieur Fry was calculating. *What am I to do? Who is this boy?*

I blurted in a loud voice, a brave voice, proudly, "I am a refugee!"

"Come here and sit with me." Monsieur Fry hoisted me up on his desk. "Jacob Julien Toledano, tell me. What do you want to be when you grow up?"

"I want to be a mountaineer."

"Excellent! I have friends who need a mountaineer. We're having a party tonight. Would you like to meet them?"

When I turned around to ask Monsieur Cardinale for his

permission, he was gone, just an empty doorway.

Riding in the front seat of Monsieur Fry's Peugeot, into the hills above the lights of Marseille, I saw an encampment of people, cooking fires, tarpaulins, families huddled, families on the move.

In a villa overlooking the city, we joined a dinner party, and when Monsieur Fry walked in, one man raised his glass and said, "*Porter un toast!*"

Wine glasses raised.

"To my friend Varian Fry. Here, from his comfortable home in New York City, to this impossible situation of desperation. To this funnel, this vice grip of people squeezed by terror and hate, he brings us hope and love."

"*Tchin tchin!*"

"*Sante!*"

"*Cul sec!* Bottoms up!"

Everyone clinked glasses together, and when I tried to toast with only water, one man filled my glass with wine, whispering, "Young man, toasting with water brings bad luck." And I sipped like my parents would.

"*Oui! Oui!* To Varain and his Emergency Rescue Committee. You welcome danger and heartbreak into your lives. Who does that? Who risks his life to save another?"

"*Sante!*"

"*Cul sec!*"

I took another sip.

Monsieur Fry stood at the head of the table. He had changed out of his suit and was now dressed for a party in a beige cotton jacket and baby blue tie. He said, "*Merci *beaucoup*. But you have the wrong man. I'm just a small thorn in the side of tyranny." He pointed to the end of the table to a small, roundish man and his wife, not dressed to party but dressed to travel. They looked nervous, their plates of food untouched. "Tonight, we bid *adieu* to our friends Marc Chagall and his beautiful wife, Bella. *Bon voyage* to a man who paints the world with eyes of wonder and bravery with colors, fanciful and real. He paints dreams and truth. Tonight they cross to freedom."

The table erupted with shouts of, "*Ja lève mon verve à la libereté!* Raise your glass to freedom!"

He continued, "And whether crossing the mountains of the Pyrénées or sailing a boat to Lisbon, we wish safe travels in all your journeys."

"Cheers!"

"*Salut!*"

I took more sips of wine sitting next to Monsieur Fry, and he whispered into my ear, introducing me to the odd-looking people around the table. They had big glasses, big noses, big ears, messy hair, and funny accents. "That's Max Ernst, another painter. That's Hannah Arendt; she writes about politics. That's Wanda Landowski; she plays the harpsichord better than anyone else in the world."

"I play the piano," said Jacob.

She overheard me and asked, "Are you a good pupil? Do you practice?"

I turned bright red and shook my head. "No." I said, "My big sister is better. She plays Mozart." The name brought a sparkle to her eyes. Her eyes were big and kind-looking, but

I could tell she would quickly lose patience with me. Maybe slap my hands. Scold me. Not like Madame Demolins, who loved teaching.

Monsieur Fry continued, "And he is Andre Breton—a surrealist."

"What's that?"

"I don't know. Nobody does. And they like to keep it that way." Monsieur Fry pointed at Otto Meyerhoff. "Do you like prizes, Jacob? He won a really big prize. The Nobel Prize for Medicine."

"Are *all* these people in trouble with the police?" I asked.

"Every one of them. Refugees, just like you. It's my job to help them."

Winking at me, Andre Breton reached into his coat pocket and brought out a praying mantis, and let it loose onto the dinner table. I giggled into my napkin, watching the insect stalk undetected among glasses and silverware until Wanda Landowski shrieked with a squeal, then I laughed until milk shot out of my nose.

After dinner, Monsieur Fry took me into the parlor where the Chagalls were checking their battered suitcases and putting on coats. They looked worried.

"Jacob, Monsieur Chagall and his wife want to take you with them tonight. To a safe place. Where the police won't take you away. They are going to America. They need a mountaineer."

"But my mother and father, how will they find me?"

Nobody answered that question; instead, Monsieur Fry said, "Do you like birds, Jacob? Marc Chagall is like a small bird with big wings. He will take you under his wing. Be brave, Jacob."

"I don't want to be brave."

Monsieur Chagall kneeled down to me and said, "You can fly, Jacob. You will see. I will paint a picture for you, and you will be flying high and brave across the sky."

How will Mama and Papa find me? How will Mama and Papa find me? How will Mama and Papa find me?

Julie woke up startled and confused. Sitting up, hugging her knees and rocking back and forth, looking around with puffy eyes, she tried to fully rouse her brain and struggled with her surroundings—her time and her place. Like an epileptic coming out of a seizure, she caught up: France. Nighttime. Lost on a country road. A flat tire.

After pumping up the tire, she listened for a persistent *hissss* and, hearing only crickets and a distant owl, wobbled a little getting on the rental bike. Topping a hillrise, she spotted the lights of Saint-Rémy and coasted toward town with conviction to be smart, be proud, be brave.

CHAPTER 10

May 2002

Franco-Swiss Border

Taking buses, avoiding train station Customs and Border Patrol, Julie chose a small highway entering Switzerland from France in the town of La Renfile, known for its lax border security. But, she had heard that the Swiss Border Patrol, with their centuries of strict efficiency, had tightened their efforts stemming a fresh wave of immigration out of war-torn Iraq and Afghanistan, and she had no passport, not even a driver's license.

Shit!

Instead of just crossing past a numbered boundary stone, she met a checkpoint and three Border Patrol officers.

"No passport? No ID?" they said.

She had rehearsed no believable lies, none that had any chance of being accepted, so she told the truth about being pickpocketed, but telling them about scattering her father's ashes in their precious country would probably get her arrested and her father's remains confiscated. *The Swiss have laws against everything.* Proffering her letter from the American Embassy in Paris, she said, "See? Signed by the American Ambassador!" and stood proudly.

All three of them scrutinized the letter as one of them read it out loud in French. Their eyebrows furrowed, then raised, and after conferring, they started laughing. The lead patrolman told her that she was denied entry: "Wait for an emergency passport." And when she asked about free travel borders throughout the European Union, "Suisse not members of EU."

Julie remembered something she thought unusual: Switzerland had just finally joined the United Nations in a close, contentious national vote. She took a last stab at it.

"But now you are members of the United Nations. You must let me in."

"UN *ist* bullshit. You go away!"

Finding herself walking along the shoulder of a small highway, dragging her carry-on through gravel, with no hotel insight, *I must look ridiculous. A tourist hopelessly lost.* With only 300 dollars left, she strategized, *I need to find a cheap hostel somewhere.* Then she had second thoughts, *Bunk beds? A shared bathroom? Shared with gross hairy men? Oh God, I hate Europe.*

Off the road, down an embankment, in a ravine, a dozen tents and tarps in different sizes and colors were pitched haphazardly. Kids were kicking a scuffed soccer ball near a smoking cooking fire. *Gypsies? No, these people are wearing drab clothes, women in black with hajibs.* The women were busy. The men milled about, shiftless, smoking. A refugee camp not in a poor country in conflict, but on the border of two countries with enormous wealth, and she had heard of one camp in Calais where refugees hopped onto trucks in the middle of the night, trying to get to England. Squalid. *This place looks like people not on the move, but a dead end of the line.* From her vantage point on the road above, she could feel their pain.

But maybe they know how to get into Switzerland?

Hidden from their view, she watched them. Refugees. Illegals. Immigrants. Asylum seekers. Displaced and unwanted. *But at least they have family.* And this made Julie feel more alone and think of her father as a little boy.

Her thoughts were broken by commotion inside the encampment. Two men rushed to a young woman bent over, trying to walk, waddling, staggering, and took her by the arms. She was pregnant. The front of her dress was wet. Her water had broken. Collapsing into their arms, the men carried her into a green canvas tent.

This is no place to have a baby!

Julie thought of the birthing suites at Oregon Health Sciences University, where she had just graduated from medical school. Fancy, designed by interior decorators. Clean. Serene. With almost romantic lighting and ambient music. But in an emergency, transforming magically: fetal monitors, oxygen, IV pumps, operating lights, trays of surgical instruments, and filling with nurses, respiratory therapists, doctors of obstetrics, anesthesiology, pediatrics, and her as a medical student.

This is no place to have a baby!

Thinking of all the obstetrical complications—umbilical cord wrapping around the baby's neck, non-stop hemorrhage from uterine rupture or retained placenta, and dangerous breech birth—a scream kept rising.

This is no place to have a baby!

Every day, babies die, she knew this. *God's will. Nature's way.* Every day in refugee camps, babies die. And tomorrow another newborn will die. *God's will. Nature's way.*

But today?

Julie walked into the camp.

Not today.

Not here.

Not now.

Not on my watch!

All eyes followed her to the big canvas tent. At the tent flap, the two men stood, an older one, maybe the young woman's father, and a younger man, maybe the husband.

"Doctor. I am Doctor Julie Tolle. American doctor," she introduced herself in stuttered English, "I can help. Let me help."

She was told they were from Iraq, "We are Kurdish." They lifted the tent flap, and inside it was dark, hot, and smelling of amniotic fluid and sweat. When Julie's eyes accommodated, she saw a girl—*a girl!* Lying on her back, laboring on a dirty mattress. The girl was flushed bright red, panting way too fast. Looking at the two women attendants, they were worried, faces roundish, wrinkled past their years, and

Julie explained she was an American doctor and knelt to the girl's face. She held her hand. Pulling hair away from her sweaty face, she said in English words she would not understand, "Let me see. Let me check you."

Julie washed her hands in a bowl of warm, soapy water and reached under the blanket to feel the girl's vagina and cervix. Her fingers found the wide-open edges of her stretched cervix, completely effaced, fully dilated, ready to push.

Pulling back the blanket for a visual inspection, looking for the baby's head, *maybe with a thick mat of black hair that all the cutest babies have,* she saw a baby's butt.

A butt!

Breech!

Oh God, no! Breech!

CHAPTER 11

May 2002
Franco-Swiss Border

I can't turn this baby; it's too late, and I don't know how.
After hours of imploring the girl to "Push!" and "Breathe!", the baby came butt-first with a gush of bloody amniotic fluid. Pink at first, the baby girl turned dusky blue. Floppy. Silent, without a cry or even a whimper.

Shit! Apgar 3.

Giving the tiny body a vigorous rub, then clearing away mucous, Julie put her lips over the newborn's mouth and nose and gave her a whisper of a breath. And another. And another. The baby darkened to purple.

"Breathe! Breathe!"

Julie continued resuscitation. The women held the girl's hands and watched, their horrified expressions blunted, masked by lives of trauma. Entering with a rush of cool evening air, the two men stood over the desperation. Hovering. Scared.

What am I doing wrong? What else? She was afraid to look at their faces. *They will see my panic.* She couldn't bear to see them all looking at her, their hopes and dreams vanishing as life disappeared from the baby.

"Breathe! Breathe!"

The baby startled with a shudder. Arms and legs spasmed. The baby gasped. Choked. Cried. And cried. And cried. Pinked up, Julie put the baby in the mother's embrace.

Pulling open the tent flaps, she stepped outside, took a breath of fresh air, and straightened her back. The sun had set, the evening star was beaming, the cooking fire was ablaze, and Julie was proud, relieved, almost in tears when a group of women met her, offered her hot soup and smiles.

Two men agreed to take her over the border into Switzerland. "We leave tonight," they told her.

Through the night, the Kurdish men told her they were exiled fighters for the KDP, and led her up a narrow valley to a mountain pass where they could see the lights of Geneva. The moon was full. The air was cool and still. The Kurds told her, "Be in city before sunrise. Arrest is no good. Jail. Deport." They instructed her to take the trails. "Roads are patrolled."

She said, "Bushwhack?"

"*Oui*, whack bush. No noise." And they pointed the way, leaving her alone. Looking to the south, she could make out the haunting massif of Mont Blanc, snow-capped, darkest of blue, and she thought about opening the myrtlewood box and scattering her ashes right here. *Say a prayer. Call it good. Go home.*

Struggling along game trails, she tumbled down a forested mountainside. When a fir branch smacked her, she face-planted into the dirt. A glint of shiny metal caught her eye, and she picked it up. Army dog tags on a beaded steel lanyard. Looking up into the highest branches, she spied ghostly shreds of an old parachute—a web of nylon strings, straps, leather bomber jacket. She tucked the dog tags into her pocket.

Descending into the valley, she entered the city as the sun was rising. *Oh no! The sun is up.* And she kept an eye out for any vehicle labeled *POLICE*, but saw only milk trucks, postmen, and delivery trucks zipping to stores and restaurants. She found a 1-star hostel near the city center.

In the shower stall of the shared bathroom, she let hot water cascade over her, washing away the refugee camp and her trek up and down the mountainside. Stepping out of the shower, a small towel barely covering her, she was surprised to see three men shaving in the sinks, their eyes following her in their mirrors. *God, I hate Europe.* In her miniature room, she combed through her wet hair, smoothed on lotion from Provence, and lay on the bottom bunk bed, pulling the thin blanket up to her chin. *Bed feels so good; up for 30 hours, like being on call at the hospital. I'm here. I'm in. Only one more step. But, it's a big mountain…*

When she awoke, the top bunk was in her face like the lid of a closed coffin, and the afternoon sun was beaming into her tiny room. She unpacked. The myrtlewood box she placed on the nightstand, and, deep in her carry-on, the gifts from Madame Demolins. The royal purple pouch, elegantly embroidered with gold and with a gold satin draw-string, was meant to hold something special. She had tasted Cognac once, just a sip, and it felt like drinking a lit cigar, a smoky burn going down, worse refluxing back up, and taking a week to eradicate from her mouth. *Yuck!* And she always felt sorry for women who had to kiss cigar-smoking husbands: Winston Churchill, Sigmund Freud, Fidel Castro, and Mark Twain—*If heaven has no cigars, I shall not go there.*

She untied the drawstring of the pouch and shook it onto the bedspread to deliver the bottle of cognac. Jewels fell out! A necklace, a brooch, a bracelet, earrings, a hat pin. Diamonds. Sapphires. Gold. Silver. Julie stood back watching the sparkly heap glisten in the sun. *What? Are these for me? From who?* Afraid to touch them, she wondered, *Are they real? Cut glass and chrome or diamonds and gold?*

Thinking a jewelry store in Geneva could tell if she had diamonds or junk, she picked up the smallest piece, the hat pin with a long needle with one stone, and held it in a sun-beam, mesmerized by the way it caught and reflected light. *I am strolling the Champs-Élysée in 1900 something, hatpin to hold my hat and a brooch to clasp my cape,* she dreamed as she pulled on her North Face hoodie and baseball hat.

Reaching inside the pouch to retrieve, perhaps a snagged earring, she found something else and withdrew a fragile slip of paper. She unfolded it:

UBCS SUISSE—GENEVA

DATE: 7 AUGUST 1939

DEPOSIT: *1,230,000 FR*

NAME: PAUL TOLEDANO

ACCOUNT: XXXXXXXXX

It looked like some kind of certificate. On closer inspection, a bank deposit document, an old one. Her grandfather's name—Paul Toledano. *A bank right here in Geneva!*

Julie formulated a plan—*first, eat something!* Then find the bank, then find a jeweler. She stuffed the jewelry under her pillow.

On the streets of Geneva, she found an old city anchored on a hillside along the lake by stolid, stern buildings. At a streetside café, she munched a baguette sandwich and gulped a Coke. She saw street signs for: The World Trade Organization, the International Red Cross, and the UN High Commissioner for Refugees. *Wow, the world comes together in Geneva.* She wanted to visit the "High Commissioner," burst into his office, take him by the lapels to the top of his building, point over the mountains and tell him, "There. Right over there, on your doorstep, people are huddled, without a country to call home. Oh, and take some supplies for a mother and her newborn baby."

The bank was on a corner, four stories, gray stone, big doors, small sign—**UBCS SUISSE est. 1889**. Inside, black granite columns trimmed with gold held up a tall tiled ceiling, and men in suits walked across polished marble with thudding taps from heavy wingtip shoes. Julie's Nikes squeaked as she approached a teller.

"*Bonjour*," she said, and when the teller answered in a stream of French, Julie raised her hands in surrender and said, "*Non, non*. English, please." Carefully spreading the old deposit certificate and turning it to face the teller, she asked, "Can you give me some information, please?" The teller bent over, squinting, but didn't touch it. She turned away and returned with her supervisor, who studied it more intently but again would not touch it.

"Come with me, madam. You should have made an appointment." Julie followed him to an empty conference room, was asked to sit, and offered, "Evian or Perrier?" She waited a long time, glancing at her Casio.

A squat middle-aged man, dressed impeccably, hair slicked, clean-shaven with skin like a Pink Pearl eraser, sat down across from her and did not identify himself. He placed a compact Leica camera on the desk. A thin leather booklet, old but unused, was placed on his side of the desk. Julie glanced at its tiny typed label, but he folded his hands upon it and asked, "How may I help you, young lady?" not in English accented in French, like she was used to hearing, but with a German accent.

"I have a deposit slip from my grandfather. He passed away. I would like some information, please."

"I will need some identification."

"I am Doctor Julie Tolle from America." She stood up and extended her hand across the table, and he shook it with the tepidness of a mollusk. "Paul Toledano was my grandfather. And you are?" With no ID, she hoped to get the bank officer off-track enough to get some answers.

"I am Herr Stueben."

"And what is your position at the bank, Herr Stueben?"

"I am Vice President of Accounts."

"Great." She handed him the bank deposit certificate, placing it in his hands. "Herr Steuben, tell me about this. Is it a deposit receipt? Is the account still active? Pardon, but I can't read French."

The banker put on his reading glasses and perused the paper, rubbing his fingers on a corner and holding it up to the light. "A cursory visual and tactile inspection. Forgeries are common," he said as he laid the document on the desk and handled the Leica. "And how did you come by this document, Doctor Tolle?" Still focusing the camera on the paper slip. CLICK.

"It was recently returned to me by a friend of my grandparents."

"This lighting is awful. Would you mind holding the paper up in your hands?"

Julie held the deposit slip, and Herr Stueben carefully focused the Leica. *CLICK. CLICK. CLICK.*

He just took my picture!

"Excuse me, do you have identification? Your passport?" he quizzed.

"It is back at my hotel suite," she lied. *Keep him talking.* "My grandfather was from Saint-Rémy." Then added, "In France."

"I know where Saint-Rémy is," he said curtly.

"He loved the Alps."

"Nice."

The banker took out a Montblanc pen, opened the leather journal only partway, and made a short notation, then closed the book and rested his folded hands, obscuring the tiny typed label from Julie's curious glance.

He stared at her without emotion. She stared back.

"Do you have a death certificate? We cannot proceed without a death certificate."

"My grandfather was killed in the Holocaust. Auschwitz, I have been told."

"I am so sorry," he said with even less emotion. "These claims require complete and accurate documentation. The highest standards. Impeccable scrutiny. Account numbers. Death certificates. Legal wills. Trust documents. Court rulings. Etcetera."

"Herr Steuben, I'm just seeking information. I'm not claiming anything."

"This is a 'Dormant Account', inactive for over sixty years. Now property of the Swiss Treasury. You come here with no appointment. No ID, no documentation. A foreigner and stranger to our bank. You waste my valuable time. I must ask you to leave."

A security officer appeared at the door.

"Thank you for your valuable time." *Asshole!* Julie rose from her chair, and Herr Stueben, with ingrained courtesy, stood up. She turned to leave but stopped. "Herr Stueben, you seem to know the geography; is Auschwitz near here?"

In a bistro, she sipped a mocha and nibbled a Swiss cookie

called a zimbtitten. "A zimbtitten bitte." She thought about her meeting at the bank. *Yikes! That did not go well. But now I know that an account does indeed exist.* She studied the deposit slip. *So. What's your story?* She tried piecing together what little she knew: The family, including her grandparents, her father, about age 7, and big sister Eloisa, traveled to Switzerland in the summer of 1939. A Swiss mountain guide took them up the Lagginhorn. Grandfather was arrested, placed in custody, and the whole family escorted back to France. *Maybe the Swiss Police thought they were Jews seeking asylum? The deposit was made in August 1939, and Hitler took Paris the next month. Grandpa is hiding his wealth just in time.*

Julie scribbled on a napkin the deposit amount—1,250,000 francs. The European Union recently established a common currency—the euro—and she knew the conversion of euros to dollars. But Swiss francs to dollars? *Maybe like Mexican pesos? 1000 pesos equals fifty dollars.* She did the calculation: Swiss francs to US dollars, *Whoa... One and a half million dollars!*

Walking the street, looking to duck inside a discount jewelry store, she found only the finest jewelers in the world. She picked a small shop and went inside, and felt totally out of place—elegance she did not know existed behind closed doors. She removed her baseball hat, saw herself in a mirror, and groaned, *Oh my gosh. I look like a... I don't have the words.*

A saleswoman approaching her with an expression of, *Are you lost?,* asked, "How may I help you?

"I have a piece of jewelry that needs an appraisal."

"Do you have an appointment?"

Julie shook her head, "*Non.*" *An appointment for every-thing in this country?*

The saleswoman brought out a jeweler, an older, round-ish man in an unbuttoned white dress shirt, silver chest hair climbing out of the collar, and a jovial face like Santa Claus, if Saint Nick was clean-shaven. With a loupe, he examined the gemstone perched on the hatpin, making notations in a ledger with a carbon copy.

"It is an antique cushion-cut diamond, approximately three-carat, clear and nearly flawless, nice brilliance. An excellent stone. The hatpin is in the Art Nouveau style, probably from Paris, popular in the early 1920s."

"It was my grandmother's."

"Was she a flapper in the Roaring Twenties? I ask because the pin itself is rather long and sharp; some women of the time used these as self-defense against rogues or mashers."

Julie laughed, "I think she was just a mom."

"For insurance purposes, a value of 20,000 francs." He handed her the appraisal coupon and a bill for the appraisal. Julie was shocked by the value of the hatpin, the smallest piece of jewelry in the heap stuffed under her pillow back at her cheap hostel.

The appraisal bill of 150 francs made red warm embar-rassment rise in her cheeks, and she said, "I don't have 150 francs, only a few euros and dollars." They settled on a "Courtesy Appraisal."

Walking downhill to the waterfront and passing stately

buildings of Rolex, Patek Phillipe, Hermès, Montblanc, Prada, she was reminded of a saying about Geneva —This city of wealth by stealth. Entering the waterfront park, a clock made entirely of flowers—twelve thousand blooms, the *l'horloge fleurie* was keeping precise time. It even had the world's largest second-hand. *Really, Switzerland? A second hand?* She checked her Casio.

Along the shore of Lake Geneva, she moved away from the site where 'Sisi', the Empress of Austria, was stabbed to death by an Italian anarchist in 1898, and found a place where swans were feeding. Julie marveled at how clear blue the water was and, pulling her legs to her chest as the sun set, a cold breeze came off the lake, a hint of pink reflecting from the surrounding mountains. She rolled the hatpin in her fingers. Her train was leaving in the morning for Visp, then a bus up to the village of Saas Fee, and from there a climb of the Lagginhorn. *I would rather be going home.* But home was no longer Oregon; home was soon to be an empty rental house with unpacked cardboard boxes on a bench above Salt Lake City and the start of her medical internship.

I need to finish this. I got this. Action conquers fear.

"Ouch!" The hatpin stabbed her hand and was bleeding bright red.

CHAPTER 12

Hugging a lichen-encrusted boulder, out of the wind, just steps from the summit of the Lagginhorn, Julie concentrated on slowing her breathing and heart rate just like Kiki told her, "Don't race the final moves to fish-flop yourself on top of a climb; arrive with style—a Sunday morning stroll." Alone on the airy summit, the alpine valley below was dayglow green, ringed by shimmering white peaks of the Saastal Alps, but the Matterhorn, one valley over, was shrouded in clouds. Wind whipped at her parka, and holding onto a five-foot iron cross wedged in stone like Excalibur, she was buffeted while extricating the myrtle-wood chest from her pack.

Clutching the box to her chest with a hug like she would give to her Daddy when he came home late from the hospital, wrapping herself around his leg, she looked to heaven. She remembered the Little Mountaineer bedtime stories of her father's escape to America. Snippets of memories of him twirled in her head.

Julie told him, "I have always felt so loved by you…"

With a small silver key, she opened the box and held it up to the sky. Ashes flew into the wind, carried off like a puff of smoke, joining the forgotten plumes of the concentration camps. She pitched the wooden box and watched it fall a thousand feet below, shattering into splinters on sharp boulders.

Into the summit log, she found a blank page and wrote:

Jacob Tolle MD 1933–2002

Tearing the page from the book, she folded it into a paper airplane and sailed it off the summit. Flying like an Alpine chough, the black crow of the Alps, the plane twisted on unseen air currents, swirling on updrafts, darting through slipstreams, soaring and spiraling out of sight. Told that each black bird represents the soul of a dead climber, she thought, *There are way too many black birds flying here.* Remembering that most climbing accidents happen on descent, she repeated a mantra taught to her when rock climbing with Kiki: *concentrate, concentrate, concentrate.* And she had used that same mantra while taking her medical board examinations.

Her concentration was sidetracked while descending the thin arete. It was like walking on clouds—a lightness of body, a freedom of spirit. She felt happy …finally. Skipping from one boulder to the next, her feet were deft, and she was balanced, maybe from all the dance lessons her father had paid for, and she thought, *He sent me here. These are the same footsteps my family followed in the summer of 1939.*

She spotted two men climbing quickly. The lead climber in a bright yellow parka looked like a stubby banana—*Chiquita.* Upon meeting, Julie stepped aside. Just like a banana is all yellow with a black stem, this man's dark complexion, black goatee framing his unsmiling mouth, and dark glacier glasses completed that image. He said nothing.

The second climber, a young man with long confident strides, stopped, lifted his sunglasses, and said, *"Bonjour."*

"Good morning," said Julie, lifting her sunglasses too. The expression on his face changed. Not the expression of an ogling young man's double-take or lustful gaze, this was a startled recognition, like the surprise excitement of seeing a dear friend halfway around the world. He stood staring.

"Pardon. Have we met before? You are familiar to me. No?" he asked in accented English.

"No. I'm sorry. I don't think so."

"But I am sure. Somewhere. Perhaps. I am thinking here in Saas or Zermatt. A party?"

"I don't party."

"Of course," he said, looking her up and down. "Are you from America?"

"Yes. And you?"

"I am from here." His gloved hand swept across the vista. "A local."

"Of course," she said, eyeing him from his red Scarpa boots, trim Gore-Tex pants, Dachstein sweater, and fleece headband. It was his tousled blond hair blowing across his handsome face, square chin, straight nose, intense hazel eyes, and engaging smile that captured her. "I think I would remember you," she said, feeling flush.

He pulled off his glove, extended his hand, and said, "My name is—"

"Johann!" called his climbing partner from above, "Schnell!"

"Hi, Johann. My name is Julie." And she pulled her glove off to shake, but he took it to his lips and kissed it, her flush growing, a warm rush.

"Johann! Schnell!"

They both looked at the yellow figure higher on the ridge, angry, waving wildly.

"The Banana Man wants you," she said.

Johann laughed and said, "He can wait. Maybe I find him next spring." He looked at her more intently, a sincere appraisal, and said, "You do look familiar. Like the 'girl next door', now all grown up. We should meet again. Where are you staying?"

No. No way. I am not going to tell this guy anything. I am on a mountainside on the other side of the world and have just buried my father. "I'm at the Hotel Strauss," she heard herself say.

"I will call on you," he said with a formal bow. Julie bowed too, but thought a lady should curtsey, so she bent her knees and ankles, turning at an awkward angle, losing her balance. He caught her in his arms, and her face turned crimson.

He turned and ascended quickly, and Julie pirouetted to descend. Dancing down a few boulders, she turned to watch him, and as she turned, so did he, their eyes meeting over a distance cut shorter and more intimate by the crystalline alpine air. He blew her a kiss. She waved her hand.

Walking through mountain meadows, she wished she were twirling a long skirt like Julie Andrews in *The Sound of Music* with wildflowers brushing her hem. She came upon a squat stone hut built into the slope with a haystack outside, and Julie could hear cowbells farther down the valley. Loitering in the warm sun, drinking down her water bottle and chomping a thick triangle of Toblerone, she thought, *What was that? There is no such thing as love at first sight. How about smitten at first sight, and smitten rhymes with zimmbitten. A zimmbitten bitte. I wonder if any of that hay is wild oats?*

Entering the forest on well-marked trails, she marveled at the yellow metal signs clearly printed with kilometers and time to destination, not the weathered planks of the U.S. Forest Service pegged to rotting posts, pointing in dubious directions.

Finally, arriving at the resort hamlet of Saas Fee on aching feet, past its little shops and restaurants, she saw him—Johann, sitting on the sunny steps of the Hotel Strauss, twirling his ice ax. Just as she did before summiting the Lagginhorn, she stopped to gather herself, but this time her breath shortened and her heart raced.

"*Bonjour!* Or is it *Guten tag?*" she asked.

"Ciao. I am fluent in four languages. But English is my least favorite. Too much American slang," he added with swagger, "Hey baby, whassup?"

"Ha, if you speak English, I will limit the slang." She sat down on the steps alongside him. "How did you get here so fast?"

"I know a shortcut—the Hohsaas cable car. And I ditched my partner. He is not, how you say, 'a happy camper'. Is that slang too?" After their talk about climbing the Lagginhorn, he faced her and became serious. "Miss Julie from America. It is 'Miss'?" And Julie nodded. "Will you be my guest for dinner tonight?"

No. No way. I don't even know this guy. A shower and early bedtime are what this girl needs.

"It is a family dinner. A birthday party for my grandfather. He is turning 93 today. My brother is the host."

More reasons to decline. Stuffed in a Swiss hut with bubbling stinky cheese and a wheezing geezer spitting out birthday candles with his last breath.

"I would love to," she said.

"I will be in the lobby promptly at seven."

How can three flights of stairs seem insurmountable? I just climbed a 4,000-meter peak, she thought, entering her little room paneled entirely in knotty pine. Pulling off her climbing clothes, leaving them in a dirty pile, she flopped onto the bed and stared at the ceiling. *I've been staring at too many ceilings lately, tracing the cracks with tears in my ears. No more tears. And what am I doing? A date tonight? My head says one thing, and my gut tells me something else. 'Sew some oats. Kick up your heels.' That's Malcomb talking.*

Instead of a rest, she fell deep asleep and woke from a dream, a dream of falling face-first off a cliff, and her eyes flew open just before she smacked the ground. The afternoon sun no longer shone through her window, and she panicked when she looked at the clock—it was late, 6:00 PM.

In the shower, working with urgency, she shampooed, conditioned, shaved her legs *and* under her arms. *I don't care what European women do. They can braid it for all I care.* She put on makeup to hide her sunburnt nose and cheeks, eyeshadow, mascara, and Lip Smacker.

Her travel dress, a black polyester knit, was hopelessly wrinkled, and she furiously ironed it with the room iron, a steam-hissing contraption from 1970.

A knock rattled the door.

Knock. Knock. "A gift for Fraulein Julie. For the party tonight," said a woman's voice.

Half-naked, she snaked her arm out the door, snatching a small gift bag, Cartier. She opened it and found a necklace with a diamond pendant and matching earrings. She snapped it shut. *Nope. Not gonna happen.* And her thoughts flashed to when Cal gave Rose the "Heart of the Ocean."

Coming down the stairs to the hotel lobby, her eyes met Johann's, and again she saw that look of excited surprise, unexpectedly seeing a cherished friend or maybe a lost lover. She wobbled on her open-toed pumps, toenail polish chipped by hiking boots.

"Oh my. You look," and he paused, took a breath, and said, "gorgeous." He kissed her hand.

"You should not have sent me this. I cannot accept this," she said, handing him back the jewelry case.

"I understand. But just for tonight. Tonight is special. I

apologize, this is much more than just a birthday party. It is a celebration. When my brother puts on a party, it is a social event. Turn around."

Placing the necklace around her neck, she felt his warm breath giving her the opposite of shivers. He turned her back around, and Julie looked into his handsome face. "And these," he said, taking each earlobe and placing the diamond studs. Anticipating a painful pinch, she grimaced, but to her surprise, only felt a gentle tug. Rubbing his fingertips together, he said, "A watchmaker's touch. We are a nation of watchmakers."

He took her hands and examined her fingers. "A typist?" She shook her head. "A teacher?" She shook her head. "A computer programmer?"

I'm going to dinner with a male chauvinist. Let's play along. "Yes! How did you know? I am the reason we survived the Y2K Global Meltdown. But I need a manicure, your granite mountains are brutal on a girl's nails."

Johann helped Julie into a trench coat and then into the sidecar of his WWII vintage BMW R75 motorcycle. He raced up the Saas Valley around tight corners to a chalet nestled in fir trees, an impressive structure of timber and stone, flying a Swiss flag on a big lawn. Two men in black parkas waved them through the gate, and they parked in between a Lamborghini and a Ferrari. A helicopter sat on a helipad with its lights twinkling red and blue. A Volvo station wagon marked MILITÄRPOLIZEI idled nearby, the policemen flicking ashes from cigarettes out the windows.

"Since your September eleven terrorist attacks, security

is much tighter, and there are self-important people here tonight."

Johann took Julie's arm and escorted her to the door. Looking over her shoulder, she spotted Johann's climbing partner, no longer a chunky banana, now dressed in tactical black, stocking hat pulled low, cradling an automatic weapon, a German Shepherd on a short leash, and speaking into a headset.

"Who is he?" she pointed.

"That is Marcel Conte, the 'Happy Camper'. He is our family security agent and accomplished alpinist. Protector and confidant."

"He looks serious."

"He takes seriousness to a new level. Off the charts. Over the top."

Inside, Julie, expecting to find a cozy mountain lodge with a big flaming fireplace, trophy mounts of exotic animals, chandeliers of antlers, old Swiss cowbells, and, for sure, a long alphorn, was amazed to find modern open spaces with exquisite carpets on rustic floors, Scandinavian furniture, and framed artwork on high white walls illuminated with gallery lighting. Checking herself in a mirror, she brushed a hand through her windblown hair and added another coat of Cherry Lip Smacker SPF 15.

"We are late for dinner; everyone is seated."

Leading her by the hand into the dining room, thirty people sitting around a long table stopped talking and laughing as they entered. In the silent pause, Julie hoped they could not hear her stomach rumbling. Among the guests, she spotted the "Bad Boy" of tennis and his American starlet girlfriend. A short Italian media tycoon, now running for president, and his third or fourth wife. 'The Herminator', the Austrian ski racer, recovering from a motorcycle crash that nearly severed his leg, causing him to miss the 2002 Olympic Games in Salt Lake City.

At the head of the table, an elderly man sat in a wheelchair, hunched over his plate, intent on raising a spoonful of potatoes au gratin to his gaping mouth.

"My little brother. The Wunderkind!" yelled a man making his way to them. "And a date? You never have a date!" He grabbed Johann by the shoulders. "Look at you. Bigger and more handsome every day. London suits you well." His brother muscled them to their seats, and the conversation began anew, louder and more raucous, corks popping and champagne flutes clinking. Stories and jokes told with flourish, laughter flowing like Dom Perignon. Julie and Johann ate in silence along with the ancient birthday boy, his face inches from his plate, scooping in cut-up veal.

"A toast!" Johann's brother rose. "Fill your glasses! To my grandfather, Walter Imseng. He has built an international empire of finance from a single humble bank. Chairman of the International Red Cross. Director of the 1948 Olympic Games in St. Moritz." He nodded to Hermann Maier with two Olympic Golds. "My grandfather has climbed the Eiger. Sailed to Antarctica. But his biggest accomplishment is the foundation of this family and the curation of influence around the world. Known in business circles as 'The Lion'. A toast to you, grandfather. To The Lion!"

"To The Lion!" echoed the party.

Cheers were shouted, and flutes were drained, and as Julie sipped her champagne, she stared at Johann's brother. *He's beautiful.* Wavy brown hair, large, friendly eyes, a smile that charms, fit like a soccer player, and where Johann was handsome in a more subtle way—like a ledger of attractive features—brother Kurt was like a musical composition. She had seen him in an article. *What was it? People magazine? He and David Beckham together chatting up the Spice Girls.*

Johann caught Julie in a double-take of his older brother, and not a kick under the table, but a whisper into her ear, "I don't party either. This is all just a show."

"What was that, son? I couldn't hear you," said an austere woman whose eyes had been burning into Julie since arriving. The woman unnerved her. Already a fish out of water, Julie had plowed through her food quietly, but hungrily.

"I was telling Julie about parties, Mother. In London."

All conversation stopped, and the entire room focused on Julie and Johann.

"Tell us about you and London, brother. How is our family bank and family banker?" asked his brother.

"A banker?" Julie said in surprise. "You told me you're a watchmaker."

The table burst into laughter. Julie flushed with embarrassment, seeing their napkins catching snow peas and nostrils spouting Champagne.

Wiping away tears from the corner of her eyes, his mother said, "Johann, where did you find this girl? How do you know her?"

"We just met," he cleared his throat. "Today on the Lag-ginhorn. This is Julie from America."

He doesn't even know my last name. This was such a bad idea.

"Tell us about yourself, dear," mother said with no sincerity. "Where is your red scarf?" The table chuckled and chortled at that remark.

Julie, nonplused, looked at the faces of the rich and famous, laughing at her expense.

The grandfather raised his hawkish hatchet face, a man who had cleaved his way through this world. He gave her an incredulous stare. A similar reaction to Johann's. A gaze like he was seeing her for the first time after a long absence—maybe a girlfriend from when he was a young man. But then his expression shifted. A frightful look. Julie felt like an unwanted apparition—Marley seeing a Christmas ghost. The elderly man toppled his wine glass, shattering crystal and spilling Chianti. Letting out a guttural moan, his head shook with a tremor, and he slumped into his wheelchair, his eyes vacant, words garbled, mouth drooling.

Johann, his brother Kurt, and their mother hovered around him and, with the help of gimpy Herrmann Maier, they carried the ancient man in his wheelchair upstairs to his bedroom. Julie trailed the entourage and, at the foot of the bed, asked, "Can I help?"

"I don't think so, dear," said mother. "It's another mini stroke. We will call his doctor in the morning."

"I am a doctor. An American doctor." *Not really, not yet. Brand new, actually.*

"You are a computer programmer. No?" Johann stood back in a head-to-toe appraisal.

"No. I hate computers."

"Me, too," chimed Kurt. "She's my type of girl. We should go to the cinema together. To Cannes." Kurt took her arm. "A Chaplin anthology is playing this summer. Your favorite, Johann, *The Little Dictator.*"

Together, Julie and Johann sat with the grandfather through the night. The revelry faded as exotic cars drove off, and the helicopter left for Milan. It was quiet. They started talking, and he asked, "Julie, why the Lagginhorn? The Matterhorn is more famous."

"My father climbed the mountain when he was a little boy with his family; he was only seven or eight years old. I scattered his ashes today from the summit."

"I don't know what to say. Amazing feat for a little boy. And my condolences. I'm so sorry. When I first saw you, tears had streaked your face, but I thought it was from the wind." "I feel much better now." She laughed a little, "Except for sore feet," and kicked off her heels. "I could ask you the same question. Why the Lagginhorn?"

"On top, did you see the metal cross anchored into the summit block?"

She nodded.

"My grandfather placed it there many years ago. To me, it seems the right gesture to honor him on his birthday. More fitting than a fancy dinner party with people he does not know or care about. I apologize, a first date should be for coffees and pastries. My brother, in an effort to secure his inheritance, throws a party to lavish on my grandfather, fawns all over him, ingratiates himself. And see what happens?" Julie watched the old man's eyes flutter as if in a dream. "My playboy brother, or as the newspapers call him, 'International jetsetter and lothario', is an asshole. He and I are different. Linked by brotherhood and nothing else. I despise him. He despises me. A sibling rivalry."

They both watched the grandfather, and Johann remarked, "It seems our families are linked in some way by a beautiful mountain."

The grandfather emitted a moan, and Julie examined him— *'The Lion'. No signs of facial droop.* Checked his radial pulse—*regular rate and rhythm.* Opening his eyelids, she looked for a pupillary response. His eyes were the same color as Johann's and still in a dream.

What are you dreaming about, Grandpa?

"Your mother mentioned something about a red scarf. What did she mean?"

"That was a rude joke at our expense. She was trying to be funny, but was mean instead. Every Swiss boy knows the story of *The Frog with the Red Scarf.* A fairytale. Once upon a time, a boy who does not go to school so he can help his poor, crippled mother goes into the forest to collect wood. He finds a frog wearing a red scarf. The frog is delighted to see him and jumps up and down. When a bird swoops in to snatch the frog, the boy picks up the frog and hides it in his pocket. He even takes the frog home and gives the frog a seat at the dinner table. Miraculously, the frog turns into a beautiful woman and later marries the boy."

"Oh, I get it. So I'm the frog. How funny." Julie smirked. "I grew up with a different fairytale from the Brothers Grimm. Once upon a time, a prince was cursed by a witch and turned into a frog. Only a kiss from a princess could break the spell. And in the end, when she did kiss the frog, he changed back into a handsome prince. Are you under a spell, Johann? Are you cursed?" *Do you need a kiss, Johann?* She thought but didn't say.

Before Johann could answer, grandfather wailed in his dream, and to Julie it sounded like an echo from long ago. A once upon a time moan.

CHAPTER 13

10 August 1944
Strasbourg, Germany
Hôtel Maison Rouge

It was a secret meeting.

Walter Imseng watched all of them grimly file in. He sat next to Willy Messerschmitt and thought to himself, *So, this is what treason looks like.* He nodded to the heads of Mercedes-Benz, Volkswagen, Zeiss, Leica, and IG Farben. Standing up, he shook the clammy hands of the chairmen of Thyssen and Krupp, producers of coal and steel and makers of armaments from machine guns to U-boats. The opulent dining room, swept of hidden microphones and guarded by SS troops, was oppressively warm, stuffy, and airless in late summer. Collars were loosened, jackets shucked, and men perspired more than the temperature warranted—a pungent sweat of bratwurst, sauerkraut, schnitzel, and cheese. Intense and stern, these were proud men, and Imseng felt proud to be invited by his friend Hermann Goering.

Germany's most powerful industrialists were here to discuss the unspeakable—Germany's defeat. Imseng knew, "Traitor!" was lashed upon those even whispering the word "surrender" *or* "capitulation," including a visit from the Gestapo. He had heard a rumor—any German town waving a white flag to advancing Allied or Red Army troops would be annihilated, slaughtered for cowardice. But today, this elite assembly had special license to outline a plan—a plan for Germany's own survival. Imseng looked around the room; desperation did not show in the solemn faces, it did not have to, the event itself spoke to desperation.

"Let us begin," said Docktor Shied, holding the SS rank of Obergruppenfüher. He offered no introduction; they all knew him, an innovator in the field of industrial productivity and the boss of their bosses. Standing tall and ramrod straight, he was imposing in his gray-green uniform, unsmiling, narrow face topped with a peaked officer's hat.

"We have been entrusted to prepare a post-war campaign. We must preserve Germany's economic, industrial, and cultural strength and not vanish before a conquering horde. Today is the beginning of a new era, a new empire, but we must plant those seeds *now*. Our task is urgent. Our cause is just. The Fatherland must endure to rise again."

The men in the room, their factories smoldering, bombed-out shells, their Jewish slave labor in short supply, were rapt. In jeopardy, not only their personal riches but, as rumors of war crime trials festered in their nightmares, their own lives were in peril. They needed no prodding. They needed a plan.

Walter Imseng, in his alpine home of neutral Switzerland, was a spectator to the bloody pummeling of Europe, and of the pillage, he enjoyed only the plunder. He did not hear the pounding roar of artillery and bombs screaming from the sky. He did not feel the earth tremble from an advancing division of armored tanks. He did not smell the acrid smoke of cities aflame, people burning, and bodies rotting. He was a busy man. He ran a bank in Zurich.

He had his own victories, not from the turret of a Tiger tank leading a Panzer Division across Poland or from a Stuka dive bomber strafing huddled British troops at Dunkirk, but from the ledgers of his own bank. His first victory—a welcome home parade in the streets of Vienna for Adolf Hitler. Deposits of the Austrian Central Bank and its wealthy Jewish citizens arriving the next day, truckloads of gold. Then, as the Blitzkrieg rolled, gold from the Central Banks of Poland, Belgium, Denmark, and finally France, overflowed his bank vaults. It excited him to visit those vaults deep within his banks, basking in the warm glow of gold bullion and gold ingots stacked to the ceiling, arousing him with pride.

He shivered in a warm reverie.

He was surprised how his bank had adeptly pivoted to the most recent war. As the Allies slogged their way towards Paris and Russia streamed across Romania, a new round of deposits came, emergent, often at night, some from the wealthy industrialists in this room, some from the Nazi elite. Safe deposit boxes jammed with jewels from European monarchies and the richest families. Artworks, too.

But paintings are cumbersome to store, difficult to appraise, and hard to sell, so he sent masterpieces to his friends in Lucerne, for a reasonable commission, of course.

He kept a few items for himself, only a few.

Walter Imseng carried a creed within his soul, a motto—*Secrecy and Neutrality.* Swiss banks, as a service to their depositors, honor their privacy with strict secrecy laws carrying criminal punishments. And as he had been taught, political neutrality is an ancient survival tool; the Swiss cling to it like an invisible cloak. Surrounded by powerful kingdoms, the Swiss, a tortoise in its shell, an ostrich with its head buried in the sand, had thrived in their mountain realm. Where the kingdoms of Bavaria, Bohemia, Pomerania, and Saxony all perished, Switzerland's deft political dance, along with impenetrable mountains, ensured its survival, a tenuous one. Imseng cultivated a masquerade of political neutrality. *But business is business. And gold is gold. Economic neutrality does not exist.*

Listening as the SS Obergruppenführer outlined his three-part plan, Imseng held his glee in check, masking his giddiness with consternation—*I am indispensable to all of this!*

He heard the plan:

"In order for Germany to survive and prosper, industry and business must partner closely with the West. Some of you already have ties to the West."

I will strengthen my personal friendships with American bankers George Herbert Walker and Prescott Bush.

"German assets must be safeguarded, hidden from those

seeking reparations and restitution. And German capital must be moved outside the Fatherland to neutral countries, quickly."

Imseng was seeing enormous inflows of German wealth into his bank and was preparing for a new surge of deposits. *I'm still in shock; the Reichsbank is sending me their gold. Unbelievable!* Just last week, the first deposits of Reich's gold. *It is happening. Germany is crumbling.* He had personally supervised the deposit of every gold bar, the most beautiful was smelted by the Nazi SS from Jewish wedding rings and dental fillings. Lustrous, shiny, and smooth, glistening with the Eagle and Iron Cross

DEUTSCHE REICHSBANK
1 KILO FEINGOLD 999.9

Gold is gold.

The Obergruppenführer paused in his speech, looking into his own hands, then into the faces of the audience. He spoke hesitantly in a sincere, softer tone. "German military leaders and industrialists will be accused of war crimes. This we know. This we know."

The whole room seemed to wobble, a hot spell of vertigo and more oozing sweat.

"The SS is preparing a network of secret escape routes to sympathetic countries."

As a board member of the International Committee of the Red Cross in Geneva, Walter Imseng was already working closely with the Vatican. After approval from Catholic priests, the Red Cross was issuing travel documents to Nazis, ensuring safe passage through Spain to Argentina, Rome to Canada, and then to South America. *I have a meeting with Adolph Eichmann this week, Himmler's righthand man.*

There were no snifters of cognac or Cuban cigars or willing women at the end of this meeting, only the spit of gravel under the tires of speeding black sedans, racing home through the night. And while the others sped away, he slept the night in the elegant hotel, dreaming of a new dawn, a new beginning, a new empire of power and wealth, of purity and order—The Fourth Reich. *I'm in a position to lead and prosper. This time for a thousand years.*

At breakfast, he dined in the hotel, an omelet, fresh orange juice, and coffee, real coffee, not ersatz coffee from ground-up acorns, then headed out for a hike. His stride, a determined one, was the fast gait of a man accustomed to scaling the Alps. He thought about the history he was witnessing—the Third Reich dying in brutal fits.

The First Reich, known as the Holy Roman Empire and as he remembered neither Holy nor Roman, birthed itself with Charlemagne in 962 AD. A true empire stretching from Italy and Germany to France and Czechoslovakia. That Empire was destroyed by Napoleon when he tricked both the Tsar and the Emperor by feigning a weak, pitiful front, then attacking, routing them into a chaotic retreat in the Battle of Austerlitz. The famous battle honored by the Paris train station Gare d'Austerlitz, where Walter departs from when traveling to the Loire Valley. The First Reich reigned for almost a thousand years.

The Second Reich, a time when Imperial Germany,

bursting with industrial and military might, colonized Africa, led by Otto von Bismarck, the *Iron Chancellor,* and Kaiser Wilhelm II. Ending in the Great War—the Great Bloodbath—17 million dead and Germany surrendering by signing the Treaty of Versailles in the Hall of Mirrors, ensuring the Fatherland's poverty forever. Walter was eighteen and an economics student at the University of Geneva.

As an economist, he thought of the big picture and how his financial world would change. Fascism to capitalism. He had been to America, studied at Columbia, and knew this to be true:

Fascism is a philosophy, a system of government that advocates the merging of state and business. Mussolini himself coined the term and claimed the first stage of Fascism should be called 'corporatism' because it is the merger of state and corporate power. Under Fascism, the individual is subordinate to the state.

In fascist Italy and Germany, the state gained control over corporations.

But in America, corporations gained control over the state.

The end result is the same to me.

Standing on a bluff overlooking the Rhine, he watched the timeless river flow north. An excavation was unearthing a mastodon. Even in wartime, paleontologists dig. Such a noble calling. He remembered his own boyhood collection of trilobites, shark teeth, crinoids, and shellfish found on trips to the Dolomites and Saastal Alps.

Oh, but a mastodon!

Conjuring in his mind, he saw the scene from an eon

ago. The great shaggy beast, surrounded by hunters, stabbing at its flank with long, sharp spears. Puncture wounds. Lacerations. Bleeding, the mastodon rearing up and thrashing his massive tusks, roaring and screaming as he impaled some men and stomped others into the blood-soaked earth. Imseng saw it all so clearly, the bloodletting strategy of the hunters. Weakening, the mastodon fought on with a viciousness only an animal fighting for its own survival can muster, the ground shaking as it leaped, festooned with spears.

Not a quick death, this fight lasting all day and into the dark night. And now, hunters brandishing flaming torches in one hand and spears in the other, moved in for the kill. They lit the furry animal on fire. The mastodon ran across the field engulfed in flames, shrieking. Collapsing in a sizzling inferno, the killing ground smelling of fresh blood, burning fur, and flesh, the great beast writhing, gasping, blood streaming from its mouth, eyes wide with fear, the men stood watching it die… slowly… in agony.

Walter Imseng turned to hurry home.

He was a busy man.

He ran a bank in Zurich.

CHAPTER 14

May 2002
Saas Fee, Switzerland

Julie and Johann watched the grandfather, sweat beaded on his forehead, snoring softly.

She learned that Johann was heading up the family bank in London and earned the moniker, *The Wunderkind*, bestowed by a journalist writing for the Financial Times.

"I'm old-fashioned," he said.

You don't kiss on the first date?

"I like old things with a history."

"Like your motorcycle?"

"Yes! You should see my boat. And I fly a vintage Messerschmitt. Now you know everything about me, and I know nothing about you."

"Everything?"

"There is one thing I should tell you. I cannot explain. I do not understand it myself. But I must be honest with you."

Oh no! He's divorced. Has kids? Drug habit? Gambling?

"I feel like I have known you my whole life. I know nothing about you, but yet here you are, right here," he said, pointing to his head. "And more than a little bit right here," he said, pointing to his heart.

Johann was sleepy, yawning, and slouching in his armchair. "Julie, go sailing with me on my boat. An overnight cruise on Lake Geneva from Lausanne to Vevey. We will eat chocolates, drink wine, and go swimming. And at night? Oh, the stars are amazing."

"Tomorrow is my last day here, then I head home. You and me? Alone? On your sailboat? Overnight? If you wear one of those skimpy euro Speedos, I will break out in uncontrollable giggles."

Eyes closed, sleep upon him, he said, "No, you won't."

Julie could not sleep. Looking at Johann, she wondered what he was dreaming about, his mouth in a smile. Wrapped in a blanket, she left to wander the family chalet, tiptoeing on tender feet, no more heels, no more hiking boots.

The first painting she came to was of a woman's face, splintered like it had been painted on glass, broken, then reassembled by a teenager with unmedicated ADHD, signed *Picasso.*

The next painting was a jumble of red-roofed villas tumbling down a hillside sprinkled with tall trees, signed *Gauguin.*

Two paintings, side by side, looked good enough to eat, ripe fruit in a bowl and a pitcher of water, signed *Cézanne.*

A triptych of intriguing paper cutouts, signed *Matisse.*

Next painting, morning fog rose like gauzy linen on a

beautiful garden, signed *Monet*. Reaching her hand to its surface, she hesitated, her fingertips hovering just above his brushstrokes. When she touched it and closed her eyes, she could almost feel the morning sun and rising mist.

At the end of a long hallway, a fanciful scene was playing out: fairy tale images of a white horse, a church steeple, a lion with the face of a boy, and a flying angel playing a flute, signed *Chagall*. *Daddy would love this one.*

Julie heard footsteps.

Oh, shit! Hide!

Johann's mother was descending the staircase wearing her bathrobe.

Julie dodged into another room, quietly closing the door behind her. Her 3 o'clock wanderings were now feeling like a cat burglar's prowl. The office was dimly lit, and the mustiness made her sneeze. An ornately carved desk and bookshelf filled one end, and a wall of photographs on another, all signed—*To Walter*. She recognized Pope John Paul. Enzo Ferrari standing with Mario Andretti and a Formula One car. Jean Claude Killy wearing three Olympic Gold medals. Prince Charles and Diana on a ski vacation. George and Barbara Bush.

Hearty and regal, a trophy mount of a chamois watched Julie with glass eyes. *I knew there had to be a stuffed animal here somewhere.*

Sitting on the edge of the desk, she looked up. On the opposite wall, a painting rose before her—a young woman in white lace, her black hair in tresses falling over her shoulders, flowers blooming around her. Colors felt and heard.

And the eyes, Julie looked herself in the eye—blue lapis.

Stunned by its radiance, the painting drew her to it like a taut string stretching from one family generation to another; strung through love and war and whispers and screams. Slumping to the floor before it, she touched her own cheek, twirled her own hair, feeling every brushstroke upon canvas.

I see her before she sees Moi. I recognize her. Imagine my surprise. I am in shock. A torrent of memories.

What are you doing here? How did you find me?!

I want to wrap my strong frame around her. Kisses to cover her face. Marie in the flesh! The flesh of little Jacob. Or is she Eloisa's? Whose is this young woman? The last time I saw Jacob, he was running for the back door as police stormed our home. The last time I saw Eloisa, she was crying, tears of terror streaming down her face. I still cannot speak of what he did to her. But at least one of them survived! That I am now sure of. *Alive.* But which one? Brave Jacob? Or pretty Eloisa? I do not know, but the proof is right here. Looking up at me. Gazing at herself. My image, her reflection.

My master has captured beauty passed from generation to generation. His genius is beyond what we can imagine. It is why he is so loved, even by young people. As boys, Johann and Kurt, playing with toy soldiers, would stop and stare at Moi. Their infatuation with me was clear in their gaze. Even today, they adore me.

It was quite the journey to arrive here. From Saint-Rémy to Paris. Oh, why couldn't I stay in Paris? A museum for Moi. Then onto Berlin by train. The sight of Marie in that cattle car is why I hang here, my heart torn into a thousand pieces. Heartbroken until this very moment. Jubilation. Hallelujah.

In Berlin, I am displayed with the others. A showing for their master, a selection for the Führer's Museum in Austria. I made it this far and not on a pyre shared with Paul Klee, Piet Mondrian, and Pablo Picasso. I should be happy, but I shudder as Hitler and Goering look at me. I am exposed for them—a pretty girl in a sunny garden. They stand, leering at Marie, ogling her, and chide each other like lusty frat boys. Rude whispers and chortling with snide laughter. They disgust me. These men stole my family. I want to choke them to death. If my master were here, he would take me up and carry me across the fields and hills back to where I belong.

Alas, I am not chosen for the Führermuseum and instead taken by Goering to his mansion, Carinhall. But I am unwelcome. Emmy, Goering's wife and First Lady of the Third Reich, hates me. I am too pretty for her. Viewing me as a competing mistress, she wants me gone. I am cast out. Ostracized.

Herr Goering takes me here, to this chalet in this mountain valley. On a trip here to visit the Third Reich's financier and his personal banker—Walter Imseng—he gifts me with the words "Grateful for your friendship and your support." The two have a successful hunt for trophy chamois, and the majestic animal hangs on the wall across from me. Goering's finely engraved Mauser hangs there, too. Look closely at the breech; his initials are there. Johann, as a boy, loved playing with it. Once, he even pointed at Moi! My daily reminders of evil.

For the next sixty years, I will hang here. Now property of the Imseng family, I enjoy none of the warm love the Toledanos exude into life; here, the austere cold creeps into every brushstroke. I am dusty. Walter Imseng no longer uses his office. No one looks at me anymore. I will never light up anyone's life, never fire anyone's imagination, never warm anyone's soul. Never. Never!

Banished to unhappiness.

How did you find me? Are you the guest of Johann or Kurt? What is your name? You don't even know Moi. You have no clue who I am. But you fall to your knees, overwhelmed. My master's masterpiece. I have touched you. Take me with you. Please. Away from this exile. Take me away from here. I beg you!

I watched the two boys grow up. Neither like my dear Jacob, curious and kind, nor Eloisa, with intense love for her little family. The older brother, Kurt, is impetuous and loud. Johann is growing into a handsome young man. Bright and ambitious, with the intelligence bestowed upon the shrewd and cunning. But he is a dangerous man with dangerous ideas. And Kurt as a teenager? I watched in horror as he tortured pets. I saw him molest his little cousin; he hurt her.

I want to warn her.

Run! Run away from here. Take me with you!

Memories burst from somewhere deep inside Julie's brain. A faraway echo. Not memory she had encoded, stored, and recalled, but a flash of memory passed from generation to generation. As if memories could be passed on the tip of a chromosome and harbored deep inside, never meant to be opened. Inherited, just as her eyes are blue.

She was young again.

A painter. An easel. Hot sun. Cicadas. Flowers. White lace sticking to sweaty skin. A hummingbird in flight. Thoughts about a boy. Papa calling, "Marie!"

Signed *Vincent…*

CHAPTER 15

May 2002
Lake Geneva, Switzerland

Life is obstinate and clings closest to where it is most hated.
Mary Shelly, Frankenstein

"I like to bring old things back to life. Restore what was once strong and beautiful. Resurrect what was once true and noble," Johann told Julie as they sailed out of the harbor and into Lake Geneva. "That is why we are sailing this old boat and not a shiny new boat of fiberglass and aluminum. This boat was built here in 1940 when petrol was scarce because of the war, and Boesch changed from crafting motorboats to sailboats. It is mahogany and teak and brass, and the spar mast is from the Black Forest in Bavaria. I put a lot of my own sweat into her."

"Your boat is beautiful. I love it. It feels solid."

"You will be my first mate."

"I don't know how to sail."

"I will teach you. Something tells me you are a fast learner. Ahoy, lassie! Hoist the mizzenmast."

"So you are a pirate? Shiver me timbers. I thought you didn't like slang?"

"Winch wench."

"Yo-ho-ho, bucko." She laughed and asked, "Where are we going? What is our first port of call?"

"This lake has been my playground since I was a little boy. I am your personal tour guide. First, we sail across the lake to Évian. To the spa. Get your nails done. You complain our mountains are hard on a girl? Wait until you see what our spas can do. While you're in the spa, I need to meet with some businessmen. Then we get a takeaway lunch and sail to the winery."

Wind. Water. Sun. Sails. A pirate's life for me.

Imagining Johann as a little boy in his sailor suit, shorts, knee-high white socks, navy blue blazer, and white cap made her smile and think, *Probably a sweet, serious boy.*

Deep blue-green water and the breeze cascading from the Alps, *maybe carrying my father,* encouraged her to pull off the hood from her sweatshirt, and she let the wind blow in her hair. *Was this your plan all along? Send me on this trek to see what I could find? Did you know? Visit Paris and the places we shared. Provence and your hometown. Madame Demolins. Climb the Lagginhorn—my footsteps following yours.*

Docking in Évian, famous for its spring water, Julie saw the majestic Hôtel Royal above the lakeshore, a place for

Europe's wealthy to cavort for the last hundred years. Inside the opulent hotel, she felt out of place—a bumpkin, but attached to Johann with his smooth confidence and impeccable manners, she almost belonged. A rough among the diamonds.

Passing the hotel boutique, he said, "Julie, after the spa, pick out a swimsuit and put it on my account."

Not the chic spas wafting essential oils and new age music, potted plants hanging from macrame, staffed with chocolate-hued teenagers addicted to tanning beds, but an old-world place of white tile and silver faucets, clean, refined, the opposite of trendy. Julie sweated in the sauna, adding in a couple of dashes to the cold showers. Next, a facial, "Your nose is sunburnt. Let me fix that." And then a manicure-pedicure with a color Johann had selected, a deep red. While getting spiffed (not unlike the Scarecrow, Tin Man, and Cowardly Lion at Oz), she read about Évian, visited by kings and queens and the Maharajas. In 1938, with Jewish persecution sweeping across Germany and Austria, the Évian Conference of 32 nations gathered at this hotel, and after 9 days of delegates expressing sympathy, only the Dominican Republic increased its immigration quotas. Britain and America cited their unemployment problems.

Doctor Frankenstein stayed here too. The newlywed doctor brought his bride here to this hotel and, worrying that his monster was on the prowl, searched the hotel to ward off the beast. Mary Shelly, aged nineteen, wrote that after "a shrill and dreadful scream," Dr. Frankenstein finds his Elizabeth "lifeless and inanimate, thrown across the bed, her head hanging down and her pale and distorted features half covered by her hair—her bloodless arms and relaxed form flung by the murderer on its bridal bier." Shuddering with a tremor, thinking, *A monster right here in Évian?*, her manicurist messed up Julie's pinky.

Emerging from the spa feeling more like a lady and not a knapsack-toting college kid, she shopped inside the hotel boutique and was shocked at how expensive the swimsuits were. Pucci and Dolce & Gabbana—just a few tiny triangular patches of fabric—were exorbitant. At the cash register, she was met with raised eyebrows when she said, "Put this on the account of Johann Imseng."

Johann came out of a meeting room into the lobby surrounded by distinguished men; older, heavier, silver hair and bald pates, dressed in expensive resort wear, golf clothes, blazers, nice shoes; from boardroom to spa hotel. They fawned over him, back slaps, handshakes, a good-spirited crew like winners of the Kentucky Derby or an IPO windfall.

He waved her over and introduced her, "Dr. Julie Tolle, this is…" and he rattled off Monsieur this and Herr that, but the companies were impressive: North Atlantic Oil, Russia Shipping Corp, Stegner Arms, Global Rare Metals, Advanced Computer Technologies, World Media, Blackstone Investment. *Is that Marcel Conte?* He had his back turned.

Johann excused himself from their adoration, put his palm in the small of Julie's back, guiding her to Les Fresnes Restaurant, and picked up lunch to-go in a box so fancy it looked like a wedding gift for a duchess. *Or a countess or a baroness. What's the difference anyway?*

Back on the boat, they set sail again, she at the helm and Johann pointing the way.

"What's that?" Julie pointed to the shoreline.

"Chillon Castle. Eight hundred years old. Home to powerful families, first the Savoy and then the Bernese, and the muse for Rousseau, Flaubert, and Victor Hugo. *The Prisoner,* a poem by Lord Byron, is a true story about a man chained to a pillar in the dungeon for four years: 'Three were in a dungeon cast, Of whom this wreck is left the last.' I was required to memorize and recite it in English for high school. It has about a million stanzas. Lord Byron etched his name inside—a graffiti artist too."

Sails full, Julie shuttled to the bow as they passed an old side-wheeler passenger ferry, LA SUISSE.

Warm sun, blue-green water, and lapping waves put her into a reverie. *Today I feel different, changed. More hopeful, maybe happy.* Questions poured in, *What was that? The painting. A dream? A ghost? The Echoes?* She could not find words for her encounter. *Who is the girl in the painting? Why does she look like me? But Van Gogh is an impressionist or a post-impressionist or whatever, his images are never totally clear, sometimes just smudges. But she is me. And I am her. And it is amazing, not only the girl, but the flowers, the clouds, I can feel the moment, see it, smell it, hear it calling. Connecting me. Where did the painting come from? Why is it here?*

Johann docked the boat at Lavaux, and they hiked up the steep shoreline above the lake through sunny, south-facing vineyards.

"These are mine," he said. "Vineyards terraced by Benedictines in the 12th century. These grapes are special vines. Hearty with roots that are resilient, weathering storms and droughts, always to bear fruit again. But they must be nurtured. Lots of, how do you say in America? TLC."

He plucked a ripe grape and popped it into Julie's mouth. It tasted sweet. She spat out the unexpected seeds.

At the small winery, a limestone farmhouse and big stone barn, Johann was warmly greeted by his staff. He gave Julie a tour of fermenting vats and a chilly cellar of big oak barrels, smelling of wine and dirt and wood.

"We craft wine in traditional ways using methods from generations ago. No stainless steel, mechanical pumps, and computers, just grapes and gravity, oak and time. Lots of time."

"What about the busty frauleins, skirts pulled up, dancing in an open vat, squishing the harvest with their bare feet?"

"We are taking applications," Johann said, looking her up and down. "Will you select a bottle for lunch? I need to check on the barrels."

A stocky man in overalls with dirt on the knees, shirt unbuttoned, chest thick with graying hair, uncorked bottles of wine—a pour, a swirl, a sniff, and a taste. "A special wine. Our Private Reserve. Close your eyes," he said to Julie. "Sip. Can you taste it? Sun shining on south-facing vines. Sun reflecting up from the lake. And limestone terraces holding the warmth of day all through the alpine night."

"Yes. I can taste it! It's good. Light, fruity, minerals, and sunshine."

"You must be very special to Herr Imseng," he said, drinking along with her. "He has never brought a woman here before."

Johann entered, dusting off his sleeves, "Did you find a bottle for lunch? We must be on our way." She held up a bottle of *Chardonnet 1996.* "Excellent. Perfect."

Johann piloted the boat along the shore to a warm, sheltered cove where they had lunch of fruits and nuts, cheeses and sliced meats, a baguette with tapenade, and a dessert of cherry tarts.

"A picnic!" exclaimed Julie, licking her fingers. "How do you say 'picnic' in Switzerland?"

"*Picknick*–German. *Pique-niqué*–French. *Picnic*–Italian."

"I know high school Russian. Enough to read poems by Pushkin and Pasternak and the Russian word for picnic is… Wait for it… *Peekneek*! Our class would visit Russian fishing trawlers anchored in my city for emergency repairs and practice our conversational Russian. We learned naughty sailor slang, not taught in class."

After lunch, the sun high and close, the wine bottle empty, Johann declared, "Time for a swim."

Julie went to the cabin below and changed into the designer one-piece swimsuit, gazed into the mirror, and was surprised how nice it fit, turning and looking at herself. *And I was going to show up in Europe wearing my Old Navy two-piece?*

On deck, Johann nodded his approval with a little smile. Shucking his pants, underneath he was wearing a bright blue racing Speedo. He pulled off his shirt to reveal the lithe musculature of an athlete. There were no '*tee-hee*' girl-ish giggles; instead, Julie turned away, hiding her eyes and blushing cheeks. *Oh my!*

Reaching for a rope hanging from the mast, Johann went to the bow and launched a long swing out from the boat and over the lake high into the air, releasing his grip, twirling a backflip, and dove deep. He did not reappear, and when Julie cried, "Johann!" he popped up on the other side of the boat.

"Julie, come on. Jump in!"

After a couple of false starts, she leaped into the lake and swam to Johann, hugging him around the shoulders. They bobbed and splashed and laughed. In tandem backstrokes, their legs kicking up white effervescence, they found themselves alone, and Julie said, "Oh Johann, look!" A pair of swans flew overhead, and Julie reveled in the scene—deep glacial lake, snow-capped mountains, and a sailboat waiting. She shivered in his arms.

Sunning themselves back on the boat, lying side by side on terrycloth towels, feeling the warm sun on their skin and the slow rocking of Johann's boat, their hands accidentally touched. Johann interlaced his little finger with Julie's, like a pinky swear, and both were left to their own daydreams.

Julie traveled back in time; she was sixteen and visiting Paris with her father. A hot sunny day, and to avoid tourists, they escaped into the middle of Jardin Luxembourg, each taking different directions. Julie found a rose garden and, like her home in Portland, the City of Roses, she wandered among the flowers in full bloom. An older boy, maybe a freshman in college, looked at her, making eye contact, and this was the first time she ever felt attractive, perhaps desirable, and certainly uncomfortable. She felt like a young woman and not still a girl.

"*Julie!*" she heard her father calling.

Questions came again. *The Painting. Will the image last with me forever? Or will it fade with time? I want to touch it. Hold it. Why is it hanging in a musty old office and not in a museum? How do I ask Johann?*

"Onto Vevey," she heard Johann call as she woke from her nap, finding him reefing the anchor with taut muscles pulling hard.

Below deck, the cozy cabin was dark, lit with two portholes, and when her eyes adjusted, she found it was clean and organized with a miniature kitchen like something Mattel would craft for Suzy Homemaker. Contrasting with the old-world craftsmanship was an array of state-of-the-art electronics: radio, GPS, radar, and a computer screen. A neatly made bed with nylon quilt and two pillows fit snugly in the bow, and she thought about Johann's offer of a sleepover.

Startled at seeing a big machine gun attached to the ceiling, she called, "Johann, what is this!" and came out on deck.

"It's a machine gun." And to her worried expression, he added, "For pirates."

"Pirates! Here on Lake Geneva?"

"I am restoring a 50-meter sloop to sail around the

world someday. The ship is old, beautiful, with good bones. My team in Holland is bringing her back to life. The world's oceans are dangerous, and this machine gun will protect us."

Us?

Retrieving the gun and cradling it, Johann proudly lectured on its history. "American soldiers had cute nicknames for German weapons; incoming rockets were 'Screaming Mimis', German hand grenades were 'Potato Mashers', mines that exploded at crotch level were 'Bouncing Betties'. But this gun, the MG-42, shooting high velocity 8mm bullets at a terrifying 25 rounds per second, was called 'The Bone Saw'."

Walking the narrow streets of Old Vevey, Johann pulled Julie into a chocolatier, explaining that milk chocolate was invented here in Vevey, the home of Nestle. "A discovery on par with penicillin."

On their stroll, each called out a new discovery, popping chocolate into each other's mouths. A morsel for each invention.

"Electricity," said Julie.

"Rockets," said Johann.

"The Beatles," said Julie.

"Soccer," said Johann.

"French kissing," said Julie. *Oh my, did I just say that?*

"Photography," said Johann as they looked into the window of the Swiss Camera Museum with cameras from the ages and their captured images. "Photographs can't lie. They portray what is truly there. With a brush and palette, an artist can indulge what his mind is seeing."

"Like Van Gogh?" *There. I said it.* A lob in his direction. A hint. A nudge. *Will Johann pick up? Confide in me about the painting hanging in his family chalet?*

"Yes! My point exactly. No one will ever see the world like he did. Multiple hues of genius and madness and love, dabbed and swirled together creating visions more inspired than any person with a camera."

Julie popped a chocolate into Johann's mouth and exclaimed, "Van Gogh!"

They ate dinner in a small bistro; candles and a Pinot noir, salad, trout, pomme frites, tiramisu, ("No way am I eating a plate of cheese for dessert."), and port wine.

"Your surname has been shortened? Toledano. That is an old Spanish surname. From the city of Toledo. No?" asked Johann.

"Anglicized," Julie said, "People make it what they want. If you don't like Latinos, it's Mexican. If you don't like Jews, it's Jewish." She shrugged. "It is what it is. I am what I am."

"I like what you are, Julie Toledano," he said with candlelight warming his face.

Walking back to the harbor, they passed a statue of Charlie Chaplin, an American expat, posed as the Little Tramp with a walking stick and clutching a flower. Julie plucked a real flower and placed it in his hand.

"Your brother says *The Little Dictator* is your favorite movie." And Julie remembered how, with his Hitler mustache, Chaplin danced, tossing a world globe, fashioned from a beach ball, high in the air.

Johann's face reddened, and he said, "My brother is an effete, narcissistic man-whore."

Oh, I'd better drop that subject.

The lake was inky black, and along the shore, lit with bright lights, was a budget youth hostel, The Vevey House. "Julie, you can stay here tonight, or I can race you back across the lake to the Hötel Royal. But I assure you that on my boat, I am indeed a true gentleman, and the stars are amazing."

She answered by taking his hand.

Anchored on the lake, under the stars, they lay on deck, each wrapped in a blanket, and Julie was no match at plucking constellations out of the night sky; Johann knew them all. A shooting star streaked across the sky, a bright light vanishing seemingly at the same instant. A chill wind descended from the Alps, rocking their boat, and they dove into the cozy cabin lit with a hurricane lantern. They lay side by side, their bodies touching, barely.

Julie turned face-to-face with Johann.

Time to ask the question.

"Johann, I saw the painting hanging in your grandfather's office, the Van Gogh. Tell me about it."

"So beautiful, isn't it? I am in love with it. Much more than a painting to me. It is a refuge, a place I go to escape the world."

"When did your family acquire it? From where?"

"I don't know. It has always been there and will always be there. It is my anchor to my family. A compass of sorts. Amazing how oil on canvas can mesmerize. It runs through me; my bloodstream. I am forever entranced by an afternoon in the life of Vincent Van Gogh."

"Who is the girl?"

A gust of wind rocked the boat.

"She is enchanting, A daydream for a growing boy."

"Johann, she looks like me."

"I know."

Their lips were so close that Julie could feel Johann's words. A silence stirred between them. They listened to the wind, to the waves, and the slow creaking of the boat. Julie could hear her own heartbeat.

Johann's eyes traveled over Julie's face, her eyes, her mouth. He kissed her. Not a tentative kiss. A kiss from a confident man who had waited for the right woman and the right time. A kiss of longing. A kiss of pent-up passion. Desire, waiting for a key to unlock it. Putting his hand to Julie's face, he caressed her cheek as he kept kissing her. Any chill from the springtime swim or mountain wind was replaced by an inner warmth welling up inside of her. She parted her lips and let Johann's kiss fill her mouth. The kiss ended with both giggling and panting for air.

Johann asked her, "What was that monumental invention right after soccer and before photography?"

"French fries," she answered in a tease. "Oh wait, no… French toast. Oh, now I remember… a French braid!"

Julie climbed on top of Johann and, looking him in the eyes, started to braid her hair, both laughing. The tease left their eyes, and a yearning replaced that sparkle. Finished with her mess of a haphazard braid, she kissed him. The kiss was more than a kiss. It was an exploration. A search of each other's hearts. A test of a man and a woman and a love that could blossom and grow, maybe ignite into wild pleasure and ecstasy, or fade with a moan, a whimper, evolve into friendship, or into a fond, distant memory recalled to oneself on cold, dark, lonely nights. The possibilities of that kiss seemed endless. A long kiss. A French kiss. More than just a kiss.

A red light began flashing on the electronics panel. The monitor lit up with a green glow. Radar detected another boat closing in—fast. Johann jumped up, shirt unbuttoned. He unlocked the machine gun, slapped a belt of bullets into its magazine, and ordered Julie, "Stay below!"

A speedboat roared to a stop and idled alongside— a throaty, high-rev rumble. From the porthole, everything was black. Julie heard Johann chastise someone, and she listened intently as the conversation quieted; it was all in German. She heard the word "*Tod*"—German for dead. She heard "*Grosvater*"—Grandfather. And an angry curse in Johann's voice, "*Scheisskopf!*"—Shithead. The other voice could have been Marcel Conte's, but how was she to know, he had only yelled a couple of words on a windy mountain.

Johann climbed down into the cabin, the boat sped away, and she asked, "Who was that? What were you talking about?"

"My grandfather has passed."

"Johann, I am so sorry."

"It was his time. Even so…" Johann choked up but kept his composure.

"What else were you talking about?"

"It was an important message." And offered, "A delicate business matter that could not be entrusted to cell phones with poor reception or a radio with open frequencies."

Important. Delicate. Meaning none of your business.

Johann pulled the blanket around them, "*Gute Nacht und süsse Träume*—good night and sweet dreams." They slept in their clothes and in each other's arms, a fitful sleep for Julie.

Waiting on the platform at Gare Lausanne, Julie and Johann stood shoulder to shoulder. They were quiet with each other. Sailing this morning to Lausanne harbor, Julie felt awkward. Unsure. Not like she had found a new friend and lover, but like she'd drunk too much and woke up with a guy from a blind date. Something was off, not right. The timing, which seemed so perfect, now seemed wrong this morning. *Too soon. Coffees and pastries would have been the best idea.*

It was just a kiss, she kept telling herself. *Wild oats and kicking heels… Thanks a lot, Malcomb.*

Thinking about movies she had watched with lovers saying farewell in train stations, (Black and white. Steam from the locomotive. The chugging engine seemingly alive. Trench coats and fedoras. Train whistling. Porter calling, "All aboard!" One lover running the length of the platform, the other lover's lips pressed to the pane of glass, fogged by her breath.) Julie wondered what their goodbye kiss would be. *A peck on the cheek? A kiss on the lips?*

Her itinerary kicked in, trump cards of train tickets and boarding passes, *TGV from here to Paris CDG. CDG to JFK. JFK to SLC and "home" to a rental house full of unpacked moving boxes.* She wanted to take a Xanax and wake up at home to smell of cardboard and coffee. *I still don't have a passport. Why can't I just click my ruby slippers?*

The train arrived, a high-speed TGV, impatient to depart.

"When can I see you again?" asked Johann.

"We'll keep in touch. Starting a medical internship will take everything I've got. Not fit for human consumption." She tried to make a joke.

"I want you to stay. We have some of the world's best hospitals here and in London. I know important people. I have influence. We could build a life together. Accomplishments neither of us could achieve on our own. We could be a team. Julie stay."

They stood looking at each other.

"Johann, I have to go. I can't."

He took her into his arms, pulling her into him, and Julie raised her face to his. Looking into his eyes, she knew this was not to be a peck on the cheek. As he kissed her lips and held her tight, Julie gave in to her own passion, and any wall that she erected was crumbling as they entwined themselves. Mouths that could not yet whisper "I love you" kept kissing longer and deeper than each other expected.

"Johann, I have to go," Julie whispered, pulling away,

then boarding the train with a look back over her shoulder.

In her seat as the train departed, she looked out her window, misted by her breath. She saw only a reflection. A young woman. Eyes blue. Hair black and falling in tresses across white lace. Her Papa's voice calling her…

CHAPTER 16

May 2002
Zurich

Johann stood at the edge of the open grave, his umbrella shedding cold rain. The ground was muddy.

Don't slip. Don't fall.

The Imseng Family plot was unique. Most Swiss are cremated, and those who choose burial are exhumed after 25 years. The dead are forgotten. The Swiss are frugal with their grief and their little land. But the Imsengs, wealthy enough to have a plot, do not forget.

The reverend spoke tersely of Walter Imseng, "A life of duty and honor. A steadfast man. A titan of business and finance…" and Johann believed he was the only person in this rain-pelted gaggle who understood this. He revered his grandfather.

Johann's phone began to vibrate in his pants pocket. He ignored it.

An elderly man in a wheelchair, blanket on his lap, an

attendant holding his umbrella, was the only other mourner listening intently, his grandfather's friend from the old days. Johann recognized him—Albert Schmidt, the Nazi in charge of armament productivity and enslavement of Jews into factories. The ancient Nazi escaped into asylum with help from his grandfather, head of the International Red Cross.

They nodded to each other.

Johann's phone began vibrating again. He ignored it.

Johann remembered the day his grandfather took him into the vaults deep under the bank. He was 12 years old. Past the steel gate and long rows of shiny brass deposit boxes. Past huge steel doors and opening a separate room and descending in a caged freight elevator to a fortified cement tunnel, a bunker. At the end of the tunnel, a circular vault loomed. Johann felt a ghostly presence—a silent scream, a grip, a curse.

Taking his grandson by the hand, he led him to the vault and, after rubbing his fingers together, and with the touch of a concert pianist, twirled the combination around one way and back around the other way, around and around and around, spinning it with a clicking hum. He pulled the lever, and the vault opened with a thudding metallic *CLUNK*. Johann, expecting a whooshing of air like discovering King Tut's tomb, felt only a chill vacuum. He shivered.

Grandfather flipped the lights.

The room illuminated with the shiny warmth of gold. *Gold! Walls of gold!* Stacked from floor to ceiling. An inside-out warmth filled Johann as he stood mesmerized. Looking up at his grandfather's face, it was gleaming, basking in the glow, eyes shining, the hint of a smile.

"Touch it," he ordered. "The most beautiful gold in all the world. Five metric tons."

Johann poked a finger at the wall of gold.

"Here, this is for you, Johann. Take it." Walter Imseng placed an ingot into Johann's hand. Shinny. Heavy. Emblazoned with an eagle clutching the Iron Cross.

```
BERLIN
DEUTSCHE
REICHSBANK
I KILO
FEINGOLD 999.9
```

Johann's phone again vibrated, and he pulled it out and checked the caller. *Tobler Eckhart? Damn it. I told him never to call me!*

A gust of wind caught the mourners, and the family struggled to keep their umbrellas from collapsing. Johann looked across the dirt chasm as his grandfather was lowered into it. He stared at his older brother Kurt. Kurt stared back. No emotions tendered in their expressions. Johann wanted to push him into the grave. Kick dirt in his face and fling shovel after muddy shovel on top of him. *Bury the fucker!*

CHAPTER 17

June 2002
Imseng Chalet
Saas Fee, Switzerland

A German Shepherd, neck fur bristling, teeth barred, raced uphill directly towards him and stopped two meters away, ears forward, waiting for a command. Lech Balzec knew this was not a guard dog.

This is an attack dog. I can't take him. I'm too old.

It froze him.

I hate dogs.

And this one had Balzec's steel nerves fraying. Instead of on this hillside pasture of wildflowers overlooking the Imseng Chalet, he was transported back to the bombed-out streets of Warsaw. The Waffen SS holding a German Shepherd an inch from his face. Vicious, hungry to bite, he could still hear the snarl and smell the animal's hot breath. He shook off those thoughts, seeing a man wearing tactical green and a holstered handgun across his chest running towards him.

Busted. Stay cool.

Lech Balzec had his Nikon on a tripod with a telephoto lens and polarizing filter to cut through the reflective sheen of the chalet windows. He was photographing the interior of the chalet and had about thirty photos.

Hired to find a looted Van Gogh masterpiece, the hunt had consumed him. Obsessed, he now devoted his life to its discovery. Retired from Israeli Mossad, he made a living finding Nazi loot instead of Nazi war criminals. But this painting was like chasing a myth, a phantom, always hiding, secluded, cloaked, but by whom?

I have been waiting for this tip. A hot tip. A credible tip

Only rumors had trickled since the end of WWII, and the possibilities were endless. Destroyed like Van Gogh's *Painter on His way to Work?* A painter with canvas and easel wearing a straw hat, strutting down a country road, incinerated in an Allied bombing run on Germany. Or like his *Seven Sunflowers?* Destroyed in the American firebombing of Osaka when 500 B29s darkened the sky and dropped incendiaries on eight separate missions.

It lives! I know it does.

And with an attack-trained beast snarling him and an armed guard accosting him, he wondered if this tip would be a bust, too. Like the ones followed into the dangerous backstreets of Moscow, Budapest, and Cairo. His network of sources and contacts extended globally, reaching major auction houses, galleries, museums, and even Interpol. He curated an investigative reporter for *The SUN* in London, and a legal scholar-attorney, Bob Bagley, in San Francisco.

The Tip: *Tobler Eckhart is secretly driving from Amsterdam to Saas Fee…*

Balzec put this together:

Tobler Eckhart, the astute curator from the Rijksmuseum and an expert on Van Gogh.

The Imseng Family, with a private collection of Impressionists, lives in Saas Fee.

Hermann Goering, the last person known to possess the painting, was close friends with Walter Imseng.

That is all he had to go on. That is all he needed. *And,* he had just glimpsed Tobler Eckhart in the driver's seat of a black Range Rover this morning.

"Heel," Marcel Conte commanded his dog. In Balzec's face, he asked, "Who are you? What are you doing here?"

Balzec's trained eye took a quick appraisal. *This man is former Special Ops.* Men trained in the dark arts of The Commando have a distinctive countenance, a bearing, a station. They carry themselves differently, walk differently, enter a room or an airport with a presence and a surveying eye. They can tell one another. Spot each other. It is in their DNA, like brothers.

Don't you give yourself up. Agent Balzec, you are an amateur aging birdwatcher.

"I am hiking and birding. Photography." He did not answer the first question.

"This is private property. No trespassing. You are paparazzi," he accused. "Give me your camera!"

Balzec relinquished his Nikon and watched him scroll through the photographs.

Disguised as a birdwatcher with hiking shorts, a khaki coat with pockets, binoculars around his neck, and a rucksack, he was confident in his costume. He had used this disguise before on surveillance. Plus, he liked birdwatching.

Marcel Conte viewed photo after photo. "Birds!" he said. *I switched SD cards…*

"I'm not paparrazi," he said. "I wander off trail."

His assessment continued. *Probably French Commandos Marine, martial arts, weapons training, and language skills. High-capacity 9mm Sig Sauer. Knife sheathed along his leg. Walkie-talkie with who at the other end?*

"Take this." He tossed the Nikon back, and not using his catlike reflexes, Blazec let the camera fumble off his hands onto the grass.

"Give me your ruck." He snatched the rucksack and dumped the contents onto the ground: sandwich, chocolate bar, water bottle, and a worn *Field Guide to Alpine Flowers.* His weapon spilled out last—a Swiss Army knife, a big fat one, with deadly tweezers, toothpick, corkscrew, and magnifying glass.

Balzec bent down on his knees and scooped everything back into his rucksack, and apologizing, said, "I saw no property signs, and I wander off. Forgive my trespass, and I will be on my way."

Feigning frailty with difficulty rising off the ground, he reached up with a hand to acquire assistance.

When he bends down, instead of taking his hand, I will take his weapon. Shoot the dog first, then him. Bang. Bang. Double-tap.

He got a hand up. But chose to fight another day. *I've got my photos.*

"Do you like dogs?" queried Conte.

"Not particularly." *Especially German Shepherd attack dogs.*

"*Fass bein* – attack leg."

The dog lunged and sank its teeth into Blazec's fleshy calf.

"*Halt.*"

The dog stood down.

"*Fass arm* – attack arm."

The dog leaped and caught Balzec's coat sleeve. Shook it. Ripped it.

"*Halt.*"

The dog stood with a broad stance, eyes wild and eager.

Balzec assumed an old man's wobbly fighting stance, ready for fisticuffs.

Marcel Conte said, "My dog also knows the German word for throat. Get the hell out of here!"

———

Balzec locked his hotel room, closed the shades, powered on his secure laptop, and opened the Nikon's SD card. Images of the Imseng Chalet popped up. The backyard patio, gardens, pool, and window after window after window. Ignoring the pain in his calf, he enlarged each window, peering inside. Furniture, a piano, a matronly woman wearing a long housedress. On the walls, he could see paintings. One stood out…

Picasso!

In a large office, he spied a solid desk, a bookcase, and a wall of plaques and photos much too small to discern.

There! On the office wall. Is that Van Gogh?

The painting was turned sideways to him and was difficult to see. When he enlarged it and zoomed in, the image lost resolution.

Smudges. Could be a masterpiece or Walter's grandchildren coloring with crayons. Damn it all to hell…

CHAPTER 18

ONE YEAR LATER
June 2003
Salt Lake City, Utah

He was stalking her.

Following Julie into the hospital, passing underneath a banner proclaiming, *Tomorrow's Medicine Today*, he noticed she was dressed to be on-call overnight, a white blouse, black skirt, flat shoes, and a long white coat—not the half-length coat sported by the medical interns—and lugging an overnight bag slung over her shoulder. He had seen this before and knew she would exit the hospital the next morning transformed: exhausted, bedraggled, no makeup, thick eyeglasses, oily bangs, dressed in rumpled blue scrubs. A reverse metamorphosis—butterfly back to larval pupae. *She could use an afternoon in the day spa.* Following her into the hospital cafeteria, she met with interns and medical students, so he grabbed a cup of coffee and a doughnut and sat at a table watching her.

She is so predictable. Early to the hospital and late coming home. Drudgery. She will be in the hospital all night. My time to pounce.

Julie and her team walked right past him, swirling white coats, armed with stethoscopes, reflex hammers, pagers (hers was buzzing), pocket protectors burgeoning with Sharpies, eye charts and penlights, carrying a clipboard or notebook, ready to battle disease and pestilence or whatever maladies awaited them.

I'll sneak into her house. Wait for her to come to me.

A busy day rounding on hospitalized patients, examining patients in her Family Medicine Clinic, admitting sick people from the Emergency Room, and always needing to be in three places at the same time, finally gave way to a respite at midnight. Entering the call room, it smelled of Lysol, tennis shoes, and dirty laundry, and Julie kicked a Domino's pizza box into the dust bunnies under the bed. As she plopped on the bed, her pager buzzed, and overhead a voice with a timbre of urgency:

"CODE BLUE POSTPARTUM MOTHER BABY

CODE BLUE POSTPARTUM MOTHER BABY

CODE BLUE POSTPARTUM MOTHER BABY"

Julie ran fast, her stethoscope bouncing around her neck. On scene, a scrum of nurses parted, letting her see a pale woman, drenched in sweat, obtunded, eyes rolled up into her head, the oxygen cannula not in her nostrils but plastered to her cheek. Between her legs, pads of unclotted blood were soaking through. Glancing around the room, she found herself the first doctor at the emergency. This was *her* Code. A newly minted resident and, *Oh shit! This is mine to run!*

Nurses calling out:

"No radial pulse."

"I got a carotid pulse. Weak and thready."

"She's bleeding out."

"BP 70 Systolic."

Julie's worst nightmare was dying in front of her, a brand-new mom, her suckling newborn whisked away. The husband arrived curious, turning horrified in an instant. Nurses tried shooing him away with firm pushes and comforting words, but like a blitzing linebacker, he swam through their defenses. He took his wife's hand that just an hour ago he held with gentle exhortations to, "Breathe, Honey. Breathe." Now her hand was limp, cold, lifeless.

"Doctor, what's wrong with her?"

I don't know what's wrong with her. But she is hemor-rhaging to death. "Your wife is bleeding after delivery. We are going to find it and stop it." *I hope, please God.*

Julie's two interns showed up bed-headed and bleary. She called for stat blood tests, six units of packed red blood cells, two of fresh frozen plasma, as she established a central IV line in the jugular vein—*a lucky shot,* all as her head raced for a diagnosis: *Torn or retained placenta. Uterine rupture. Uterine atony is the most common, but this seems like way too much blood!* She called for Pitocin and massaged the uterus.

The OB darted in. Dr. Susan Newcombe, her practiced calm, collected expression was betrayed by a wide-eyed glance at the situation. She gave Julie a look, an *Oh my God!* look that physicians pass from one to another, saying more in a flicker than in an entire lecture. Nurses barked out another set of fresh vitals, and Dr. Newcombe said, "Start Pitocin and type and cross for 6 units of blood."

"Dr. Tolle already got that goin'," said a nurse.

"Alright, let's get her over to the OR. Julie, scrub in. You're first assist."

Julie, her white-knuckled interns squeezing bags of packed red blood cells over their heads, pushed the woman's gurney to surgery while Dr. Newcombe spoke with the husband, her hand on his shoulder.

———

Before dawn, he picked the lock of Julie's backdoor, pushed inside, and began searching her home, a small Craftsman-style 1930s bungalow in the Avenues district of Salt Lake City. Not a ransack, he was methodical and meticulous. In her refrigerator (a forlorn place of takeout Chinese food, yogurt, and wilting lettuce), he found an apple, took a bite, and kept perusing. *I'm just getting to know you, my dear doctor.* An old record collection, including Louis Armstrong and Ella Fitzgerald, he recognized as belonging to her father. On her desk: a monograph from the New England Journal of Medicine, something titled *Cardiac Arrhythmias…* And, *Tolle, J.,* as one of three authors.

He picked up a picture of her father as a young doctor and placed it circa 1962. Another photograph showed

Julie and a young man in climbing harnesses, helmets, and a coiled rope, standing atop a cliff. *Boyfriend? Perhaps not. Hands on hips and not around each other.* The young man was handsome, hair wildly sticking out of his climbing helmet, a goggle-faced tan, a big smile, a leather necklace, muscles stretching a dirty T-shirt. On the back was scrawled, *Pingora—Wind Rivers, Wyoming.* Somehow, he imagined her with a more sophisticated, more prosperous young man, with more prospects, perhaps a young lawyer, not this grungy outdoor athlete.

Perusing her bedroom, apple in hand, it was tidy, bed made, no dirty laundry, a Roots beret from last winter's Salt Lake City 2002 Winter Olympics. On her bedside table, a clock radio and a short stack of books: John Grisham's *A Time to Kill, The Lovely Bones* by Alice Sebold, *Bush at War* by Bob Woodward, open book face down, Rick Steves' *LONDON.*

Her closet was tidy too, and blouses, skirts, pants, jeans, and tee shirts were orderly. Sweaters folded. *Not much for dresses. Nothing for a party. Oh, here's one: A little black dress and heels to match. Ooo la la! Oh, if I were a young man.*

At sunrise, he made himself a cup of Starbucks French Roast. At the kitchen table, sipping from her mug, *Timberline Lodge* on one side, an orange snowcat on the other, enjoying a glass of orange juice and buttered toast with orange marmalade, he examined the stack of Julie's mail. Tossing aside an REI catalog, *Outside Magazine,* JAMA, *New England Journal of Medicine,* and a utilities bill, he stared at a personal letter—*AIR MAIL.*

From: *Joahnn Imseng, London, England.*

Imseng? Imseng! What the hell?

He sliced it open and read it. Then read it again. *This is unbelievable!*

The lock turned in the door.

She's here!

———

Julie dropped her overnight bag in the foyer and headed for the kitchen. *Orange juice, granola, and nosedive into bed.* Her patient had made it. A retained chunk of bleeding placenta was removed with a scope, and needing six units of blood. Less than a hundred years ago, the woman would have bled to death, her baby motherless, her husband a young widower raising a daughter all on his own. *Kinda like my dad.* She shook her head, releasing her ponytail and letting her black hair fall around her shoulders, kicked off her Nikes, tossed her thick glasses onto the coffee table, pulled her arms through her bra, and flung it onto the couch.

She walked into the kitchen.

A MAN!

She screamed! And screamed again.

Turning to run, she saw an old man sitting at her kitchen table holding a photograph of her and her father together. Standing in the doorway, ready to bolt, a sprinter's mark, she grabbed a butcher's knife. Holding the knife with both hands, she shook with fear and screamed, "Get out of here!"

He took a bite of toast and a sip of coffee.

"Good morning, doctor. My name is Lech Balzec. I work for your father."

"My father is dead," she yelled at him.

"I know. I am so sorry. Truly. But I am still on the job. He hired me many years ago."

"How did you get that photograph?"

"It's mine. I took it with my own camera. Don't you remember? You were 13 years old, a gangly girl with braces and pimples and a pout. I came to your house in the hills above the medical school in Portland. Your nose is sunburnt after climbing Mount Hood with your father. See?"

He tossed her the photograph, and she raced through her memory of a meeting: a memory of a strange man with an accent talking with her father way past her bedtime. She thought he was a European research scientist collaborating with her dad, but it was strange when he left via their back door, and she'd glimpsed a holstered gun.

"You're a scientist?"

"I am a soldier."

"You're too old to be a soldier, Mister…"

"Balzec. Lech Balzec." He rose and tried to shake her hand, but almost had his arm sliced off. "I was a friend of your father. Let me explain. But please sit. Have a cup of coffee."

"I'll stand. You talk."

"Your father came to me twelve years ago, enlisting me to find a painting. A painting he believed was stolen from your family during the German occupation of France. A Van Gogh portrait of his grandmother, Marie. The Nazis stole it. Every day I search. It has become my obsession. My reason to live. And now it brings me here. To you."

"How about a phone call? A letter? An email?"

"I must be discreet. My search requires diplomacy and secrecy."

"I hate secrets, Mr. Balzec. I don't want to hear them. And I don't like to keep them."

He looked at Julie, feeling him taking her measure; a man who could quickly tell friend from foe. Appraise character. Trust or distrust. But what shook her the most was that she saw in this old man a person who could easily save her life or take her life. She gripped the knife tighter.

"I guess we are done here then." He stood. "*Adieu*, my young doctor." Julie saw that he was shorter than she, fit, strong, with the posture and countenance of a soldier, moving slow, but not "old man" slow, more cat-like, a grace and purpose belying quickness. "Your father trusted me. Trusted me to hear and keep all his deepest secrets. I was hoping you would trust me, too."

"He knew you better than I." She acquiesced, "Perhaps a formal introduction and a resumé would charm better than your cat burglar antics, Mr. Balzec." Julie looked at the photograph; she and her father side by side, he smiling, she brooding, and indeed a freckled sunburnt nose. "How about a deal? You sit. I keep the knife. You tell me who you really are and why I should trust you."

"Where would you like me to start?"

Adept at taking medical histories, Julie said, "Childhood."

Change came over him. A loss of composure. He was

shaken. This was not going to be a reminiscence of an idyllic Norman Rockwell boyhood, she thought.

"I will start with my most vivid boyhood memory." He paused, and Julie watched as he traveled somewhere within himself.

"When only rats and a handful of Jews with knives and clubs and no God and no chance of escape were left in the sewers of the Warsaw ghetto, Stuka dive bombers came to obliterate what vermin remained. That is when I made my escape. No Nazis in the street to kill me, only bombs screaming, buildings exploding, bricks flying, and thick clouds of smoke. I took my chance. My only chance. My last chance. And I ran through fire. I ran through Hell. Through Hell. And I lived. I lived!" His finger stabbed the air. He looked directly at Julie, a fierce glint. "I was eleven years old. *That is my childhood, doctor.*"

"Oh my God, then what?"

"I made my way into the forest, stealing food, foraging snails and mushrooms, and was found by a man who took me to an encampment even deeper in the forest where Jews hid and starved. An American pilot was brought there, too. We rescued him from the Germans after his bomber crashed. A captain. He had a pistol.

"Then the Russians came. We crawled out of the forest. I rode on top of a tank!" His expression turned to triumph.

"As the war ended, everywhere, people were on the move. I lived with gangs of orphans on the streets of Budapest and Belgrade. Made my way to Athens. When I was 15, I came to Israel and worked on a kibbutz. I was good in school.

Studied art at the Hebrew University in Jerusalem. At age 19, I was conscripted into the Israeli Army. Turns out, I was a better soldier than artist. And as it turns out, a better spy than soldier. I worked for Israeli intelligence, Mossad, for twenty years. But that is a secret, and you don't keep secrets, do you, Dr. Tolle?"

Julie grimaced.

"My work included hunting Nazi war criminals."

"Like who?" asked Julie.

"I captured Adolf Eichmann, the architect of the Final Solution. His chilling confession, '*Ich bin Adolf Eichmann,*' still echoes in my brain. I interrogated him. I knew him, 'The banality of evil', as Hannah Arendt called him. I have had successes. Just as many failures. I searched for Josef Mengele."

Doctor Josef Mengele, the "Angel of Death," Julie knew, conducted heinous human experimentation. Eugenics research on twins. One twin selected as a control, the other twin was subjected to forced insemination, injections of chemicals and diseases, and amputations. He autopsied the surviving twin, sometimes still alive.

"Mengele was never caught," Julie said.

Lech Balzec bristled, "He died of natural causes. A stroke while swimming at a Brazilian beach resort."

Stowing his anger, he said, "Now I am retired. I live in Paris. Every day, I search for Nazi loot. I have witnessed horror, now I search for beauty. I have had successes, just as many failures. Recently, I returned a Monet to the family of Paul Rosenberg. I am working full-time for your father's estate, dedicating all my focus, all my resources, and connections with Interpol and your FBI. Just last month, one of the biggest art heists in history happened when Saddam Hussein fled Baghdad, and the Iraqi Museum was robbed of 15,000 pieces. The authorities want my help. I told them, 'No, I am too busy.' Julie, your painting is the most difficult and haunting. It is like chasing a ghost."

My painting?

He pulled out a chair, saying, "Please sit with me. It is a long story. A story of beautiful genius, a family's love, a remarkable woman, and your father's amazing journey. A story of the darkness cast upon them and the theft of all they hold dear. A story of deceit and murder. It is *your story.*"

He poured her a cup of coffee.

"Sit, my young doctor, and let me tell you a story."

CHAPTER 19

June 2003

Salt Lake City, Utah

"This story is true."

Lech Balzec closed his eyes and said, "Our world is built on plunder."

When he opened his eyes, Juile saw a glint of weariness, a man who had seen too much, knowledge gleaned from experiences that break most men.

"Ancient Greece and Alexander the Great, the Roman Empire and the campaigns of the Caesars; they pillaged their way through the known world, hoarding treasures of other nations. When Europe plunged into the dark poverty of the Middle Ages, only a vast new round of pillage brought enlightenment—the Renaissance. Christian Crusaders marauding through the Holy Land. Then the Conquistadors murdered the Aztecs and Incas for gold. Colonization of the Americas, India, China, and Africa. The Slave Trade. Europeans have sacked the world. Sucked the wealth from all its peoples. Vampires bleeding the Earth.

"Three thousand years of the Earth's treasure hoarded onto one continent, then along comes Adolf Hitler and his henchmen. They systematically rape *everyone* of *everything*."

Moved by his voracity, Julie commented, "That's not quite the textbook version, Mr. Balzec." And added, "What does this have to do with a painting?"

"Ah, yes…" He refocused. "*Your painting.* It has vanished. Lost. Gone. Van Gogh painted it when he was at the asylum in Saint-Rémy."

"I've been there. Last summer. A beautiful place."

"Van Gogh painted when lucid. He painted your great-grandmother Marie when she was a young woman, really still a girl, in the family estate garden. A wheelbarrow full of flowers. The painting is true. We know of this painting from letters Vincent wrote to his brother Theo. The summer of 1889. A year later, Vincent was dead. Killed by a gang of misfit teenagers. Shot in the stomach. Murdered."

Murdered. The word slapped Julie in the face.

"The painting is blood money." Agitated, Balzec stood, his eyes flashing with anger. "The blood of your family. The blood of your people. Europe has never hesitated to shed blood for money, especially Jewish blood. Julie, *you* are the rightful heir. We must not forget." He slammed his fist on the table. "We must *not* forget!

Those words echoed throughout the old house.

Balzec shifted gears and went to stand over the turntable. "May I?" Pulling Louis Armstrong from the collection, blowing dust off the record, he placed it carefully on the platter.

With Louis Armstrong playing blues trumpet he sat back down and explained, "Your father was a witness to this painting. He grew up under its magic. He watched as it was stolen when the French Police arrested his mother and father. The French Police," shaking his head in disgust, "rounding up their own citizens so the Nazis could send them off to camps.

"But Julie, the painting is a phantom, a shadow. A beautiful dream more difficult to recall with each passing generation. Its existence, ephemeral. The flight of a hummingbird. A dandelion blown to seed. Stolen from all of us. Leaving only a faint trail, breadcrumbs."

"What breadcrumbs?" she asked.

"I have evidence it was transported to the Jeu de Paume, a museum in the middle of Paris where Germans sorted their looted bounty."

"I've been there! Not inside, but I sat on the steps. An art museum with photography." Julie flashed back to those steps, a tear turning to fury when she spotted the thief with her backpack and father's ashes.

"That is where the trail ends. It ends in Paris. Germans sorted artwork to include in Hitler's dreamed Fürhermuseum in Linz, his hometown in Austria. Goering had a fine eye, too, and an insatiable appetite. Art and artists the Nazi's deemed an affront to their ethnic purity were purged: Picasso, Dali, Otto Dix, Paul Klee, Edvard Munch, and Vincent Van Gogh, all *Entartete Kunst*—Degenerate Art. Some were sold. Many were burned. Burned!" Balzec shook his head.

He took both of Julie's hands, held them across the table, and looked her in the eye. "We must assume the painting survives. It lives! Agree?"

Julie nodded her head. "Agree." A pledge. *So now I'm in this, too?*

"Recently, a new lead has emerged. Rose Vallard, a French woman and assistant curator working under the Germans, kept secret notes of paintings at the Jeu de Paume. She recorded that Van Gogh was shipped the day after Hermann Goering visited the museum. I think to his mansion, Carinhall, in the forest of Germany. From there, the painting disappears. Never seen again. Never in a gallery. Never in a museum. Never in an auction. The master's masterpiece vanishes. Beauty denied to the eyes of the world. One of the world's most valuable paintings, a priceless treasure like a Leonardo, a Vermeer, a Rembrandt, is not *lost*. But *hiding*. Hiding somewhere."

Balzec drew his face near Julie's and, as if someone could hear, whispered, "But I am closing in on it. I can feel it. I am so close!" He pinched his thumb and forefinger together in front of her eyes.

He took a photograph from his inside coat pocket and placed it on the table.

"Your father gave this to me many years ago. This is *your* family. This is *your* painting."

Julie gazed: her father as a boy, her grandmother, her grandfather, her aunt Eloisa, all posed in fine clothes, maybe on a special Sunday. A family portrait.

"Oh my God, I have never seen this photo!" She squinted.

"My dad looks five years old. He is so cute."

"Now look behind them. On the wall. Use this." He handed her a magnifying glass.

In crisp black and white detail, the painting—a girl wearing white lace, black hair, and a wheelbarrow of flowers.

Julie's jaw dropped, her eyes flew open; collapsing into the chair, she clutched her chest.

"I have seen this painting before," she said in a breathless whisper, hand covering her racing heart. "I've seen it."

"What? What! Where?" Balzec jumped to his feet, the pounce of a leopard, his body vibrating, twitching.

"Last summer. I saw it. In the chalet of the Imseng family. In Saas Fee, Switzerland."

"I knew it! I knew it! I knew it!" he cried. Sitting down inches from Julie's face, he asked. "What does it look like!"

"Oh… It's amazing. Stunning. Alive. Colors that transcend. It makes you feel new and vibrant, like a flower in the sun. And the girl… the girl… I don't have the words."

"That is your great-grandmother, Marie." Lech Balzec was tearing up. "I promised your father *I* would find it, and now, a miracle, *you,* his daughter, finds it. A miracle. Julie, do you know what this painting is?"

"It is a Van Gogh portrait of my great-grandmother as a young woman."

"No! No! It is so much more." He knelt down, hand on her shoulder. "It is *all* of Van Gogh's genius and *all* his passion poured onto one canvas. It is the love of living life. Discovering *all* the beauty in a God-given day."

Lech Balzec sat down across the table, and Julie felt him

taking her measure, again under his scrutiny, eyeing her with the perception of a man who interrogated Nazi war criminals and Muslim terrorists.

"The Nazis stole this painting from your family and then murdered them," he said, pointing to the family in the photograph. "And now it is hiding with Hitler's collaborators. Hidden by his bankers, his friends—the Imsengs—rich and powerful." He pulled the airmailed envelope from his coat pocket. "Dr. Tolle, how do you explain this?" He held the letter like a dirty diaper. "This letter. This… *love* letter. From Johann Imseng?"

"That's mine!" Julie swiped it out of his hand. "This is none of your business." She buzzed at him like a hornet. "You break into my house? Eat my food. Read my letters. What the fuck?"

Balzec took another bite of buttered toast. Julie slapped the toast out of his mouth.

"What the fuck!"

Balzec calmly wiped the crumbs from his mouth. A silent faceoff, Julie's mind racing, *I owe this man nothing. No explanations of anything.* And, *What did Johann write this time? Still obsessed with me? God, I hope not. What should I do?*

The silence was broken when Balzec said, "My methods transgress. I apologize."

A "but" hung in the air, and the silence continued until Balzec clarified, "Johann Imseng is the heir to a huge fortune, a financial powerhouse. He is in charge of the family banking business worldwide. The Imsengs are wealthier and more powerful than most of the royal families of Europe. Johann Imseng is resurrecting a Fourth Reich. Political and industrial power that will again reign across Europe. How did you meet him? Tell me."

Julie folded her arms across her chest, lips tight.

"I am your friend in this. Trusted by your father," he implored.

"Leave my father out of this," she snarled.

"Oh, but he is why I am here, Julie. He is looking down on us from heaven, here as we sit and talk.

"We met climbing in the Alps."

"And?"

"He asked me to dinner with his family. A birthday party."

"And?"

"We ate dinner at the chalet, and that is where I saw the painting."

"And?"

"We went sailing on Lake Geneva."

"Yes. And?"

"None of this is any of your business. It's personal."

"You don't see it, do you? Or are you turning a blind eye?" He held the family portrait.

"What?" Julie asked.

"You are the image of Marie. You are her reflection. The embodiment of her allure. Both your father and Johann were raised under the splendor of this painting. Under its magic. To Johann Imseng, you mirror true beauty. The incantation of a spell. Something to possess."

Still mystified by her first encounter with Johann on the Lagginhorn and his surprise, his amazement still resonating, Julie recalled, *What could elicit such wonder in a man?* She replied, "You're delusional, Mr. Balzec."

"Am I? You think Johann Imseng loves you? A man like him is incapable of love."

"You don't even know Johann!" *He is my mistake and none of your business.* "It's time for you to go. Get out! Get out!"

"Yes. It is time for me to go." He stood over the turntable as Louis Armstrong finished singing, *"This song has ended, but the melody lingers on,"* and the needle swung to the middle around and around with pops and clicks.

Balzec opened the back door and peered around outside.

"We will meet again. Before I go, you must remember two things. First, there are no coincidences. *None.* And most important, absolutely no police, no law enforcement of any kind." Julie could tell there was something more he wanted to say, but he was hesitant, searching himself. A secret too precious, too scandalous, too salacious to share. Something he may regret telling her. "And, I believe…" he paused, his eyes searching hers, "Your father did not die by accident. I believe he was killed. Murdered."

CHAPTER 20

7 July 2003
Paris, France

If I do not get out of this rain, I will never get over this flu, Lech Balzec thought at the entrance to Pied Au Cochon illuminated by a neon pink pig. Entering the restaurant, his closed umbrella left a pink puddle reflecting on the white tile. Tonight, he was celebrating. Across from his booth, a table of raucous Parisians were partying, but their elation was no match for his joy. He had orchestrated a one-man coup d'état.

Soon, newspaper headlines around the world will ring—

VAN GOGH MASTERPIECE FOUND!

He raised his glass of Beaujolais and said out loud, "Vincent, I have finally found you!"

And a second silent toast to the empty seat across the bistro table, *to Miss Julie. Be brave, my young doctor.*

Huddling over a scalding bowl of French onion soup, he recounted his accomplishments:

I have a video deposition from the only living eyewitness to the Van Gogh, Madame Demolins.

His career with Mossad had given him prestige and access within Interpol, Scotland Yard, the FBI, and the CIA. *Interpol will secure the painting at the Imseng chalet.*

Attorneys will file a lawsuit in the American Federal Court. He retained the San Francisco law firm Bagley & Grover, his adversary in a new case, helping actress Elizabeth Taylor retain her family's Van Gogh arguing that *A View of the Asylum and Chapel,* bought by her father in 1964 for $257,000 and now worth $15 million, was not looted by the Nazis but purchased legitimately.

Bob Bagley is the best attorney in America. We will win!

He continued to review his careful strategy. *I am tipping off the New York Times, London Evening Times, and Le Monde.*

Wine fueling his reverie, he thought, *Maybe Julie's painting should hang down the street in the Louvre or perhaps across the Seine in the Musee d'Orsay where the other Van Goghs shine?*

Poking his spoon into the thick layer of Gruyere blanketing his bowl of soup, it became entangled in the gooey cheese, twisting it one way then the other, he finally extricated it. The hot soup burnt his tongue. He slurped and drank and drank some more. Strawberries and crème fraiche for dessert.

The bottle of Beaujolais now empty, fortifying him against a stormy Paris night, his waiter called, "Monsieur, un taxi?"

"*Non*, the rain has stopped."

"It is still wet and chilly, monsieur."

"*Merci*, but I will walk home."

With wine warding off the cold night, humming a song, he danced down the street with a little Gene Kelly jig, splashing into a puddle of rainwater.

Behind him, he heard the throaty roar of a motorcycle. Over his shoulder, he spied a rider in wet black leathers astride a Ducati. Homeward, he crossed the Forum de Halles, bypassing a plume of marijuana smoke from a cluster of Rastas. Emerging from the other side of the park, waiting for him, the same motorcyclist, engine revving. Wine afforded no protection from this chill—a glimpse of a gun barrel inside his black leather jacket.

With a stumbling pirouette, he walked, then started to run back across the Forum towards the hulking massif of the Church of Sainte Eustache. The church, named after Saint Eustache, a Roman general burned at the stake along with his wife and children for converting to Christianity, rose high and stolid with flying buttresses. Lech Balzec opened the door. It was colder inside. He knew services were no longer held here; no longer a place of worship, no one came here to find God—he was no longer here.

Reaching for his gun, he found only an empty pocket. *Damn!* He looked for something to fight off an attacker and tore a big metal crucifix from the wall. *Hit him from behind.* Armed with only a crucifix, he was more ready to battle a vampire than a trained assassin.

Three flickering candles in the vestibule gave him just

enough light. He went fleeing into the cavernous Gothic cathedral, past the nave and into the engulfing black dank of the east transept, then finally crawling on his hands and knees in webs of musty dust, he hid behind an elaborate crypt.

Hearing the motorcycle roaring up the cathedral steps, bursting through the door and racing around in circles, the headlights flashing maniacally on tombs of French artists, writers, generals, and clergy, the engine filling the church with gas fumes, and a deafening echo in a sacred place where Franz Liszt and Berlioz had performed symphonies. The soldier, too old to fight, dove into his deepest memories—hiding, a muscle memory, he curled into a tight ball.

They know! Van Gogh lost forever? Is Julie Tolle still alive? It can't end here. Not like this. Not like this...

Bootsteps approached the crypt. He stifled a sneeze. He did not pray. God had been wrenched from him as a little boy concealed in the dark depths of the Warsaw Ghetto.

Orphaned, Stuka dive bombers pounding the Ghetto, huddling in the sewers with a hate-filled remnant of men determined to fight and die, young Balzec prayed, "Dear God, help me find a way. Help me find a place. Help me..."

"Ssshh! Hush, boy!" A dirty hand smothered his mouth, and a fighter put fingers to his lips and said, "If you pray too loudly, God will know there are still Jews left alive in Warsaw."

He remembered what a concentration camp survivor told him, "In Auschwitz, lying on a fetid bunk, a trainload of Gypsies arrived in the middle of the night. Families screaming and wailing, and praying all through the night. I have never heard such an uproar. *Surely God will hear them?* In the morning, I watched the guards herd them all into the gas chambers, their cries silenced forever."

Living without God, Lech Balzec became an artist, then soldier, then spy. Filling the void in his heart with the beauty of art. Art—a solace and salve. *God is dead. Art lives!*

Concealed in the great Gothic cathedral, he listened to approaching bootsteps and thought, *Satan walks the earth.* The bootsteps stopped with a shuffle near his head. *He has found me. Again.*

He heard the cocking of an automatic pistol. Rising like a spectre from behind the crypt, Lech Balzec wielded the metal crucifix above his head like a giant broadsword.

BANG!

A bullet tore into his chest. Then another and another and another.

Dying, his life flashed in front of his eyes as a series of beautiful paintings: dancers of Degas. Tahitian girls of Gaugin. Rosy cheeks and cherry lips of Renoir. And flowers. *Flowers everywhere!* Water lilies of Monet. Poppies of Georgia O'Keeffe. Bouquets of Matisse. Irises and sunflowers of Van Gogh. And a girl in white lace with a cart brimming full of blossoms, signed—Vincent.

His last image came with clarity. Every detail, every color, glowing brighter and brighter—Michelangelo's ceiling of the Sistine Chapel. The outstretched hand of God, searching… reaching… for his own. Touching.

CHAPTER 21

7 July 2003

Imseng Chalet, Switzerland

He is *not* a friend of Moi. I have *never* seen this man before.

"Oh, my God! Vincent, my old friend, you have outdone yourself. I am stunned. Look what you have created."

Wobbling onto his heels, hands over his mouth, tears welling in his eyes, this stranger with a Dutch accent stares at Moi. Taking me in from afar, then close up, then from afar again cocking his head one way then another as if… what? What? This is something different. Not an admirer, he is something else. *Who are you? What are you?*

Taking me down off the wall and placing me on an easel with good light near a window, we come face to face, each taking the measure of the other. He is of pale complexion, a squatty face, scrunched and fatty, never seeing the sun, like puffy bread dough. But his eyes are intense, filled with wonder as he blinks away tears to see me clearly. I have that effect on men. I have seen it before.

Apron on, sleeves rolled up, he brushes me free of dust, the old man's office cobwebs. It feels good, I have to admit, I start to sparkle.

He sniffs me, tastes me with a long lick of his fat tongue, and mutters, "Excellent! No varnish." Next, with cotton swabs swished into his mouth, collecting saliva, he dabs and swirls at me. *Gross!* With moist linen, little by little, swab after swab, my dingy patina is removed. I remember each dirty layer: my home in Saint-Rémy with smoky home fires, the mistral carrying wind, blown from the north. I remember the diesel smoke from trucks and trains clinging to me on my journey from Provence to Paris and on to Berlin. Goering's cigar smoke as he puffed and admired me. And now here, in the Swiss Alps, with clear alpine air but in a dusty office vacated by Walter Imseng.

All day, he cleans me. Brushing off my verso—my backside—he is surprised and happy, saying, "Excellent! No labels." I have no labels. Or stamps. Or stencils. None. Not from a gallery or auction house or museum. He twists my frame. Paul Toledano himself handcrafted this for me from strong French oak.

By evening, I am clean, gleaming, even the ochre and the yellows are vibrant. I feel like an aging diva arriving on stage for a comeback performance.

The squatty man stands back and says, "Clearly a special day for you, Vincent. Fresh paints. Clear head. And a good heart. Where did you find this young woman? Who is she? Did you fall in love with her? *All* of you is on this canvas. Vincent, *this* is your masterpiece!"

At daybreak, the squatty man arrives again, assuming a different persona, no longer the fawning admirer and inquiring examiner; today, he has bravado.

Hey, I recognize that blank canvas! From Paris, Figure 30, the exact size, same linen and primed with a single layer of lead white, just like Moi. Theo would send these canvases from his colorman in Paris. An old blank canvas. *How did you find that?*

Watching him prepare his palette, squeezing old tubes of paint onto his painter's palette, I am transfixed. Transported. *You have all my Master's oils!* Zinc white. Emerald green. Viridian. Sienna. Chrome yellow and orange. Vermillion, red lead. Red ochre and bone black. All the blues are here too: cobalt and Prussian blue, even ultramarine, usually too expensive for Theo to send. Curiously, the palette contains no eosin red. It is a fugitive color fading with time, and I have none. *You know that, too? Who are you? And what do you want with Moi?*

Donning a painter's smock, he straightens, trying to stand taller and flexes his flabby, stubby arms. I laugh. *Are you trying to acquire the courage to paint Moi?*

No hesitation. Brushstrokes, strong and thick. Sometimes painting straight from the tube with little mixing. Clutching four or five brushes at a time.

He hums Wagner.

Painting deliberately, intensely, focused like my master, he paints all day. Concentrating on the image of Marie, I see his eyes sparkle; the gleam is disconcerting. I have seen that look before, and it always unnerves me.

The light is gone. He is done. Smug, arms folded across his chest, jowls upturned, he surveys his creation with pride.

From an envelope, he removes a handkerchief and holds it delicately in front of his painting. *What are you doing?* Simultaneously, he shakes the cloth and blows a breath across the wet canvas. It is like fairy dust. I smell a whiff of lavender and olive and cypress, pollen fragrances like perfume, taking me home, to my Provence.

He turns the painting around. I can see myself. We are face-to-face.

I am beautiful!

He signs the painting—*Vincent.*

CHAPTER 22

13 July 2003
Maussane Les Alpilles
Provence, France

Marcel Conte jimmied the lock and popped the door. The small house smelled of lavender and urine; he stifled a sneeze. A streetlight and table lamp penetrated the dark, and he could see a wheelchair in one corner and a baby grand piano in another. Pill bottles were aligned on a tabletop with an assortment of photographs in tarnished frames. Porcelain figurines dotted all about, watched him, following him with their painted eyes. One room was emitting soft snores. He crept closer.

There she is! Make this quick.

Entering her bedroom, he felt a surge of power. She looked like a ghost, her white hair tumbling across her pillow and her ancient but smooth face translucent with purplish veins spidering like a road map. Grabbing a pillow with both hands, he held it just above her face and watched her as her eyelids fluttered in a dream.

What are you dreaming about? A cherished pet? A secret lover from your youth?

A nightmare?

Her eyes flew open.

He silenced her scream with a pillow. "Hush!" he whispered.

Smashing the pillow over her face and pushing with powerful hands, he smothered her.

Securing her twisting head, his grip tightened. Her flailing legs kicked off blankets. Her hands scratched at him. He thrust harder, snarling curses at her.

When she stopped thrashing and fell limp, he hugged her to his chest, squeezing the last remnant of air from her lungs, an exhaled long squeal, like slowly closing a squeaky door. Dead, he pulled her arms and legs under the blankets, tucking her in. Tenderly, he brushed her hair away from her face and closed her bulging eyes.

Sleep well, Grand-maman.

CHAPTER 23

July 24, 2003
Camp 4
Yosemite National Park

"Feet. Feet. Feet. Think with your feet. Put your left foot high on that lip and get a toe on it," said Kiki from the base of a massive granite boulder.

"I can't do it!"

"Not with that attitude. Move to your right. Shake it out."

Julie rested, dangling one arm then the other, trying to return strength and blood flow to her hands. The first day of her vacation, and she was more gripped than when running CODE BLUE.

"This is the Kor Problem—the test piece. If you can climb this, the rest of Yosemite is a piece of cake. But you gotta go. You can't hang out."

Reaching into her chalk bag hanging off her butt, she dusted each sweaty hand and crimped her fingers on a granite nubbin as her other hand searched the stone like a blind person reading braille.

"Stop scratching and clawing this poor boulder. That's it. Nice move. You're getting it. Okay, now here's the crux."

Strands of black hair escaping her ponytail were plastered to her sweaty neck, and her bangs stuck to her forehead. Her tank top clung to her torso, back muscles taut, and her legs began a sewing machine tremor as she readied herself. Licking her lips, huffing breaths, she focused.

"This is a dynamic sequence," Kiki called to her. "You must move without stopping. First, put both hands together on the same flake high above your head. Then pull yourself up while placing your right foot on that knob and power up, reaching for a big jug with your left hand. You can't see the jug, but it is there. Julie, look at me… Trust me. It is there."

Julie looked down at Kiki. He was standing in the last sunbeam hitting the valley floor as afternoon cumulus gathered. He looked strong. Ready. *I trust you. Like a precious friend.*

Their friendship was special. A friendship forged by bonds of shared trauma. It could have been more than friendship; it could have been a relationship, like a stack of Jenga blocks, each block a dinner date and movie, picnics, study hall footsie under the table, day hikes, bluebird ski days, popcorn on the couch with old movies (they both loved Hitchcock). When she first met him in college, she dismissed Kiki as a boyishly handsome ski bum, climbing bum, wasting his parents' money at school. She had turned him down four times when he'd asked her out, and almost reported him to Campus Security. Worse, they were paired together for a biology assignment, and when he did not complete his part of the project (*I've been busy, putting up a new route in American Fork Canyon*), Julie got her only B grade that semester, ruining her perfect 4.0. *I'm still mad at you.*

But when she needed help, when things got crazy and dangerous, he saved her. Rescued her. And took her on an unplanned trip to Washington, DC. It was not a breezy, itinerary-free, two-lane highway, feet out the windows, wind in the hair, road tunes, open container, car camping, hot springs, road trip. This was what they called their *The Road* trip after Cormac McCarthy's apocalyptic novel of a father and his son traversing a dying Earth and dodging human cannibals. It was meant to be a joke between them, but it was not funny, and they never talked about it.

On that trip, Kiki got arrested. Busted by the FBI. But that is a whole other story. *Maybe I'll write a book about it someday,* she had told herself.

"Trust me," Kiki called again.

I trust you… with my life… not my heart.

"Will you catch me if I fall?"

"I got you. I'm right here. Now go. Go! Go!"

Lunging… Stretching… Flying… Every part of her committing to this move, fingers poised to clinch, her feet kicking in mid-air, she whiffed. Catching nothing, granite shredding her palms, she fell backwards, peeling off the boulder. Kiki caught her. Cradling her breathless body, her eyes flashing, her hair covering her flushed face, she looked like a wild child.

"Damn, I almost had it!"

Kiki did not release her. Wiggling to free herself, he held her tighter. Brushing hair out of her eyes, he gazed at her. Their eyes met. He brought her mouth to his and kissed her… hard. Julie, twisting her face away, struggled free of his arms and brushed herself off. Wiping his kiss from her lips with the back of her hand, she stood, stunned, hands on hips.

"What the hell was that?" she barked.

He did not answer. Instead, turning Julie around, he reached into her chalk bag, clapping his hands together with a loud SMACK, engulfing them in a white puffy cloud. Leaping onto the block of granite, he climbed swiftly with power and grace. Flying to the hidden handhold, he caught it and dangled freely with one arm. After crunching ten one-arm pullups, he dropped to the ground next to Julie, opened his water bottle, drank it down, and walked away.

Camp 4, the climber's camp recently saved from the bulldozer, was settling down for the night. Colorful tents like a multi-hued hobbit hobo encampment nestled together in darkening woods of tamarack and ponderosa. A shirtless boy, his body twisting and arms flailing in a genuflecting ballet, navigated a slackline stretched taut between tree trunks. Muggy air, fragrant of pine and wildflowers, clung to Julie as a thunderstorm brewed. *The air feels like lotion.* But she was not soothed. *Kiki, where are you?*

Darkness insinuated itself between the tall trees, and the moon peeking from behind Half Dome was gobbled by a dark cloud. Julie sat alone. Other climbers huddling around picnic tables with wine bottles and candles flickering in their faces, recounted climbs of the day and planned climbs for tomorrow. Laughter broke out. Climbing gear jangled—an off-tune ding of carabiners, chocks, cams, hexes, and pitons. Thunder rolling into Yosemite from the Sierra high country sent her into the tent: a four-season North Face VE 25, veteran of Kiki's Alaska ascents. She took off her clothes. Lay down on her sleeping bag. Reading *All the Pretty Horses,* by headlamp, she put it down, realizing she had read five pages and recalled none of it. Her mind was elsewhere. Her thoughts on Kiki.

He tried to kiss me! We're friends. Not girlfriend and boyfriend. What's he doing? What does he want?

But she knew what he wanted. The kiss was not a surprise. Although the venue certainly was.

Their friendship had been deepening. Always attractive to her, Kiki had a confidence, an easy charm, and an engaging smile. No longer a college boy, his face had earned lines from river rafting and mountain climbing. Now, when he smiled, all those wrinkles were recruited into his smile, genuine and warm. *Not just buddies anymore. He makes me feel special.* Kiki had been laying out his case, *"I've changed,"* he told her. And he had. Progressing from adrenaline-fueled, Red Bull-sponsored outdoor athlete to a nine-to-fiver. The Director of the University's Adaptive Sports Program, he was charged with teaching handicapped people outdoor sports like skiing, fishing, and kayaking. *"I got a 401k, health insurance, and two weeks paid vacation,"* he'd proudly told her.

And now spending his valuable vacation time with me. But I hurt his feelings. Kiki, I'm sorry. Where are you?

Kiki swirled an ice cube tinkling in a glass of Wild Turkey. The Yosemite Valley Lodge had a small rustic bar, and he sat on a stool looking at nothing.

Stupid. Trying to kiss her. She needs a romantic dinner, not a gritty granite boulder. And somebody else, not me. It's gotta stop. She's been driving me crazy since college. "'Let's be friends. Can't we just be friends?" she says. I don't need another friend. I can't do this. Let it go. Let her go. After this trip, it's adios, *Julie Tolle.* Vaya con Dios.

"Fuck it!" he said out loud.

A man sat on the stool next to him and ordered a beer, introducing himself as Philippe, a French climber. "Kershaw Kenyon," said Kiki, and he wiped chalk off his hand to shake with the man. They chatted about climbing, the Frenchman about the Alps, and Kiki of Yosemite. And Kiki gave him the beta on his favorite climbs in The Valley. After the second round of drinks, Kiki told him of his grandfather climbing here in Yosemite in the 70s, "My grandpa returned from Vietnam a misfit 'Baby Killer' and found a home here in Yosemite. He fell into a group of rock climbers putting up some of the hardest routes on El Capitan."

"The Stonemasters? Jim Bridwell?"

"Yes! You know? They were a group of bad ass climbers, true hard dicks, taking over from Royal Robbins and Yvon Chouinard. My grandpa told me that nothing in Vietnam was scarier than being roped in with Jim Bridwell when 'The

Bird' was tripping on LSD on the high pitches of El Cap. He later admitted the Asshole Bandit, a punji stick booby-trap laid by the Viet Cong, 'totally scared shit out of me.'"

Excited to find out both their grandfathers had served in Vietnam, Kiki's with the US Army, 1968, and Phillipe's with the French Foreign Legion at Dien Bien Phu, 1954, they toasted to their "*Grand-père.*"

"Cheers!"

"À la *vŏtre!*"

Philippe asked, "Girlfriend?"

"Let's have another drink," answered Kiki. "A friend who happens to be a girl." And added, "Unfortunately."

"Meaning what? She is not your lover?"

"No. More like a thorn in my side."

"*Oui.* A thorn in your heart."

"*Oui.*"

When Julie switched off her headlamp, a bolt of lightning flashed far away, and she counted, "one thousand one, one thousand two, one thousand three, one thousand four, one thousand five," before thunder rumbled down the canyon. *Lightning will hit the high cliffs and not down here, right?* Lying in her sleeping bag in the I-can't-see-my-hand-in-front-of-my-face blackness, she thought about bears. This was her first time at Camp 4, and the rangers told her that bears were pilfering food from campsites, "Last night they stole a bag of Cheetos and a package of Oreos." And she knew what all Girl Scouts know—"bears attack girls on their periods."

Also, a serial killer was loose in Yosemite, abducting women and slitting their throats with a hunting knife. *But that was two years ago. He's in San Quentin heading for the gas chamber. Isn't he?*

Her thoughts circled back to Kiki. *He tried to kiss me? Am I leading him on? He'll want to get married and have kids. It's all I can do to come home late and microwave Cup Noodles. Best I keep Kiki in the "friend zone"?* Her thoughts shifted. *And what about Johann? He thinks he loves me!*

Fat drops of rain splattering the tent with an intermittent *Dap… Dap… Dap…* that, with a windburst, became a loud staccato of a torrential downpour. Shuffling steps approached the tent and stopped. *A bear?*

A long screech startled her as the tent door zipper opened. Kiki piled in, flopping clumsily on top of his sleeping bag.

"We're climbing GIVE PEACE A DANCE tomorrow," he announced, pulling off wet clothes and adding, "One of my grandpa's first ascents."

"Where have you been? Are you okay?"

"I've been at Yosemite Valley Lodge. Grandma met my grandpa there. She'd say, 'I was a waitress, and he was always hungry.'" Kiki added, "I've been chillin' at the bar."

"Who with?"

"Talkin' to a French guy. Philippe. He climbs in the Alps. Trad. Old school."

"Have you been drinking? You don't drink."

"I don't have to drink to have fun, but why take the chance?"

Julie chuckled.

Kiki undulated pupae-like into his mummy bag and lay face to face with Julie. She could smell alcohol on his breath. She asked, "Can I ask you a question?"

"No."

"You kissed me."

"That's not a question." He answered, "It was impromptu. Impulsive. Impestuousness. Is that a word? You wiped it off, so it doesn't count. Anyway, I ain't gonna apologize."

"I get it. I'm a girl and you're a boy. Apology accepted."

"You know, you really aggravate me."

"Aggravation accepted."

A flash of lightning and one thousand one—BOOM, followed by a microburst, shook their dome tent. They cuddled closer.

"Can I ask you another question?"

"No."

"Why climb your grandfather's old routes?"

"I'd rather talk about kissing you."

"Sorry, that topic is now off limits."

"I'm connected to him; more than just sharing his name, we share a soul, and when I feel that connection slipping, I can renew those memories and recall those lessons. He is with me on every pitch. I place my hands and feet where he did."

"What lessons?" Julie pressed him, never knowing Kiki to be this talkative. Loose. Tipsy.

"How to shake another man's hand and look 'em in the eye. How to tell the truth. When to throw a punch. Other stuff too. Stalk a bull elk. Cast a dry fly. Shoot an arrow.

Dutch oven cooking, frame a house. I'm building a log cabin for us. Swedish cope design. Logs from Canada. A bedroom loft and a Norwegian soapstone fireplace, it radiates heat all night. Ten acres on a spring creek in Wyoming. Native trout…"

Us?

Julie interrupted, "I met your grandfather. Remember?"

"I do. He picked us up when we came down from hiking Grandeur Peak, and my car wouldn't start. He drove you back to campus in his Ford F350 dually. He always asked about you—'how's that Brainiac Babe?'"

"I always wanted to have a grandpa like him. A little rough and a lotta love."

"You follow in footsteps, too. You climbed the Lagginhorn. The same route as your dad."

Julie did not answer, collating a mixture of emotions with memories and thoughts. A sifter, sorting through images.

"He sent me on that trip. His wishes. But he knew I would discover things about him and our family and about myself. A grand design or scheme of some kind. But Kiki, everything with my father is fresh and confusing. I'm still angry and sad. I can't figure it out. He died of an insulin overdose. How can that happen? He was organized, meticulous. Sometimes I wonder if he did it on purpose. An intentional overdose. Killed himself. He left me with questions and no answers."

Julie could not forget Lech Balzec's parting shots, *"Your father's death was not an accident. He was murdered."*

"Murdered," the word felt like a cancer in her brain, and

she could not let it grow and metastasize, a malignancy she kept sequestered. *But what if… Then who? And why?*

"You romanticize your grandfather for good reason. All I do is cry and feel lost. I could have been a better daughter. Taken better care of him."

Wind from the crest of the Sierra Nevada, down from Tuolumne Meadows, funneling into the valley, shook their sturdy tent. Thunder rolled closer. Julie stifled a little sniffle and another and another. A tear rolled down her cheek. She snuggled into Kiki, and he kissed her forehead. Put his warm lips to her temple. A kiss on her cheek and a salty tear. He whispered, "Don't cry."

Julie turned, raising her mouth to meet his lips. First kisses. Tenuous kisses. Warm ones. Tender ones. Each kiss exploring, seeking purchase in the other's heart, kisses tasting of sweet whiskey and minty Carmex. Each kiss bolder than the last. Each kiss pushing a new boundary. Testing limits of what passion would allow. Kisses not knowing when to stop or where to end. Julie didn't care where these kisses would lead. Lost in a new way on a path she did not know. And surprised—*not scary at all.*

Julie kissed him with an open mouth, a never-ending kiss that left them both breathless. Kiki panting said, "What the hell was that?" She kissed him again.

Lightning flashed overhead, and for a moment, Julie saw a longing and a need in Kiki that warmed her, and she let herself be pulled into his strong arms and nestled into his muscled body.

Kiki whispered, "I love you…"

With the storm filling Yosemite Valley and thunder and lightning chasing, from Half Dome to El Capitan to Glacier Point to Washington Column and echoing into Royal Arches, Kiki kissed her with the full passion she'd awakened.

All night, the storm raged on, sometimes it quelled, quieted as clouds paused, gathered, and intensified only to storm and rage again. Finally spent, the thunder passed into the night, tumbling down from the High Sierra and spilling out of Yosemite Valley and over foothills with distant rumbles and roars.

CHAPTER 24

Marcel Conte waited at the base of the climb. GIVE PEACE A DANCE was secluded, tucked high, and far away from other popular climbs. *Perfect! An accident waiting to happen.* Reading from the climbing guide, "Three pitches of 5.7 and 5.8. Thin hand cracks, a narrow chimney to an exposed summit. An overhanging rappel. First ascent—Kershaw Kenyon & Jim Bridwell, 1971." Kiki had described the climb, parlayed the beta, and his plans to climb it last night in the Lodge Bar. Conte bought the drinks, and Kiki told him stories. Looking up at the towering granite and stroking his new goatee, he worried about the weather. *Another storm is gathering.* He cursed when he checked his Tag Heuer. *Americans—always late. A nation of interbreeding mongrels. The Melting Pot. Negroes. Jews. Slant eyes and Hispanics. More like a fetid ragout.*

He tied his climbing shoes and cinched his pack, wishing it held his Beretta 9mm auto. But the new airport security made traveling with weapons difficult. *My Beretta would make quick work of this. Damn Muslims, all of them terrorists. They are responsible for the new airport security. Now French and American soldiers are dying in Afghanistan.* Recalling his service with Commandos Marine, France's equivalent to US Navy Seals, and his covert assassinations of Negro politicians in Algeria and Congo, he muttered, "I've killed my share."

He thought about Julie Tolle. *I can see why Johann is infatuated with her. Kershaw Kenyon, too.* He had first seen her photographs the night he killed her father. While Jacob Tolle fell unconscious after Marcel hit him in the head, Conte administered a lethal dose of insulin. Checking out photographs of Julie playing lacrosse, prom, hiking, and graduation. *A young beauty.* He also remembered Jacob Tolle's slow death, flaccid pale body on the kitchen floor, gasping at ever-increasing intervals, and just when *this has to be his last gasp,* another shallow inspiration and an even longer pause until the next gurgle.

And now she is prettier than the French and Italian starlets that older brother Kurt tramps around with. Johann, beguiled and bewitched by an American Jew Bitch. Sorry, Johann, all that ends today. And all because of a painting? Of another Jewess? He shook his head. Checked his watch.

She will not recognize me. Only a passing glance on the arête of the Lagginhorn, he thought, scratching at his new black goatee.

Conte looked to the sky; he knew mountain weather and how afternoon storms build quickly, catching climbers unprepared. He checked his watch again. *Maybe their plans have changed, and they are rutting in their tent all morning?*

He heard boots scraping on rocks and laughter.

They're coming!

He readied himself.

Pulling from his pack a rope and donning a climbing harness, sling racked with climbing gear, he prepared to free solo the climb, just starting out at the moment of their arrival. But this was his ruse. A plan to climb *with* them and not ahead of them. All he needed was their invitation.

"*Bonjour*," he said, giving them his friendliest smile.

"Philippe, this is a surprise," Kiki said. Behind his Julbo sunglasses, Conte watched both of them scrutinize him head to toe, from his knit hat to his Mammut rope, Millet pack, and Scarpa shoes. "You are climbing solo?"

"*Oui.* When you told me of this climb last night, I just had to give it a, how do you say it? A shot. A go. You inspired me with stories of your *grandpere* and Jim Bridwell. But I worry about afternoon storms."

"If it rains, this climb will be like slithering up the sides of a wet, moldy shower stall," warned Kiki.

Conte watched as Kiki and Julie conferred, exchanging looks between them and glances back at him. He overheard, "An accident waiting to happen," and "Search and Rescue."

"Phillipe, rope in with us. Climb with us."

"Perhaps you are right. 'No old bold climbers' and I hope to be climbing my Alps as an elderly pensioner."

Kiki said, "Okay, then. This climb has three long pitches and a big, airy rappel. I will lead. Julie, you are in the middle, and Phillipe, you are in the rear."

Don't order me around, shithead.

As Kiki stepped into his climbing harness, racking it with carabiners and slings, chocks, quickdraws, and cams, he said to Julie's worried look, "Relax. It's a dance."

"Belay on."

"Climbing."

Kiki wedged his hands inside a dark crack, moved his foot onto a flake, and pulled himself upward. Moving fast and confident, he placed protection and clipped the rope into it.

"He is very good, smooth and strong," Conte said as he played out lengths of rope through his belay ring and chatted her up. She told him she was a doctor doing heart research. "Wonderful. The heart. So much more than just a pump. How do you know each other?"

"Friends from college."

"Are you his girlfriend?"

Julie's cheeks rose crimson red. "That's personal."

"Oh, but of course. Excuse *moi.*"

Conte could feel her eyes upon him and sensed her unease, guarded. Perhaps recalling a father's words of, "*don't play with strangers.*"

Julie asked, "You look familiar to me. Have we met somewhere? Maybe in France last summer?"

"Belay on!" Kiki's echo from somewhere up high fell upon them.

"Your turn, doctor."

"Climbing," she called with both hands cupping her mouth.

"Wait!" said the Frenchman, turning her around, yanking hard on her harness, cinching it deep into her crotch, doubling it safely back through the buckle, and reefing on the figure-8 knot. "I would not want you to get hurt, my young doctor."

CHAPTER 25

On the last pitch of GIVE PEACE A DANCE, the granite smelled different; gone was the gritty smell of hot summer, now it was cool, mossy, and Julie caught a whiff of the Pacific and a zing of charged ozone.

Don't look down. Don't look down. Don't look down. Julie looked down. Way below in a dizzying swirl, ponderosa pine trees looked like shrubbery, massive boulders like broken marbles, and Phillipe, a muscular rodent.

Concentrate. Concentrate. Concentrate. But she couldn't. It amazed her how rock climbing always took total concentration, but now on this climb, other thoughts crept in.

I kissed Kiki last night. Big mistake. So much for the "Friend Zone." What happens now? Can I keep it just friends? And Johann Imseng is still sending me love letters. This is so confusing. Should I tell Kiki about him? He needs to know. But he gets so jealous.

Clinging to rock with sweaty hands and a tenuous toe-hold, her leg beginning the sewing machine tremor, she told herself, *focus!* The next handhold was a chickenhead of protruding granite, a cluster of quartz crystals and feldspar—a long reach. There was nothing for her feet, just blank, smooth rock. Gripped. Frozen. Hugging the cliff, she did not want to move.

Don't look down. Concentrate. Action conquers fear.

Stretching for the chickenhead, her fingers found it, crimped it. With just a slight move, her foot buttered off the toehold, and she slipped.

"FALLING!"

Snatching her, the rope caught her, held her, and she felt a steady pull—Kiki.

Just before the summit boulder, she stopped to gather herself, wiping away a tear with a chalky hand, smearing her face with snot, Cherry Lip Smacker SPF 15, and streaky mascara. *Really, you wore mascara today?*

"You made it!" said Kiki.

She stood on the airy summit buffeted by gusts of wind, hair whipping about her messy face, and before she could say anything, she caught her breath, drank from her water bottle, and gathered her thoughts.

"We need to talk. Kiki, I have something to tell you…"

"I have something to *show* you," Kiki interrupted, talking above the howl of wind, "I found this! It's a Lost Arrow piton from grandpa's first ascent. He left it. I wiggled it free. Yvon Chouinard himself made this. It's still sharp. A good luck charm for you." And he clipped the knife-like piton into her harness.

"Kiki, there is something I need to tell you. There is someone else…"

Marcel Conte's paw slapped at the summit boulder, and he pulled himself up, bracing against a blast of wind. "*J'hal-lucine!* Look at this storm!" Spit from ominous black clouds, lightning struck a peak above Tioga Pass. The temperature dropped. Wind tore at the climbers. A zap of electricity buzzed from the metal of their climbing gear.

Kiki efficiently set up the rappel anchor. "We gotta motor."

Conte unclipped from the rope. Off belay, he crept to the edge and peered down to the base of the climb 400 meters below. Julie watched him and called, "Be careful."

"*Oui. Oui.*"

Conte dug from his pack a canary-yellow parka, and Julie watched him pull it over his head, then zip it up to his bearded chin. She startled. Shuddered. A cold shot of adrenaline. A thump to her chest. A stab in her gut. Flashing to an image from the Lagginhorn, she saw a climber in a canary-yellow parka looking like a stubby banana. The Banana Man calling—"Johann Schnell! Schnell!"

Conte? Marcel Conte! A coincidence? What a coincidence!

Then she remembered what Lech Balzec told her, *"There are no coincidences. None."*

Conte's eyes met hers. Julie expressed recognition, shock, and surprise. His eyes narrowed, and nostrils flared.

"What! You?" she yelled at him.

Conte glared. A menacing snarl, curled lip.

He charged her. A bullrush. Shoving her. Flinging Julie off the cliff.

Flying. Screaming. Somersaulting, she careened into empty air. Blind for a split second, she felt her body in a slow twist, a weightless tumble past jagged rock. In a headlong plunge, Julie saw the ground rushing towards her. A jolt snapped her. The rope caught her, smashing her into the cliff face with a grunting *WHUMPFF.* Dangling, dazed, and breathless, she twirled in an abyss of an approaching storm.

CHAPTER 26

Same Day, July 25

Tuolumne Meadows

Yosemite National Park

Twisting in slow circles, hail began pelting her, sharp stings of BBs hitting her face and hands, icy pellets jumping, bouncing off everything all around her like she was miniaturized and in a popcorn maker in a movie theater, this one cold and frigid. In a dizzying kaleidoscope, Julie could see Kiki hanging directly above her, their rope snagged on a shrubby, gnarled pine. Tied together, he had been pulled off the summit, too. Looking down, trees and boulders swirled in a nauseating vertigo. When a stone pinged off an outcrop, zipping past her head, she looked up to see Kiki climbing down to her. He settled on a narrow ledge just to her left.

"He pushed me! He's trying to kill me!" she cried.

Kiki did not answer and reached out, trying to pull her over to his ledge.

"Swing over here."

Swinging back and forth like a pendulum, she got closer to Kiki's outstretched hand. Adding a kick off the rockface, they touched fingertips.

"Come on! One more swing. You got this."

Like a metronome toppled by a frustrated piano student, her motion stopped. Conte was down-climbing and trying to free up their stuck rope. Julie could feel herself slipping with each knot he unsnarled. With a last kick, she swung to Kiki, and he caught her, clutching her to him as the rope whipped past them with a whistling *WHOOSH*.

"You're hurt," she said; Kiki's arm dangling, flapping like a broken wing—a bird fallen from the nest.

"My shoulder's out."

With a clattering shower of rocks, Conte came at them.

"He's coming!"

An angry hornet, he lit on their ledge; the size of a pool table, stripped of its felt, now slick slate dusted with hail.

Hitting Kiki in the face with a stone-wielding fist, Kiki could not fend off the blows. Landing with sickening thuds, each punch struck with ferocity. Julie jumped on Conte's back, but he shrugged her off and kicked her in the stomach, doubling her over, leaving her gasping for air and retching.

Writhing into a ball, she watched Kiki knocked to his knees and then pounded into the ledge. Astride him, Conte delivered blow after blow, pummeling Kiki with fists and elbows. Blood splattered the hail. Kiki seemed unconscious. Conte wrapped his arm around Kiki's neck in a chokehold, winching, reefing tighter and tighter. Julie could see Kiki's face, eyes glazed and bulging, mouth gaping. She screamed, but no sound came out.

Julie stood up. Staggering to Conte and unclipping the Lost Arrow piton, she raised it high above her head. With all her strength, she struck, plunging it deep into Conte's back. Like a bowstring stretched by a powerful archer, he stood impaled, roaring into the hailstorm and wobbling at the precipice.

Kiki regained consciousness, rolled onto his side, and delivered a kick to Conte's knee with a crushing pop. He buckled, stumbling off the ledge. Falling, he grabbed the lip, holding the edge firm, legs flailing, kicking in empty air.

"Help me! Doctor, please! Help me!"

Julie watched him. He was frantic. Wild. Kneeling to him, his pleading eyes searching hers, he whispered, "Doctor. Please. Help me!"

"Here, take my hand," she offered.

As Marcel Conte lunged for her hand, Julie snatched hers away.

He fell. Backwards, arms and legs in circles, screaming until he thudded on the ground. Bouncing, his body lay wracked, splayed, twisted, obscene.

After a slow, treacherous downclimb on slickened rock, they lit on the ground, exhausted and overcome with relief. The storm was passing, congregating up in the mountains, and left hailstones sprinkled on the green ground. Hurting, adrenaline tapped, Kiki sat under a ponderosa, his back against the mighty tree. Julie put his shoulder back in place; she'd done this with him once before. "Sorry, Kiki, we have no pain medication this time." He almost passed out. She fashioned a sling out of 2-inch nylon webbing.

She left him groaning and clammy to find Marcel Conte's body—a glimpse of a bloody yellow parka. Having seen victims of multiple trauma, examining them, resuscitating them, their skulls crushed, jagged bones protruding from open wounds, she steeled herself. Searching, she found nothing. *Nothing? Gone? Wait! What's that?* Tossed into pine needles, she spotted it—the Lost Arrow piton dripping with bright red blood and shredded muscle.

CHAPTER 27

Same Day, July 25

High Sierras

Tioga Pass

Kiki drove the Toyota truck not back down to Yosemite Valley but up to the crest of the Sierras into the dark storm.

"Kiki, where are we going?"

"The hell away from here!"

Shoulder in a sling, deftly using his knee to steer, he shifted through gears, driving fast on wet asphalt. Windshield wipers unable to keep pace with the deluge, he squinted into the foggy rain clouds. His truck hydroplaned.

"Look out!" Julie screamed. A Dodge Ram 4x4 almost side-swiped them, the driver honking and flipping them the finger. "Are you okay? Let me look at you." His left eye was swollen shut, and the other just a narrow slit. "Oh, Jesus. Pull over. You can't drive."

Swerving into a parking lot, the truck skidded to a stop, the headlights illuminating a sign:

TIOGA PASS
ELEVATION 9945 Feet

Kiki shut down the truck, and the Toyota exhaled an exhausted wheeze. Wired, on edge, they exchanged places, Kiki collapsing into the passenger seat. They sat there, windows fogging, wind rocking the truck, and rain pelting the cabin with a tinny rat-a-tat.

"Who is that man? Where did he come from? Why did he try to kill you?" Kiki flooded Julie with questions.

"I don't know."

"You don't know? What do you mean, you don't know!" Kiki screamed at her, shaking the bloody piton in her face. "What's happening? What the hell, Julie!"

"I don't know what's happening," she screamed back.

They sat in silence.

Julie finally said, "It's a long story. I only know fragments. And may have it all wrong."

"Tell me."

"My father laid claim many years ago to a painting stolen from his family when the Nazis invaded France. He was the rightful heir. He's gone. So it falls to me. Now I'm the only heir. It's supposed to belong to me."

"You?" Kiki raised his eyebrows, his eyes purplish slits. "Don't stop. Keep going."

"The family that has the painting wants to keep it."

"They would kill to keep it?"

Julie did not answer. A blast of wind rocked the truck. *Could Johann do this?* She recalled his attachment and reverence for the painting, *like blood running through my veins.*

"It must be worth a lot of money," Kiki probed.

"It's priceless.

"A masterpiece?"

"It's a Van Gogh," and she repeated what Lech Balzec told her, "The master's masterpiece."

"Start the truck. We gotta get out of here. To the police. There's an FBI office in San Francisco."

"No police, Kiki. No FBI. I have to think this through. I gotta figure this out. Kiki, I looked all over for a dead body in a yellow parka, and all I found was the piton and some blood. His name is Marcel Conte, and he works for the family that owns the painting. What happened to him? Where is he?"

Kiki thought for a moment and said, "My first bow hunt with my grandpa, I shot a bull elk not in the heart and lungs but in the guts. We trailed it for two days. When we finally found it in a stand of thick timber, it was dead. Meat rotten and half-eaten by coyotes and magpies. Julie, look at me. The guy is dead. Dead. Cadaver dogs could find him next spring." They agreed to the rudiments of a plan. No police, and "We gotta find Lech Balzec."

When Julie started the truck, pushing her foot on the accelerator, the Toyota lurched forward, a series of leaps, sputtering and stalling out, more like a porpoise and not a truck.

"Push in the clutch. It's the pedal to the left."

"I know where it is. I'm not stupid."

Grinding the shifter into first gear and simultaneously releasing the clutch, the truck again jumped, bucking onto the highway. It stopped, stood idling, huffing, awaiting proper commands as an old horse would do with a neophyte rider.

"Kiki, there is something you should know about me."

"You're full of secrets."

"I can't drive a stick shift."

Staying in third gear and riding the brakes until they smoked, Julie drove down the steep backside of the Sierra Nevada from Tioga Pass to Lee Vining, telling Kiki about the painting. About how Van Gogh gave her family the portrait and how the Nazi's stole it and lost it. And how Lech Balzec came to her, searching for the painting and wanting to file a lawsuit on behalf of her father's estate. *Should I tell him about the Imsengs and Johann?*

"All this is going on around me. I feel like a marionette hanging off to the side while the real players are pulling strings and dancing all about. And I am so sorry I got you into this mess. And now you're hurt, and it's my fault."

She rehearsed how to tell Kiki about Johann: *Kiki, I met someone last summer in Switzerland. A guy. He's involved in this, too. It's his family that has the painting. Kiki, he likes me.* When she turned to tell him, Kiki was holding his shoulder, eyes just slits of purplish contusions, and lips fat and split. *It can wait.*

A sign:

Lee Vining

Pop. 187

A mining camp that should have blown away in the Dust Bowl, scratching an existence as a tourist wayside on the shore of dying Mono Lake, desiccated by water diversion, the slurping sounds coming all the way from thirsty LA. The town (with numbered streets all the way to 3, four motels, an RV park, Gas & Groceries, and tufa) had the smell of brine shrimp riding the wind of dust devils.

They stopped at the Shell station.

A diesel Chevy Silverado with a hay bale and Queensland blue heeler in back, parked ahead with a bumper sticker—Yosemite Sam, six shooters blazing in both hands—*"If God didn't want us to have guns, he wouldn't have given us Trigger Fingers."*

Kiki ordered, "Please, a big bottle of ibuprofen. A liter of Coke. Ice bag. Gas up with premium, cash, not card." And Julie disappeared into the gas station.

Inside, her senses were assaulted: the smell of nacho cheese in a warm vat, shriveling wieners on hot rollers, popcorn, old coffee. Just out of the Yosemite backcountry, she entered a world of snack food, Slushees with colors never seen in nature, tourist trinkets on stand-up twirling displays, and tee shirts caught her eye, "Go Climb a Cactus" with a giant saguaro and "Yo Semite—Go Hike."

Back at the truck, Julie administered four Ibuprofen and a jumbo Coke.

"I'm so lucky to have you," said Kiki as she secured an ice bag around his shoulder and a smaller one he held to his face. His words came out slowly and slurred.

Julie said, "Look at me." She studied his pupils, held up

fingers for him to follow. "I think you're concussed. Let me put your seat down. You need to chill."

I'm the worst luck you can have.

Julie dodged back into the gas station to pee.

On her way out, she grabbed a knock-off Swiss Army Knife, a big fat one made in China, and at the checkout counter, a stack of newspapers, the San Francisco Chronicle.

Big bold print. The headline shocked her.

"Oh my God. No!"

CHAPTER 28

Bob Bagley sat down at his desk, coffee, fresh-squeezed orange juice, a blueberry muffin, and the San Francisco Chronicle ready for his consumption. Excited, he had a special client visiting today and stirred a package of Metamucil into his juice; he took two lithium tablets for bipolar mania and drank it down.

Headlines proclaimed:

FOUND! LOST VAN GOGH

"Not 'LOST'. Stolen!" he shouted out.

He read:

A painting from artist Vincent Van Gogh, only rumored to exist, was discovered in Switzerland. FBI authorities working closely with Interpol announced, "A contested work of art allegedly looted by the Nazis with potential heirs now in the United States has been located and secured. It was found in the collection of a prominent Swiss banker."

Local art historian from SFMOMA, Chelsey Westover, claims, "This Van Gogh has never been documented, never exhibited. Mentioned only in letters Vincent sent to his brother Theo, it is a mystery. Said to be a portrait of a Jewish girl in their family garden, it was painted in 1889 while Van Gogh was in an asylum for the mentally ill. There, Vincent alternated between madness and genius, his creative powers sometimes catching fire. His most iconic work, like Starry Night, is from this era. But this painting is a myth, a fanciful legend. I have my doubts. I'll have to see it to believe it."

A lawsuit was filed in US District Court by local attorney Robert Bagley, an expert in art restitution, representing the family estate. He declined to comment for this article, saying, "This is pending litigation. We have an excellent case. The murderous sins of the past must not be rewarded. Justice will prevail for my client's family regarding everything stolen from them, including the lives of loved ones."

The claimant could not be reached for comment.

A preliminary hearing is set for next week in New York City.

A painting from artist Vincent Van Gogh, only rumored to exist, was discovered in Switzerland.

FBI authorities working closely with Interpol announced, "A contested work of art allegedly looted by the Nazis with potential heirs now in the United States has been located and secured. It was found in the collection of a prominent Swiss banker.

Local art historian from SFMOMA, Chelsey Westover, claims, "This Van Gogh has never been documented, never exhibited. Mentioned only in letters Vincent sent to his brother Theo, it is a mystery. Said to be a portrait of a Jewish girl in their family garden, it was painted in 1889 while Van Gogh was in an asylum for the mentally ill. There, Vincent alternated between madness and genius, his creative powers sometimes catching fire. His most iconic work, like Starry Night, is from this era. But this painting is a myth, a fanciful legend. I have my doubts. I'll have to see it to believe it."

A lawsuit was filed in the US District Court by local attorney Robert Bagley, an expert in art restitution, representing the family estate. He declined to comment for this article, saying, "This is pending litigation. We have an excellent case. The murderous sins of the past must not be rewarded. Justice will prevail for my client's family regarding everything stolen from them, including the lives of loved ones."

The claimant could not be reached for comment.

A preliminary hearing is set for next week in New York City.

Bagley thought, *I love it. First, decline to comment, then let 'em have it.* He then remembered, *My clients. Damn. If I could only find them. Both Lech Balzec and Dr. Tolle are not returning my calls. Where is that girl?*

Elizabeth Taylor sat opposite Bob Bagley. She was seeking his counsel on a totally different Van Gogh painting. Spellbound by the beautiful woman in his office, he failed to listen; instead, he tried puffing out his chest and sucking in his paunch—Pooh Bear, grizzled and ripe in old age.

"My father bought the painting at Sotheby's for $257,000. Now worth millions. It has been hanging in my living room in Bel Air ever since. There are absolutely no ties to the Nazis. The ownership is clear. Those descendants are wrong. It was sold in a straight-up deal. No coercion and not sold under duress. It's mine. Mine!"

Dazzled by the actress sitting in his office, her violet eyes flashing like the impressive diamond on her finger, Bagley's thoughts wandered; *she is far prettier in person than on the movie screen. Be cool. Professional.*

Taylor continued, "*View of the Asylum and Chapel at Saint-Rémy* was painted by Van Gogh in the spring of 1889. His only painting depicting the Asylum and the surrounding fields. He was dead less than a year later. The family claims their grandmother sold it under duress while fleeing the Nazis. But that is not true."

"And that will be our defense," Bob Bagley declared. "Sold, in a 'good-faith' transaction. Not stolen by Hitler.

The claimants have waited far too long, and the statute of limitations expired decades ago."

He continued, "You know, Miss Taylor, my grandparents were victims of the Holocaust. Communists; they were arrested and forced to work in German factories. They did not survive. My hatred runs deep. We must not forget. We must not forget." Agitated, Bagley's bushy eyebrows furrowed, and his nostrils flared with a thicket of nose hair.

Taylor, flashing her diamond ring, the ring Richard Burton bought her, said, "This 33-carat diamond was once owned by the Krupp family, arms makers for Hitler. And now look—it is on the finger of a Jewish girl."

"It fits you well." The diamond sparkled with a deep blue iridescence like Elizabeth Taylor's eyes. Face-to-face with one of the world's most beautiful women, Bob Bagley was lost, mesmerized. Wanting to say something flirtatious, a master of legalese and lawyer jargon, eloquent in the courtroom, he searched for something to say, remembering, *she is currently single.*

A commotion outside his office escalated into shouts, his secretary screaming, "He's busy! You can't go in there!"

The door burst open.

Standing in his doorway, Julie Tolle held this morning's newspaper:

FOUND! LOST VAN GOGH

CHAPTER 29

August 7, 2003
One Week Before Trial
Law Offices of Bagley & Grover
San Francisco, California

"Julie, this is a preliminary hearing, but *everything* is riding on this." Bob Bagley was sitting at his desk, and Julie in a high-back leather chair.

"You know I have a daughter, smart like you. See, I was a good father, doting, happily wrapped around her finger. Dance lessons, violin lessons, just her and me on a Disney Cruise—my most memorable vacation. Best time of my life. But although a good father, I was not a good husband to her mother, and now she holds bitterness like a knife. I reach out and nothing. Ever."

"Keep trying. Don't give up."

"Like a daughter, I will represent you. Fight for you. We do this together. But it won't be a Disney Cruise."

Bagley adjusted the photograph of his daughter, about age six, on his desk and said, "I bet you were a good daughter."

"I could have been better. Taken better care of him. Be there when he needed me."

"Don't feel guilty. We all have regrets, our love enduring somewhere alongside them."

Julie wanted to change the subject. "Was that Elizabeth Taylor?"

"Yes! She is fighting for a Van Gogh, too." He straightened his paisley tie. "I think she likes me. Told me she is 'done with those Hollywood Types'."

Julie saw a glint in his eye, and for a moment she let him have his miniature daydream.

He rallied and said, "Let's get down to brass tacks."

Sharp pointy metal. What does that have to do with anything? She recalled Scrooge's perplexity with Marley being, *"Dead as a door-nail. The deadest piece of iron mongery in the trade."*

"Yours is a difficult case. Barriers that are daunting but not insurmountable. First, we are filing in America. We would have zero chance in French or Swiss courts. *Zero.* They will argue that American courts have no jurisdiction over foreign citizens, and that is true. But... the Imseng Family has business holdings within the U S of A and are indeed subject to our laws. So there. *Gotcha!*

"Second, the Statute of Limitations. It's a law that sets time limits on when a legal claim can be filed, and for-ty-five years is way beyond any conceivable limit. They will argue we have not acted promptly. But... there exists a clause—The Discovery Rule: the time may start when the injury is *first discovered*. That's what we cling to."

Bagley shucked his suit jacket, loosened his tie, eyes widened.

He's getting all fired up.

"If we can get past those hurdles, then we must prove ownership. *Provenance.* It is like a birth certificate for an art piece. The foundation of trust. Where was the painting born? Where has it been? Who has owned it? What is its journey? Collections. Galleries. Exhibitions. Museums. Listen, and a painting will tell you. Sometimes only in whispers.

"And easier for a masterpiece painted in the spring of 1889 than for the Peter Paul Rubens painted in 1617, I recently restituted. But I will articulate a methodical, clear, and convincing argument on your behalf."

Julie quizzed, "But this painting has no gallery stamps, museum marks, or anything."

"We have three lines of evidence:

Vincent's letters to his brother Theo, a photograph of the painting in the home with the Toledanos, and an eyewitness."

"Madame Demolins? But she has dementia," said Julie.

An alarm chimed from his watch. "Excuse me. I must take my medicines. Sometimes I forget." He got up and went to his mini fridge, swilled a bottle of water, and swallowed his pills. He brought back a bottle of Aqua Calistoga for Julie and sat down next to her.

"Madame Demolins, your grandmother's best friend," stated Bagley.

"I met her."

"I know."

"She has advanced Parkinson's and doesn't remember much. I didn't ask her about the Van Gogh. I didn't know about it."

"Ah, but Lech Balzec did! And he interviewed her on videotape. The tape is being translated with English subtitles, archived, and transcribed." She is the only eyewitness. Your father has passed. His big sister…"

"Eloisa. My aunt."

"Your Aunt Eloisa, next to inherit and an eyewitness. But she is lost to The War. Perhaps in a fairytale, she lives on the beach in Majorca."

"That would be nice."

Both took a moment to embrace that fable. Then Bagley bent his bushy eyebrows in sincerity, the opposite of a frown, and looked Julie in the eye.

"Julie, you do not have to proceed with this claim. Cases like this have their own momentum. Like the boulder Sisyphus is pushing up a mountain. It can crush you. In my heart, I know, a great injustice was done to your family. That wound is gaping open. But it may never heal and forever gash you. Maybe never meant to heal and always fester in pain. A pain you must endure so we never forget. Never forget.

"We may not win. Are you willing to lose?

"If we lose, your wounds will have dirt cast into them and rot you from the inside out. I have seen it happen. This is your life, a promising life with a noble career. Are you ready for that?"

"Before you answer, I have subpoenaed both Madame Demolins and Lech Balzec. Their testimony is crucial." Bob Bagley paused, then said, "Madame Demolins died in her sleep last week. She was almost 100 years old."

"Oh no! Oh my god, no. She is so sweet. Like family. That can't be. I should send flowers or something. I wanna cry…"

Bagley pushed a box of tissues in her direction.

"Julie," Bagley put his hand on hers. "Lech Balzec is dead too. Killed in a random street crime per Paris Police. No one has been arrested."

"What! Lech Balzec killed? Oh my God! It's not true. Tell me this is not happening. He can't be dead. He can't be dead. It's a mistake."

Bagley put his arm around her heaving shoulders as she sobbed and said, "This is not a coincidence. Julie, I will keep you safe."

CHAPTER 30

July 2003

Imseng Chalet

Swiss Alps

I am on the move.

Stripped of my solid oak frame crafted just for Moi by Paul Toledano, swaddled in acid-free paper, then linen, and carefully crated, I wait.

Where am I going?

I remember my last trip, traveling in the trunk of Hermann Goering's Mercedes-Benz 770. A long trip from Carinhall to here in the mountains, a gift for Walter Imseng. I was a welcome present, and the Old Man made me feel at home, but I felt more like an orphan taken in by well-to-do strangers. My home is in Provence with the Toledanos.

Walter Imseng is dead. And I feel the loss. Really, I do.

Blind in this dark crate, I wait.

I can hear someone giving orders. But who? It is faint, and I struggle to listen in. Johann? Kurt? I don't trust them.

Kurt is reckless. Johann conniving. Who do I belong to now that the Old Man is dead? What is in his will? Who inherits me? And I fantasize that I hang in the Louvre, my attribution tag: *Bequeathed by Walter Imseng.*

Someone picks me up and jostles me. *Be careful! What are you up to? Where are you taking Moi?*

Kurt, are you selling Moi?

If I am yours, my future with you is a big question mark. Taking me to London, to the auction houses of Christie's or Sotheby's? A rich and famous collector? And I dream of going to America. Or is this one of Kurt's secrets? He owes money to casinos all over Europe. Will I hang in a smoky backroom of the Casino de Monte Carlo? Or banished to an estate of the Saudi Royal Family?

I have no idea what Johann would do with me. He is too shrewd to fathom.

Excited. Nervous. I worry about Julie Tolle. She is my Marie. She is my connection to my master. My only link to my family.

Julie, how will you ever again find Moi?

CHAPTER 31

August 14, 2003
U.S. District Court Lower Manhattan
New York City

B*agley is late.*
Waiting in the empty courtroom, Julie jumped at the crisp snap of opening shiny leather briefcases. Intimidated by the courtroom with its rich wood paneling, black marble columns, and tall judge's bench, she straightened, trying to sit taller. An armed bailiff stared at her. Opposing attorneys, shuffling documents and doodling on legal pads, eyed her too, whispering, scrutinizing, strategizing. Both well-dressed in white blouses, navy blue and gray skirts and jackets, stylish and business-like, ready to do battle. Julie felt more at ease in an overwhelmed Emergency Room with sick patients crashing all around than in this court that had ruled on cases since 1789. Called the "Mother Court," there was nothing maternal about it. Squirming in her chair, she knew the Blind Sheik, responsible for bombing the World

Trade Center and plotting to bomb the UN and FBI, sat in this exact… same… chair.

The judge arrived in a swirl of black satin, and she sat down already with a scowl on her face.

Where's Bagley?

"All rise," called the bailiff.

Julie stood and, looking over her shoulder, saw Bob Bagley bustling into the courtroom in a suit that fit ten years ago before being hunched by osteoporosis and weight gain from his love of food and wine. He looked like some kind of hedgehog-badger and plopped down next to her, his face flushed and wearing strap marks from his ill-fitting, too-tight CPAP mask. He was clean-shaven but had nicked his chin, and a dot of blood clung to the second of his double chin, another tiny dot on his collar. *He needs a haircut, too.* And with a double-take to his eyes, they were bulging and bloodshot. He opened his battered briefcase, and Julie spotted a bottle of lithium used to treat Bipolar Disorder, but without its cap, the pills had spilled all over.

The court clerk called, "In the matter of *Imseng versus Tolle—A Motion to Dismiss.*"

The judge addressed the courtroom, "This is a preliminary hearing. We are here only to decide whether this case has legal merit and can proceed to full trial."

"Your Honor, good morning. This is a motion to dismiss," said the woman attorney standing before the judge. About forty, wearing modest gold jewelry and stylish glasses, she looked competent, adept, with presence to capture an audience. "This litigation is a misguided attempt to appropriate my client's property. The artwork in question, without any doubt, belongs to Kurt Imseng. Its provenance is secure, and his ownership is legal. This action is frivolous and predatory." The attorney walked to the center of the courtroom and continued, "The defendant's claim is based upon letters Vincent Van Gogh wrote his brother Theo over one hundred years ago. Letters he wrote while being hospitalized in an insane asylum. He was mentally ill, unsound, and in the words of his doctor, suffering from 'Mania and Lunacy'. And the defendants are not clearly named in these dubious letters written by a man in the throes of serious mental illness."

Julie remembered the letters. *They are thoughtful, articulate, and heartfelt.*

Bob Bagley stood and said, "Your Honor, these letters are lucid and honest. We submit both letters as evidence. The letters in Van Gogh's own handwriting tell about gifting the painting in his words to repay their kindness. Read them yourself."

The woman attorney continued, "The defendant also proposes that a grainy, unfocused photograph taken over seventy years ago is documentation that this painting is their property. This photograph allegedly depicts the Toledano family in their home with the Van Gogh painting in the hazy background. We can prove that this photograph is not an original; it is a reproduction and declared by our expert, 'prone to all manner of fakery'.

Bob Bagley stood up and said, "Your Honor, we disagree. This photograph will be proven to be authentic and clear in its detail. We submit this photograph as evidence and have our own expert witness who will testify to its authenticity." Then he sat down.

"Objection. Your Honor, Mr. Bagley's interruption of my opening statement is rude and calculated. May I please continue without interruption?"

"Objection noted." The judge nodded, darting a finger and knitting a frown at Bagley.

"The statute of limitations expired decades ago. There is no due diligence in this case. A claimant who fails to exercise her cause of action loses her claim."

"Your Honor, how can my client claim a painting no one knew existed until just recently!"

"Stop interrupting me," the attorney shouted directly at Bob Bagley. "Your Honor, there are absolutely no statutes in place and no precedent to justify this bogus attempt to confiscate my client's property."

"What about the Washington Principles!" yelled Bagley.

The Judge reprimanded, "Mr. Bagley, you will have your turn. Respect the decorum of my courtroom. I will *not* warn you again." To Julie, the judge looked like a terrier, alert, stern with razor-thin lips painted with lipstick, her hair dyed brunette and eyebrows penciled in, and somehow moving independently from each other; she wore an expression of, *don't piss me off.* A face that could soften and warm into a smile at the sight of a new grandbaby—maybe.

"Your Honor, the Washington Principles on Nazi Confiscated Art of 1998 is a consensus of 44 countries and art museums and auction houses. They outline eleven general guidelines for the restitution of Nazi-looted art. These are suggestions. A wish list. The Principles are only advice to countries and their art museums. There is not one legal statute among them. And importantly," she looked directly at Bagley, "they have *no* application to private individuals."

Bob Bagley was flustered, sweating, and loosening his tie.

"In addition, Your Honor, we can prove conclusively that this artwork was *not* stolen but a good-faith transaction. And that is what we have here: a family of foreign citizens, the Imseng family, acting in good faith."

"There is not one shred of good faith on display here!" shouted Bagley.

"I will ignore your ill-mannered insults, Mr. Bagley, and continue. My final argument is the most important," she pronounced, walking closer to the Judge's bench.

"This court has a storied history. Since the birth of our nation, it has ruled on some of America's most important cases without prejudice. It is highly respected for good reason. But… but with all the respect it richly deserves, this court has no jurisdiction over the citizens of Switzerland. None. I cite the ongoing litigation of the *Republic of Austria vs Altman* and the painting, *Lady in Gold* by Gustave Klimt.

"Your Honor, the country of Switzerland has its own set of laws; fair laws, crafted and enacted over centuries. We ask you to dismiss this ill-conceived action. It has no merit, and you have no jurisdiction. Thank you."

Oh my God. We are in trouble, Julie thought.

Bob Bagley rose by pushing off Julie's shoulder. He straightened his wide tie and extended his hands out of his ill-fitting suit as he approached the bench.

"We contest everything that has been said, Your Honor. This court should reject the Imseng family's attempt to portray this case as something other than it is—a straightforward cause to recover property from someone who wrongfully possesses and refuses to return it.

"The horrors of the Holocaust have not passed, have not been addressed, and are not forgotten. For the Toledano family, the Holocaust meant the loss of home, livelihood, and valuable property. Then… their murder. The continued wrongful possession of this painting and their denial of its true ownership, Your Honor, is the final indignity to the Toledano family." He turned, nodding to the opposing attorneys and sat down.

That's it? Julie wanted to jab a sharp elbow into his ribs. *We're sunk. Get up there and say more!*

The courtroom door swung open, and Johann Imseng entered.

Julie turned and saw Johann sit down behind her. Like when she was a kid at the top of Sky Rush, the colossal roller coaster, all the blood left her face, and, lightheaded, she sank into her chair, gripping the armrests. She could sense his warm breath on the back of her neck. The attorneys continued to argue, but Julie only heard fragments as her recurring nightmare of thoughts re-entered her mind, thoughts she tried to keep at bay. *Is Johann behind all of this? Is he a monster? What happened to Marcel Conte? Where is he?*

"Again, Your Honor, we urge you to dismiss," the woman attorney continued to plead her case. "The statute of limitations has long expired. There is a failure of due diligence. And—"

Bagley interrupted, "How can my client pursue an action she did not know she had? This painting was stolen and then hidden!"

"We can prove my client legally procured this artwork in good faith. Your Honor, the Imseng family has a long history of charitable endeavors, including serving as chairman of the International Red Cross during World War II. Now they sit on the board of the World Health Organization, UNICEF, and the International Monetary Fund. The unfortunate events that befell the Toledano family cannot be righted by this misguided lawsuit. My clients are not Nazis—"

"They are worse than Nazis!" screamed Bagley, pounding the table. "Unfortunate events? You portray this as a case of bad luck? Whoops? Sorry? These people conspired with Hitler. Financed Hitler. Made fortunes from Nazi atrocities. The Swiss Red Cross during the War was a cruel joke; blood brothers to the Gestapo. The Imseng family has no creed except that of pure evil greed."

"Objection!" shrilled the woman attorney. "Your Honor, we will not tolerate the slanderous lies spewed by Mr. Bagley. Shut this man up!"

"I am warning you, Mr. Bagley. Your behavior is unprofessional. Control yourself. You are close to being in contempt of this court," admonished the Judge.

"I will not be silenced." Approaching the bench, face flushed, jugular veins popping, a fist clenched, his words came in a frothy spittle. "If you dismiss this case, victims of the greatest crime against humanity will be muzzled, their cries extinguished. Don't close your eyes. Don't close your ears."

"This is not a war crimes trial, Mr. Bagley," proclaimed the Judge. This is *not Nuremberg*. I warned you." The judge rapped her gavel, turned to the bailiff, and ordered, "Mr. Bagley is in contempt of the U.S. District Court of Lower Manhattan. Cite him."

Julie watched her attorney unravel, a spinning top wobbling off the table. *Something's wrong with him. Did he forget his lithium? He's off his meds. My attorney is losing it. I need to help him.*

"Contempt? Contempt? You label me with your pissant word. My hatred for this proceeding and my despicable opponent far exceeds mere contempt." The bailiff took his arm, and he and Julie helped sit him down in his chair, Bagley saying, "Never forget! Never forget!"

The courtroom took a breath. The bailiff stood behind him.

Bob Bagley whispered in Julie's ear, "We're losing." Unwound, he tried to compose himself. Drinking a glass of water with a shaky hand. Shuffling files inside his briefcase. Scribbling on his legal pad.

Bagley finally rose and said, "Your honor, excuse my forthright behavior. We have an eyewitness who can testify to seeing the painting in the Toledano family home. An eyewitness who will accurately place the painting in their home as a treasured possession. She saw the Van Gogh painting on many occasions in my client's ancestral home. Her name is Madame Demolins. Let me tell you about her."

"Objection. Your Honor, we cannot depose this witness."

"Overruled. Continue, Mr. Bagley."

"Madame Demolins is nearly 100 years old and was a dear family friend and neighbor. The children's piano teacher. We have a video deposition taken by Lech Balzec, a well-respected researcher in finding Nazi-looted art and its restitution—"

"Objection, Your Honor!" The opposing attorney leaped from her chair. "This video is not admissible evidence. We are aware of this video. What it shows is an elderly woman with Parkinson's dementia vaguely recalling history from forty years ago. Your Honor, Lech Balzec is not an attorney; he has no relationship to any court. He is a privateer who, in his retirement from the Israeli Secret Service, profits from finding Nazi loot. The video is not a deposition; the witness is never sworn in, and it is entirely in French. And importantly, we cannot cross-examine this witness."

Bob Bagley said, "We acknowledge the limitations of this evidence, but it is important to the truth of this case. The truth will become clear if we hear from all who can express it. Is it not crucial to hear from an eyewitness? We request the court admit this video as evidence."

"We cannot cross-examine these witnesses," said the woman attorney. "Madame Demolins passed away in her sleep recently. And your Honor, Mr. Balzec was killed; a casualty of street crime per the Paris Police."

Julie turned around and looked at Johann Imseng with disbelief and loathing.

"Both my star witnesses dead, killed," shouted Bagley.

"I want both counsels in my chambers *now,*" called the Judge.

Bob Bagley extricated his arm from Julie's clutch.

"Please don't leave me alone," she pleaded. He left her alone. Alone, with Johann Imseng.

CHAPTER 32

Same Day
U.S. District Court Of Lower Manhattan
New York City

Julie heard footsteps approaching as she sat, eyes forward, staring at the judge's empty bench. Johann sat on the edge of the defendant's table, and she glanced up at him in his tailored suit, now wearing glasses. She was seething.

"Hello," he said in his accent. She did not reply. "Hello?" She ignored him.

He moved in front of her and knelt in front of her face. "Julie?"

"I have nothing to say to you." A torrent of emotions ran through like flash flooding in a desert arroyo.

"I was hoping we could work together."

"What kind of monster are you?"

"I am not a monster. I'm just a man."

"People I love are dead because of you." Julie caved. Ever since Lech Balzec told her, "Your father did not die by accident. He was murdered," she had built a wall around that idea. Cloistered in disbelief. Imprisoned by doubt. Incredulous. *Murdered?*

"I can explain. Let me explain."

"Marcel Conte tried to kill me!"

"Conte. Where is he, by the way?"

"I don't know where he is. Rotting in hell, I hope. I should've gone to the FBI with all of this. Everything you say is lies. All lies." Tears welled in her eyes. "You said you *love* me."

Johann took a deep breath. "The sins of the father are not those of the son. My family wields enormous power…"

"And greed."

"And greed," he conceded. "But now I am in charge. Chairman and CEO."

"Oh yes, I forgot, *The Wunderkind.*"

"I am charting a new direction. I know what is right and what is wrong. I don't need judges and lawyers to tell me." He sighed, caught Julie's gaze, and said, "I want to offer you an apology. An apology from my family to yours."

"My family is dead, Johann. Murdered."

"I know," Johann said in a whisper. He took her hand, and she gave it to him. Johann's hand felt safe and warm, and she thought about how she had snatched her hand away from a pleading, lunging Marcel Conte. Julie wiped away a tear.

"Look at me." She looked. "I have loved you from the first time I saw you. The painting? It is the most beautiful painting in the world. But Julie, it is not mine. My grandfather gave Kurt the painting. My brother Kurt inherited it."

Julie looked at Johann but could offer no words.

"Kurt is behind *all* of this. I know the painting is yours. I will make this right. Trust me." He took both her hands and said, "I do not want your painting, Julie Tolle. I want your heart."

<hr>

"All rise," the bailiff called as the attorneys and the judge reentered the courtroom. Bob Bagley looked angry, a simmering pot ready to boil over, unhinged. When he sat, Julie put her hand on his arm with a calming gesture, and she could feel he was tense, twitchy. *We lost. What should I do?* Part of her wanted to talk to the judge herself.

The judge spoke, "Let me make this perfectly clear." Her expression had changed from *don't piss me off,* to, *you have really pissed me off.* "I will not let this hearing go off the rails. This is not a circus. This is not a war crimes trial—"

Bagley shouted, "No. This should be a murder trial! My two most important witnesses dead within a few days of each other?" Red-faced and jowls wobbling, he pointed a shaking finger at the attorneys and accused, "This is not a coincidence!"

The two opposing attorneys looked at each other and sat silently.

"Mr. Bagley, control your outbursts. Your case is unraveling with each tirade."

"I will make my case, Your Honor, as I see fit."

"Not in *my* court."

"If I am unable to make my case in this court, then I will

present all the damning facts to the people. To the media. I will seek reparations in the billions from the Imseng family bank. I will bring a class action lawsuit on behalf of Holocaust life insurance beneficiaries cheated out of their rightful claims. I will leave the Imseng family tarnished forever. And cripple their bank into default. They won't be able to make change for a ten-dollar bill!"

The opposing attorneys conferred in whispers.

"Speak up," the judge told them.

"Your Honor, we again request dismissal of this claim. This case has devolved into libelous accusations, bizarre threats, and no evidence."

The judge pronounced, "The ruling of this court, U.S. District Court of Lower Manhattan in the matter of Imseng vs Tolle: Motion to Dismiss." She looked at each person in the courtroom, and her eyes landed on Julie. "The motion to dismiss is denied. Dr. Tolle, you may proceed with your legal action."

Then her scrutiny fell on Bob Bagley. "But not with Mr. Bagley as your counsel." Addressing him directly, she said, "Mr. Bagley, you are not fulfilling your duties to this court. You are not adequately representing your client. You are unprofessional in your conduct. Your antics and behavior leave me no choice but to recuse you from this case. Bailiff, escort him, please."

The attorneys for the Imseng family asked to approach the bench and confer with the Judge. Julie watched their discussion, sitting alone without representation; she tried to listen in.

The judge spoke to her, "Dr. Tolle, the Imseng family would like to meet with you tomorrow morning in my chambers. A proposal for a resolution of this case. If you agree, then meet with me in my chambers at 9:00 am."

Numbed, perplexed, Julie nodded.

"Is that a yes?"

"Yes, Your Honor."

CHAPTER 33

Same Day

Battery Park, Manhattan

Julie walked home. Evening rush hour was fading. Taxis and taillights. The law firm had put her up in a sailing yacht moored in Battery Park Yacht Club just eight blocks from the courthouse. "Tight security provided only to the rich and famous," Bagley said. The yacht owner was a life-long friend of Bob Bagley, a classmate at boarding school and Columbia. Both accomplished sailors. This would be her second night on the yacht that JFK and Jackie had piloted around Hyannis.

On her walk to Battery Park, her thoughts were racing. She worried about Bob Bagley. Her diagnosis: acute mania. *How will I find a new attorney? Why is Johann here? Brother Kurt inherited the painting? He is behind all of this? Brother Kurt, international jet-setting playboy. The "effete man whore" as Johann called him.*

Dread crept inside of her like the cold fog that was

trickling upstreet from the Hudson River. The fog, not wafting kelp, barnacles, and mussels like the Oregon coast, but an industrial chemical odor, strangely sweet. Julie walked past remnants of the World Trade Center. A memorial was being erected, and floral arrangements in varying stages of decay and rot were scattered around. A fresh bouquet of spring flowers caught her eye, making her wince at the pain someone was feeling, a wound that would never heal. She caught a whiff of burnt jet fuel. Looking up, she saw a ghost on fire careening out of the sky. She hurried along, looking over her shoulder.

When she got to Battery Park on the shore of the Hudson River, a ferry boat disappeared into the fog rolling upstream. Colder and darker, city lights flickered on.

At the guard shack of the yacht club, she rapped hard on the window to get the guard's attention from whatever engrossing website he was immersed in, and he unlocked the gate. At the far end of the dock, she unlocked another gate to enter the slip where the boat was moored. The *Fitz, a 52*-foot sailboat, "safe for a president," is what Bagley told her, sat proudly with a slow, almost imperceptible rocking.

Showering off the layers of sweat from the courtroom and hustling down canyons of gritty city streets, Julie let the day roll away in the steamy teak bathroom. Donning a hoodie, she sat cocooned in the cozy cabin with a hot cup of Constant Comment tea and helped herself to a tin of Walker's Shortbread cookies. Ferry boats were blowing their deep bassoon foghorns, and the city lights cast an eerie glow across the Hudson River. She thought about Kiki somewhere on the Colorado River, *guiding in the middle of the Grand Canyon on your oar-rigged rubber raft. Kiki, you should see my boat. Wish you were here. Always safe with you.*

She thought about Johann. *Why are you here? What is your part in all of this? My night on your boat… You were right, the stars were amazing. We kissed each other—oh my. The Fitz is bigger than your boat.*

Shifting from one guy to the other, her mind played a pro vs con trick with her. Life with Johann would be privileged. He offered her work with UNICEF or WHO. She could run the winery on Lake Geneva. Live in London? Sail to French Polynesia?

Where would a life with Kiki find me? Continuing my heart research or a family practice clinic in Steamboat Springs or Jackson Hole? Running rivers, skiing powder, raising a raucous gaggle of kids?

When her head started bobbing with sleepiness, she crawled into bed. Now, among her diagnoses, her therapist added, psychophysiological insomnia—mind racing and thought rumination. When her head hit the pillow, her head spun. *Did JFK make love to Jackie in this same bed? Or with Marilyn Monroe?* She said a prayer for Bob Bagley. A prayer for Kiki running dangerous Chrystal Rapids in the Grand Canyon.

At two in the morning, it was her heart keeping her awake, tugging, aching. She turned on her phone. She knew where her heart lived, where the promise of her future brightened, where her world was warm and safe. Proud to be on his arm. Excited to be in his embrace. With her laptop in bed, Julie composed an email: *Dear Kiki,*

I have been falling in love with you forever, I just never knew it. Falling for the boy and now the man you have become. Hold me. Love me. I'm yours. Will you be mine?

Julie

She hit the *SEND* button. *NOT SENT. NO SERVICE.*

In her last fragment of wakefulness Johann's voice, *"Julie, I don't want your painting. I want your heart."* And… *"Marcel Conte. Where is he, by the way?"*

Gently rocking and creaking the boat lulled her into sleep.

CHAPTER 34

Marcel Conte grimaced and stifled a groan, slithering upon the yacht. Using both hands, he lifted his injured leg over the gunwale. Zipping down his wetsuit, pain shot through his back, radiating into his leg as he wiggled, extricating his broken body out of the skin-tight neoprene. His healing vertebral and rib fractures jabbed him, and the festering stab wound in between his shoulder blades felt like a hot poker.

He unsheathed his dive knife.

Enshrouded in night fog, he crept along the gunwale thinking, *This is my last assignment. I will never follow anyone's orders ever again. Orders and commands my whole life. French Army and Special Ops. The Imseng Family. No more. Never again. But this time it's personal—the Jew Bitch. Rape her. Kill her.*

Julie woke up feeling a shadow cross the porthole. A shiver, she pulled the covers up to her chin and listened. *A creak? Footsteps? Did I lock the transom hatch?* She looked at her cellphone—3:25 am. Abandoning the tug of her warm bed, she pulled on her hoodie sweatshirt and tiptoed out of the sleeping cabin into the main galley. She checked the transom.

Oh good. It's locked.

As she turned to crawl back into bed, the hatch shuddered. A tug on the hatch from the outside.

Oh my God. Someone is trying to get in!

Silently, she found a fillet knife and stood shaking at the bottom of the ladder. The hatch rubbed, grinding as it was being tested, twisted, and pulled. Then silence. The lap of waves. A distant foghorn. Her heartbeat. Wind through her pursed lips, breathing. A faint wheeze at the end of expiration.

Gone?

Gone?

Suddenly, pounding fists and kicking feet pummeled the hatch. Banging, thrusts, and grunts. Curses. Made of thick teak, it was built to keep out a stormy ocean.

"I am here for you, my doctor. No place for you to run. No place for you to hide."

Marcel Conte!

Flooding with adrenaline, she grabbed her cellphone and punched in 911. *NO SERVICE.* Then one bar flickered.

Then *NO SERVICE*. Standing silently in the dark cabin, she hoped he could not detect her, worried her pounding heart would give her away.

Inside her chest, her airways tightened. Throat closed off. She could not breathe. Coughing erupted from deep within her lungs. She tried to cover her mouth. Coughing and wheezing doubled her over. *I need my inhaler!*

"Get out of here! The police are on their way," she shouted, but it came out as a breathless babble.

"No, they're not."

"What do you want?"

"I want my revenge. Sweet vengeance."

Oh my God. "Who sent you?"

"I have my orders."

"Kurt or Johann?"

"You claim a painting that is *not* yours."

She thought about giving up her claim. Canceling her case. *You can have it. I don't want it. Go away. Leave me alone.* But she could not utter those words. Too many lives lost. Too much injustice. *Fight for it.*

"It *is* mine. My family."

"Ugh, your family," he spoke through the hatch. "Dirty Jews with a priceless painting. That must not happen. Your father was the first to die. Oh, yes. I killed him. A sweet death. That bump on his head? Not from a fall but from my club. Knocked unconscious, I injected him with his own insulin—a triple dose. He never woke up. His brain, starving to death for sugar. A slumber. A dreamy death. Not like yours."

Julie slumped to the cabin floor. She could not believe what she was hearing and remembered what Lech Balzec said, *"Julie, your father was killed. Murdered."*

NO SERVICE lit up on her cellphone, but she dialed 911 anyway.

"Go away! Leave me alone. I beg you. Please."

"You beg me? You beg *me*! When I pleaded for your help, clinging to a cliff. Your hand? You pulled it away. You let me fall. Left me to die. Crawling in the mountains for days. And now, my doctor, I live with a body wracked with pain. Pain! Forever constant pain. I will have my revenge! Vengeance is all I think about."

Hammering at the wooden hatch began with something metal. Thud after thud. It did not splinter. It did not budge. Pounding and cursing, he could not break in.

Julie powered on the marine radio, and it lit up with colored LEDs and a warm buzz, Channel 16 illuminated. She called into the microphone, **"MAYDAY, MAYDAY, MAYDAY, 911, SAILBOAT FITZ MARINA, MAYDAY, MAYDAY!"** and repeated over and over.

Pilfering the cabin, she started collecting: fire extinguisher, baton flashlight, box of Drāno Kitchen Granules, and opened an emergency kit containing a strobe light, foghorn, and flare gun. She piled them onto the table. She found her inhaler and took two hits.

Radio static filled the cabin.

He's gone?

Footsteps padded above her head. *He's still here…*

The radio crackled, *Fitz. This is the US Coast Guard*

Cutter Sailfish. What is your emergency? What is your location? How many persons on board? Over.

Before she could answer, the plexiglass ceiling hatch caved in, shattering with a screech. A long gaff hook swung wildly into the cabin and caught Julie across her scalp, tearing out a chunk of hair. *Swoosh*, she ducked another swing. Dodging other swipes, the sharp hook raked through the cabin seeking to sink into her flesh. Catching her hoodie, Conte yanked her towards the skylight hatch.

Fitz. What is your emergency? Over...

Sticking his head through the jagged plexiglass, Conte looked at her. Upside down. Maniacal. Evil.

Reaching for the radio mic, she screamed as Conte grabbed a fistful of hair and, along with the gaff hook snagged into her hoodie, he started pulling her out of the ceiling hatch. A powerful tow tugging her through the splintered plexiglass. Stretching, her fingertips found the tabletop, and she snatched the Drāno granules.

Conte and Julie were face to face, his teeth broken, his breath vile.

She threw a handful of Drāno at him.

Screaming, Conte recoiled, leaping out of the hatch. Julie landed flat on her back, all the air knocked from her, and she lay there, gasping, hungry for air, with the boat rocking with Conte's jumping and shrieking.

Gathering herself and a weapon, she unlocked the transom and slinked outside, peeking. There he was—standing at the bow, tearing at his eyeballs.

Julie approached, "Johann or Kurt?"

"It's Kurt! It's Kurt! Johann thinks he loves you. Help me! My eyes are on fire!"

"Burn in Hell," she whispered.

Julie loaded the flare gun with a cartridge, aimed at Conte, and pulled the trigger. The flare exploded into his abdomen. White-hot phosphorus ignited, burning furiously. Conte tumbled into the water, writhing as the flare disemboweled him, searing his guts from the inside out.

Julie watched the glowing body float into the foggy river, bright white and ghostly, then sputtering, flickering on and off, then it vanished.

Fitz. What is the nature of your emergency? Over.

CHAPTER 35

When Julie called Bob Bagley's cellphone, a nurse from the Psychiatric Unit of Columbia Presbyterian Hospital answered and refused to let Julie talk to him. "He's medicated and sleeping. He has not slept for days," she said.

The sun was rising, a pink grey over the skyscrapers of Manhattan, and fog was clinging to the water when she got on deck. Looking for a floating charred body, she saw bits of styrofoam and a dead seagull wrapped in fishing line. The sailboat was the same, stoic, except for the hammered teak hatch and the broken plexiglass ceiling hatch, a clump of her hair dangling from one shard, and she touched her tender scalp. *Clean all this up? Leave it as a crime scene? Yellow police tape all over the dock? A body? Marcel Conte, a burned-out shell of a man, eviscerated, incinerated. Good luck finding him.*

Walking to the Courthouse, all these thoughts came in a jumble, a random flight of ideas.

She thought about going to the police. *But Balzec said, "No police." But he's dead.* And running through her brain was a story, The Story. She tried rehearsing it. It sounded crazy. *Where would I start? Vincent Van Gogh 1889? The Nazis and World War II? Or "I just killed a man." And to whom? Flag down a patrol car? Is there a precinct station around here? Walk into the FBI Headquarters? I know Special Agent Franklin Hill.* She could hear him say, "Why'd you not come to me first? What's wrong with you?"

Just as her thoughts flipped to the agony on Marcel Conte's face, the smell of phosphorous and burning bowels, she rounded the street corner, and the huge monolithic courthouse smacked her in the face.

Just like on an on-call night in the hospital and leaving a Code Blue after an hour of resuscitation, the talk with the grieving family in shock, in tears, left devastated, and then on to the next patient and the next, she compartmentalized. *I'll do this first. Then to the FBI.*

At the courthouse, she rode the elevator to the 21st floor, gathering herself, composing herself, and when she stepped out, there he was. Silhouetted. Johann Imseng stood at the far end of the hall, tall and trim in his suit, looking out the big window.

She lost it.

Steps breaking into a full-on sprint, Julie rushed him. Her push in the back flattened his face into the glass. When he turned around, Julie hit him in the face and continued to punch him until he corralled her flailing arms.

"Let me go!" she started screaming. Two bailiffs arrived, pulling them apart and restraining her.

"Stop it. That's enough," they said.

Escorted to the judge's chamber, the judge said, "What the hell is going on here?" Both Julie and Johann were flustered and sweaty. A welt rising on his cheek, he tucked in his dress shirt and straightened his tie. The bailiffs stood behind them, unruly schoolmates marshaled in after a playground scuffle.

"What's this all about?" asked the judge, inspecting them.

Julie did not answer. She didn't know where to start.

When there was no answer, the judge asked a simpler question, "How is Mr. Bagley?"

"He's in the psych unit at Columbia Presbyterian," Julie answered tersely.

"I am sorry to hear that. He was first in his class in law school. Shortlisted for the California Supreme Court. I hope he gets better." With a scowl, she said, "Are you two going to behave? Can I dismiss the bailiffs?" She motioned for them to leave and told them, "Thank you."

"Sit," she said. "We are here to explore the possibility of a resolution to the ownership of the Van Gogh painting. I'm willing to mediate. I have seen a photograph of the painting and admit I am touched by it and feel a duty to find it a proper home and ownership. The Imseng family is open to negotiating."

"Julie, I have a proposal," Johann said.

"Before we get to that, I need to address the realities.

Julie, you have no counsel, and Mr. Imseng has a whole legal team at his disposal. Nothing we decide here is irrevocable. This is a non-binding mediation. You both have legitimate claims to this painting, worth a fortune, and in a court of law, one of you will win, and one of you will lose. It will take years and money."

Julie thought to herself, *And there is someone not at this table. Someone who has no voice—the Van Gogh painting. You are here, my friend. Here in my heart.*

"I also need an answer to a personal question. There is more to this case than what has been presented. And now you have a fistfight?" said the judge. "What is the relationship between you two?"

"We don't have a *relationship*," said Julie.

"Friends," said Johann. "Maybe more. Hopefully more."

"More? More what! More lies?" yelled Julie.

"Let me explain," said Johann. "We met in my hometown in Switzerland. Hiking and sailing. We have a connection." He paused and looked at Julie. "And… a misunderstanding."

"A misunderstanding? Oh my God. A misunderstanding!" said Julie.

"Your honor, let me continue." Johann got on his knees in front of Julie and looked her in her eyes. "The painting is yours. Julie, the painting belongs to you. I want *you* to have it."

Fuming, Julie had her arms folded across her chest.

The judge raised her painted eyebrows with skepticism.

"My family to you. Restitution. I don't need lawyers and courts to tell me what to do. Nothing can right these wrongs. It's only a gesture. But Julie, it is heartfelt." Johann put his hand on his own heart.

Johann stood and took both Julie's hands in his. "I have a proposal. You and I together gift the painting. Donate it. A historic gift. We cross this chasm together. Building a bridge from the horrors of the past to a brighter future. Let beauty light the darkness. Heal scars. Right wrongs. Imagine the delight in the eyes of young people as they experience the magic of an afternoon your grandmother spent in her garden with Vincent Van Gogh. Let that moment shine for all to see."

"I need some clarification," the judge interrupted. "Your older brother, Kurt Imseng, is listed as the sole heir to the painting. I have it right here: the Last Will and Testament of Walter Imseng clearly designates: '*The eldest grandson…*' The court will need—"

"My brother died yesterday. A car crash. A steep mountain road."

"I'm so sorry. My condolences," offered the judge.

"We were not close."

Julie sat stunned. *Kurt dead? An accident? Not an accident. No coincidences. Did Johann do this? And what about Conte?* Her hands in his, Julie wanted to believe, she wanted to trust.

"Julie, let's do this together. You and I. We donate the painting together. Our gift to the world. What do you say?"

CHAPTER 36

September 2003
Metropolitan Museum Of Art
New York City

"**J**ust as the *Mona Lisa* anchors the entire Louvre, your gift will be The Met's beacon to the world," Alain Ulrich proclaimed, standing at the head of the boardroom. The curator buzzed like a plucked guitar string dipped in espresso, a blank screen behind him. Julie looked at him dressed in a black sports jacket with a light grey T-shirt underneath, rectangular black-rimmed glasses, *his forehead is so tall it could be used as a gallery space.* He had become her friend, gushing professionally all over her, like the drug reps at her hospital trying to sell her on the latest, most expensive medications. She looked at the other three gathered around the table, interesting strangers: art historian Grace Varga from Yale. Wilson Brockbank, an art conservation scientist from the Smithsonian. Tobler Eckhart from the Rijks Museum in Amsterdam is an expert, *The Expert*, on Vincent Van Gogh.

He was dressed in tweed and a scarf, graying blond hair combed longish and covering his hearing aids.

Also in the room, Van Gogh's painting now finally with a proper title bestowed by default by the experts in this room—*Girl in Garden with Flowers*. The painting stood on an easel, covered, draped in black nylon. Julie felt its presence. She noticed the others did too. Like an unexpected guest celebrity, watching silently. But for Julie, the painting had a pull, a force of nature, a magnetic draw, gravity.

Alain Ulrich continued, addressing Julie directly, "Dr. Tolle, your donation has astonished the art world. Forgoing a lengthy legal battle with an uncertain outcome, your generous gift, along with the Imseng family, is a staggering achievement. Indeed, the legalities of recovering a looted masterpiece are stacked in favor of the current owners. Countries and their museums have rigged the system and have the financial resources to protect what they believe is rightfully theirs."

"True. True," chimed Tobler Eckhart. "A museum in St. Petersburg recently told a family, 'We will torch the painting before giving it back.'"

"Mr. Imseng is unfortunately unable to attend. He gave us authorization to proceed," said Ulrich.

Julie was conflicted; one part of her was relieved Johann was not there, the other side dressed in a nice blouse and pleated skirt, new shoes, and forgoing Lip Smacker SPF 15 for Crushed Rose Lancôme.

"We are here to discuss the authenticity of our newest acquisition. A masterpiece has been found, and the whole world awaits." All eyes turned to the shrouded painting at Ulrich's shoulder. "We are tasked with establishing the provenance and attribution of this masterpiece. Simply put, where did it come from? Where has it been? Who owns it? And who painted it?"

At the mention of, "Who painted it?" Julie saw a nervous squirm from Dr. Brockbank, the Smithsonian scientist.

"This is a presentation of rigorous research and a thorough investigation. We plan to exceed the Washington Principles that governed art ownership from 1935 to 1945. Dr. Varga, you are first."

The art historian was an elegant, 60ish woman, not the bookish librarian Julie expected. She stood next to the shrouded painting, wearing a wool navy blue dress, white cashmere sweater over her shoulders, silver necklace, matching earrings, and ladies' Rolex, giving off a stylish aura, perhaps a Vogue model as a young woman.

"Vincent Van Gogh painted this painting in the summer of 1889. Probably the last painting before he fell into a deep psychosis. Painting this masterpiece may very well have undone the man. First slide, please."

The big screen illuminated with an image of the painting. An image of a young woman holding a wooden wheelbarrow brimming with flowers. Olive trees and the Alpilles rose dark blue in the background with a swirling sky of afternoon cumulus. The colors were stunning—the unmistakable palette of Vincent Van Gogh depicting a summer's day in Provence. The room fell silent. Everyone began staring at Julie and back and forth from her to the young woman on the screen. Pulling a wayward strand of hair behind an ear, she blushed.

"The resemblance is amazing. Uncanny," said Tobler Eckhart. "Remarkable how beauty from one generation can travel to the next."

"DNA," said Dr. Brockbank, matter-of-factly.

"Next…"

The blank expanse of the back of the canvas, the verso, appeared.

"Art historians rely on labels, stamps, and handwritten notations to guide the provenance. What gallery was the piece purchased from? At auction? Dates? On the verso of this painting, there are none. Nada. No clues to be found here," said Varga. "Next…"

On the screen, a handwritten letter from Vincent to his younger brother Theo, one sentence highlighted.

"Letter to Theo dated July 1889. He describes the setting, the scene, and the model, then writes, '*Today I gave the painting to her father…*' This is clear evidence that the Toledano family were the original owners." She let that notion sink in for dramatic effect. "Next…

A black and white photograph filled the screen. "A portrait of the Toledano family circa 1939. This is an original and not a reproduction. Not a copy, as some have insinuated. The painting is seen in the background, clear in its detail."

"The Smithsonian concurs," added Wilson Brockbank. "Not a copy."

Julie stared at her family as the art historian addressed

her directly, unemotionally droning, "We see your grandparents, your aunt Eloisa as a young woman, and your father Jacob as a little boy. They are seated, dressed formally in their Sunday best. The painting stays with your family until..." Varga paused, looking around the room, then said, "1942. The Vichy regime governing the Unoccupied Zone of France are puppets to their Nazi overlords. The Vichy Police arrest husband and wife and imprison them at Drancy Internment Camp, north of Paris. And on to Auschwitz, where they perished."

"Murdered," corrected Julie, and she remembered what the old librarian, righting headstones in the cemetery, told her.

"Murdered," Grace Varga repeated. "Your father, Jacob, escapes the Nazis by traveling to Marseilles, then to Lisbon, then here to New York City, and is taken in by a family living on the Upper West Side. As a remarkable footnote, your father traveled on the same boat as Marc Chagall and his wife, Bella."

"He was eight years old," said Julie, looking at him in the photograph, determined, serious, brave even as a little boy. "He grew up in New York City, not far from here, and loved this museum. He would spend every Saturday here and wanted to be an Egyptologist and work at the museum."

Julie continued, "When the Imseng family and I came to an agreement about donating the painting, they wanted to donate it to the Louvre. But I insisted, I was adamant, a deal breaker—and with another round of mediation, we gifted it to the Met."

"We owe a great debt to you and your father," said Ulrich.

The art historian rubbed her temples. "Now we come to our problem. A big problem. Eloisa Toledano, your aunt. The teenage girl in this family photograph."

All eyes in the room looked at the image of Eloisa. A pretty face. A teenager's smirky smile, framed in wavy black hair. Wearing her finest dress. Engaging. Haunting.

"Eloisa is next in line to inherit this painting. But she is lost to history. We have no records that she survived the war. She vanishes. A ghost."

"The 'English Sister'. My father's nickname for Eloisa, because she went to boarding school in England. What do you think happened to her?"

"A young woman alone, caught up in a world at war? My mind races to all sorts of conclusions. From the horrors of concentration camps to heroism in the French Resistance. But she is nowhere to be found. And if she is still alive, then she does *not* want to be found. Believe me, I have looked *everywhere*," said Varga.

"My father was sure his sister died in the war."

"I am not so sure. She may still be alive somewhere. Next…"

"Wait! Can I have a moment?" Julie watched the distinct faces of her family; they were all looking directly at her, expectant, calling to her. *My family, I am all that is left.* They blurred as her eyes filled with tears. "Next," she said.

Her family disappeared, and another photo flashed on the screen. A black and white of German soldiers in a tall, long lobby with numerous framed artworks.

"Then our Van Gogh arrives at the Jeu de Paume, a grand palatial structure built by Napoleon in the heart of Paris. Here, the Germans warehoused riches stolen from across western Europe."

Julie's mind traveled to the steps of the Jeu de Paume, fighting with the thief, spitting on her and screaming, *"Putain!"*, and she muttered, "I've seen that building." She looked to the painting. *We've been traveling the same path, you and I. Paris. Swiss Alps. Even your little hospital room in Provence. And now, finally, here together.*

"Next…"

A black and white picture of a mousy woman, her hair pulled back into a bun, wearing small, round glasses and a plain woolen scarf.

"Who's that?" asked Julie.

"Madame Rose Vallard. An art curator from the Louvre. An assistant to the Germans, she was the only Frenchwoman allowed inside the Jeu de Paume to help with their larceny. A complicit traitor? No. She is a spy! Unbeknownst to them, she is fluent in German. She sees and hears everything. Don't let her 'Plain Jane' appearance fool you; she is a lion. Alone and in great peril, she secretly catalogued hundreds of masterpieces. Recording where they arrive from and who they departed with."

An image of French, hand-scribbled in tiny lettering, appeared, translated:

*Arrived—18 August 1942. Provence. Van Gogh—
Girl with wheelbarrow and flowers*

Then another image:

*Departure—30 August 1942. Berlin. Van Gogh—
Girl with wheelbarrow and flowers*

Selected—H. Goering

"We know the date of each of Hermann Goering's visits to the Jeu de Paume. He personally selects artwork. Some of which he shows to his friend Adolf Hitler for his planned Führer Museum in his hometown of Linz, Austria. Some he keeps for himself. Others he sells. Our painting leaves for Berlin the day after Goering visits.

"But the trail grows cold, lost in the chaos of World War. Is it sold? Burned? Destroyed in Allied bombing? Looted again by conquering hordes of Russians? Maybe Goering keeps it? We have no records, and the painting is never seen again.

"But Julie, your father must have believed the painting was hiding somewhere. And like a miracle, Van Gogh is found in a chalet in the Swiss Alps."

Tobler Eckhart interjected, "Dr. Tolle, when you first saw the painting, what were you thinking? What did you feel?"

Shaking her head and waving him off, she answered, "I'm sorry. I don't have the words, Mr. Eckhart. I fell to my knees."

The art historian continued, "The Imseng family claims ownership. They claim the Van Gogh was sold to them in a good-faith transaction. Yet they produce no bill of sale. A family of fastidious bankers can't find a receipt? A ledger? They only own the painting by possessing it. But possession is a powerful legal entity. Hard to pry loose. As you know, Dr. Tolle.

"Next, I will show you an excerpt from a video recording by Lech Balzec, renowned for his work in art restitution. He was a colleague of sorts," said Grace Varga. "But as I honed my skills with a degree in Library Science, an MFA in Art History, and an Internship at Sotheby's, Lech Balzec acquired his skill set on the battlefields of the Middle East and years with Mossad. We will miss him."

"Wait, I need to back up. Julie, some years ago, we don't know exactly when, your father retained Balzec to find the painting. Your father must have known, somehow, that the painting was hidden. Did he ever talk to you?"

"Dr. Varga, my father was a man of secrets, with a past he never shared with anyone, and he never mentioned the Van Gogh to me."

"Roll the tape," called Varga.

At her kitchen table, Madame Demolins sat while Lech Balzec interviewed her. She told a story about her friendship with Clara Toledano, teaching both Eloisa and Jacob how to play the piano. And she reported seeing the Van Gogh painting on the wall of their home a "hundred times." *Joli tableau*—A pretty picture.

Julie was rapt; this was the conversation she was hoping to have with the old lady.

Varga paused the tape and said, "Often in dementia, only the past is remembered, but with exacting clarity. Roll tape…"

When Balzec questioned the old woman about the Vichy Police and about harboring Jacob, sending him off to Marseille with the Maquis, the Resistance, her tremor intensified. Her agitation built, and her masked facies grew red; a tear welled. And when Lech Balzec asked about Eloisa, the old woman wailed, *"Elle vit! Elle vit!* She lives! She lives!"

The tape ended in a freeze frame with Balzec's hand on Madame's shoulder and her conjuring a faint smile through the pain.

Julie looked at them, engaging in a smile, through a history of tragedy, the human spirit and compassion still flickered. *Both dead. Not a coincidence. Is this painting a curse?*

"Unfortunately, Mr. Balzec does not ask any more about your aunt Eloisa, and she remains an important mystery."

Alain Ulrich said, "Thank you, Dr. Varga, for your diligent research and your hard work." Dismissing any mystery, he concluded, "May Aunt Eloisa rest in peace. Hopefully, she is no longer turning over in her grave."

"Now onto attribution," said the curator. "Who exactly painted this painting? A moot question, I believe."

"Yes. Yes." Tobler Eckhart gave an agreeing nod.

Nervously, the Smithsonian scientist Wilson Brockbank stood. "I may have some bad news. Next slide, please…

CHAPTER 37

Wilson Brockbank stood up alongside the shrouded painting, a bead of sweat across his forehead. The room took a chill. Dressed in a short-sleeved dress shirt, his black tie too short, horn-rimmed glasses, and a buzz haircut, Julie thought he belonged at NASA mission control for the launch of a 70s moonshot; on edge and nervous.

"Wilson, tell us what your research shows," said curator Alain Ulrich, grim and hesitant.

"Let's not start with the painting but with its frame," he said, pulling back an edge of the black nylon to reveal part of the frame, a dark, rich wood. "It's French oak. Handmade with great care. Strong. The nails used are the same found in French fruit crates from the same era."

Tobler Eckhart said, "Julie, your grandfather could have crafted this. I think he made this! Touch it."

The painting pulled her to it, reaching for her, and she rose from the table and touched, then stroked, the frame. The wood was smooth and warm, alive feeling, and Julie felt a glow inside. Brockbank added, "The bottom underside of the frame is roughened owing to its difficult journey." Rubbing her hand underneath, Julie whispered, "Ouch," when a tiny splinter poked her finger.

"Now, onto the canvas," said the Smithsonian scientist. "Next slide, please…"

An enlarged portion of the painting near its border showed threads of fabric incompletely covered by a brushstroke. "The canvas size is Figure 30, made of flax, thread count 11.6 by 17.6. Prepared with a double ground layer of calcium carbonate and lithopone by Tasset & Lhote of Paris. The canvas is not similar to what Van Gogh used while in the Asylum; it is the *same* canvas. *Exactly* the same. Now onto the painting itself."

Julie saw a sliver of glee return to the faces, but more sweat on the scientist's.

"Van Gogh often used an underpainting to guide him. For this work, he sketched with charcoal. It's faster than oil, needing no drying time. Next slide, please …"

A vague image appeared, white and gray and black, rough and spartan.

"This is an infrared photo of what lies beneath. Sometimes we find an entire painting hiding underneath."

Julie squinted at the hidden charcoal draft, incomplete lines of mountains, trees, clouds, and a woman. Ghostly.

"Next slide, please… Grazing light is used to bring out the surface of a painting. A strong beam illuminating at a severe obtuse angle."

The surface detail was cast in shadows, rutted and craggy.

"Oh, my! The unmistakable impasto of Vincent Van Gogh," Eckart said in reverence. To Julie's puzzled expression, he explained, "Impasto is a technique of artists using thick brushstrokes to imitate texture and create three dimensions; they can even be sculptural, adding volume and depth. Vincent uses brushstrokes to impart emotion unlike any other painter, ever."

"And no varnish," added Brockbank. He continued, "We humans see only a narrow spectrum of electromagnetic wavelengths. We can't see long wavelengths like infrared. Or short wavelengths like ultraviolet."

"Like bees," chimed Julie.

"Yes… Bees." Brockbank paused, wiping his face with a handkerchief.

"Next slide, please…" Two images side by side. "UV and infrared can help us see later restorations, repairs, and underdrawings. There are no repairs or restorations."

"Next slide, please…"

"An X-ray," Julie said, looking at the familiar image.

Ulrich said, "X-ray tells us about technique, structure, and pigment, and will elucidate tears and repairs. This painting is pristine. Absolutely pristine."

A proud, beaming smile returned to Curator Ulrich.

"With spectroscopy, we can identify individual pigments. What paint is used. I won't go into detail about what spectroscopy is and how it works. Scientific. Much too technical. Boring stuff."

"I'm not easily bored, Dr. Brockbank. I have a degree in Biochemistry. What kind of spectroscopy did you use? Vibrational? Elemental? Or Fournier IR?"

"All three. Next slide, please. Here's the list: Zinc white, Lead white, Cobalt blue, Ultramarine blue, Prussian blue, Emerald green, Viridian, Sienna, Chrome yellow, Chrome orange, Vermillion, Red ocher."

"This is Van Gogh's summer palette, not similar; it is the *same* palette. *Exactly* the same. Next slide, please…"

The painting in its entirety filled and illuminated the screen.

"Look at the style," marveled Tobler Eckart. "All in line with his other paintings from the Asylum. Efficient. Specific. And yet exploratory and experimental, emotional. Bravo, Vincent! Bravo!"

All through Brockbank's presentation, a "but…" hung in the air. A hammer poised to fall. A rug ready to pull. Julie could tell they all sensed it.

Alain Ulrich stood behind Brockbank as he continued with his presentation. With an intermittent twitch of an eyelid, he said, "Scanning electron microscopy shows the minutest detail down to the level of the tiniest microbe. Next slide, please…"

The image was of an intricately patterned sphere. Beautiful all on its own.

"Pollen!" exclaimed Julie.

"*Ambrosia artemisiifolia*—common ragweed. Highly allergenic. Pollen is evenly distributed across the entire painting," said Brockbank, and he loosened his tie. "Importantly, even on the face of the model."

"As it should be," countered Ulrich. "Van Gogh painted outside—*plein aire*. Indeed, his painting *Cypresses* has bits of sand embedded as if a gust of wind sent the canvas flying to the ground."

"Next slide, please… This is a photo—micrograph. A magnified pinhead of pigment from the girl's cheek. A pink brushstroke of vermilion derived from cinnabar and zinc white."

"What's that?" asked Julie, spotting a lacy black speck.

"This is the partial wing of an insect. *Apis mellifera*—the common European honeybee."

"Brockbank, where are you going with this?" questioned Ulrich. "Van Gogh is in a flower garden. Bees are all around him. Surprised he was not stung himself."

"Last slide, please… I return to Vincent's handwritten letter to Theo:

July 1889.
The girl herself I completed in my room.
I could paint her now or in one hundred years.

Everyone stared at Van Gogh's written words. Julie watched their faces, minds churning with this difficult information. All the boxes check except this one unfathomable outlier.

"Are you insinuating that someone else painted it? Added pollen?" With difficulty, Ulrich uttered, "A forgery? A fake?

Preposterous. Absolutely preposterous!"

The Smithsonian scientist sat down. Grace Varga looked rattled. Tobler Eckhart looked confused, and the curator defiant. All silent, trying to break an impasse within their thoughts.

Julie broke the silence, "I have visited the Asylum in Saint-Rémy. Stood in Van Gogh's room."

"As have I," said Eckhart. "His room is on the second floor with an open window to the courtyard. Multiple paintings, including *Irises,* which Sotheby's sold for $54 million ten years ago, are from this courtyard. No doubt swirling with pollen and buzzing with bees."

"No doubt," echoed the art historian. "No doubt."

"Can we please move on from bug parts?" asked the curator.

Tobler Eckhart echoed with his own, "Please!"

"You don't know something about me," said Alain Ulrich, now standing next to the perspiring scientist. "An admission. Something I am not proud of." He let suspense fill the room, then grinned. "I am a season ticket holder to the New York Jets." Everyone chuckled. "And when a referee makes a call, that call cannot be overturned unless there is 'clear and convincing evidence'. Today, we are here to make a call.

"As you *do* know, I am an expert on the life and work of Marc Chagall. Our collection of his work is second to none." Seriousness took hold of the curator, a frown furrowing his tall forehead and his fierce gaze tracking around the room, boring into Julie, then moving to Varga and fixing

Tobler Eckhart. "When I am asked to testify to the authenticity of a Chagall painting, my call stands. It stands!" He raised a clenched fist. "What we say here is more than a wobble in the art world; it will be earth-shattering."

CHAPTER 38

October 3, 2003
Metropolitan Museum of Art
New York City

Kiki, in freshly-pressed Levis, a dress shirt, bolo tie, and a splash of Polo Sport, bounded up the stairs of the Metropolitan Museum of Art, a rose in hand, his new Tony Llamas heavy on the steps.

Lit with a glow, the museum was both inviting and imposing, with burnt orange banners exclaiming:

VAN GOGH

VAN GOGH

VAN GOGH

VAN GOGH

VAN GOGH

Joining the queue of tuxedos with black ties, black dresses, and heels, he gave his name, "Kershaw Kenyon."

Peering inside the museum, a jazz band was playing, and people were gathering with champagne flutes in hand. Two women at the door flipped pages of the guest book.

"Sorry, sir. We can't find you on our guest list."

"Check again. Kershaw Kenyon or maybe 'Kiki'?"

Squinting and running her finger down the page, she said, "Oh, here you are!"

Kiki exhaled a sigh of relief.

"But, sir, your name has been crossed out. And a note: *NO ADMITTANCE, Johann Imseng.* Sorry, sir." She motioned for SECURITY.

Kiki descended the stairway and stood on the sidewalk, fuming mad, as taxis and limos dispatched New York City's elite into a scrum of rubberneckers, paparazzi, and NYPD. A policeman approached and told him to "Move along." When a catering van pulled up, and the delivery man struggled carrying a huge silver platter, Kiki picked up the other end, and they both entered through a different door.

I'm in!

The Great Hall was decorated as if he were standing in a town square of Provence. Marble columns twined with climbing garlands of cypress, sunflowers, and irises were everywhere. Fresh lavender wafted across the massive room, mingling with notes of a jazz quintet playing John Coltrane. A self-portrait of Van Gogh in a straw hat projected across an entire wall, and Kiki looked into Vincent's eyes; they shone wary and unsure, uncomfortable with all this attention.

Kiki felt claustrophobic, even in this huge hall. Just off the Colorado River, guiding the Grand Canyon, not pale like New York socialites or sporting golden tans from vacationing on St. Maarten, he was sunbaked and windblown. He spotted the flamboyant owner of the Yankees, the mayor of New York, Tom Hanks, and his wife Rita. The Secretary of Defense, rumored to be running for President, worked the room like a campaign fundraiser. Barbara Streisand looked him up and down, smiling, perhaps thinking of her leading man—a young Kris Kristofferson in *A Star is Born.*

The star of this gala was displayed on a podium atop the hexagonal marble information center in the middle of The Great Hall and surrounded by sunflowers. Museum lighting illuminated the shrouded masterpiece, hidden from view.

In a corner off by themselves, Kiki saw Julie with Johann Imseng. He was tall and straight, dressed in a tuxedo. She was in a casual dress with a light sweater over her shoulders. He watched them, Johann making her laugh, Julie touching his arm. They were in their own little world. Jealousy shot through him like an arrow.

Julie startled when she saw Kiki. Then blushed. Then smiled and waved him over.

"Johann, this is my friend Kiki Kenyon," Julie said. *Not boyfriend.* "And Kiki, this is Johann." They did not shake hands, and Johann put his arm around Julie's waist. "He and I are donating the painting together. Can you believe all this hoopla? A big shindig."

To Johann's puzzlement, she said, "Hoopla is a…"

"I know what *hoopla* means, it's actually French, but *shindig?*

"A folksy big party." To Kiki, she said, "Johann is fluent in *four* languages.

"But not American slang," added Johann.

"You two have something in common," she said.

A girlfriend?

"Kiki is a mountain climber," said Julie.

"I happen to know of your exploits, your new route in Yosemite, and first ascents in Alaska," said Johann. "I climb too, in my Alps, but never enough time for such expeditions as yours. Perhaps we can share stories? Share a climbing rope someday?"

I don't share.

A server with a silver tray of champagne approached, and Johann took one for Julie and offered one to Kiki.

"I'm good," Kiki declined.

Johann sipped and said, "Moët & Chandon. Maybe you want a beer, Kiki?"

"Oh my gosh!" Julie said, looking at her watch. "I gotta get ready. *Excuse moi.*" She gulped her champagne, handed Kiki the empty glass, and added, "You guys okay? Good?" she asked, walking away with a worried glance over her shoulder. Both men watched her leave—a confident sashay.

"I don't know what she sees in you. You have nothing to offer her," said Johann. "Why don't you just walk away?" He pressed. "You give her backyard barbecues and Bud Light. Me? A winery on the sunny shore of Lake Geneva.

"You? A rubber raft and a bumpy butt down a muddy river. Me? A sailing sloop cruising French Polynesia.

"With you, she will be overwhelmed in a family clinic treating snotty noses, ringworm, and scabies. With me? An influential position with the World Health Organization or UNICEF."

Johann stood in Kiki's face and said, "Kiki, this is mathematics, basic arithmetic that even *you* can understand. One, plus one, plus one, equals three. Why don't you just walk away?"

"Why don't you just *fuck off!*" Kiki shoved him.

When Johann righted himself, squared his shoulders, and crooked a fist, Kiki pushed again. Johann swung at him. Ducking, Kiki came up with a right hook, smashing the side of Johann's head. As Johann spun, Kiki had a moment. *Fuck him up? Teach him a lesson? Or hold back. Pull my punches?*

Kiki crashed another fist caving Johann's side then hit him with a vicious uppercut. Johann landed hard on the floor. A woman screamed. The jazz band stopped. The room hushed. SECURITY scurried.

Sprawled, stemming blood from his lip, Johann yelled, "Kick 'is fooking ass out of here! He is not supposed to be here."

<hr>

"Johann, give me your arm," Julie whispered. Wobbling on high heels, teetering at the daunting precipice atop the Grand Staircase, she did a double-take at Johann. "What happened to your lip?!"

"A squirmish with your friend Kiki," Johann said, touching his fat lip.

"A skirmish," Julie corrected. "He did that?"

"Security kicked him out."

A camera flash stunned her, blinding her, and when her vision returned, she scanned the crowd below: curator Alian Ulrich waiting on the last step. Bob Bagley, jumping up and down, craning his neck, trying to get a peek. Grace Varga standing with Tobler Eckhart. Her father's friend Malcomb Sussman, the new editor of the New England Journal of Medicine, was watching. The Secretary of Defense and his wife were pandering with celebrities. *Oh no, not the Defense Secretary!*

Dressed in a sleeveless designer gown, she touched her diamond necklace, no longer a setting in her grandmother's hat pin; the cushion-cut diamond sparkled. Taking an unsteady first step, she repeated the climbing mantra Kiki had taught her: *Concentrate. Concentrate. Feet. Feet. Feet…*

Applause grew as they descended, and the band played *What a Wonderful World.* Julie felt like a bride. Alain Ulrich, beaming like a proud papa, escorted them to the podium right next to the shrouded painting. Julie thought about her father, wishing he were here, and a random thought entered her head: *Who will give me away at my wedding?*

"Cavemen painted their caves. Sometimes exquisitely," announced the curator to the crowd. "Art is what makes us human. Art is in each of us; it is our nature, our human nature. Tonight, in an astonishing act of generosity, two families come together to gift a masterpiece created by a genius with a troubled mind and a tender heart—Vincent Van Gogh. This magnificent work of art bridges dark chasms when the world lost its way, when evil plunged us into unspeakable horror. Tonight we cross a bridge. Tonight we stand in warm sunshine. I introduce to you, Julie Tolle and Johann Imseng."

"Good evening. Apologies do not come easily for me." Johann took Julie's hand. "Tonight is but a gesture. From my country to your country. From my family to your family. From my heart to your heart." He gave Julie a kiss on the cheek, his lip swollen.

Blushing, hand to her necklace, she said, "My goodness. Thank you, Johann, and thank all of you. My father loved this museum. He would be so happy to see this painting finally find a home. And Vincent, too. Let's see it! Shall we?"

The room dimmed. People drew closer. The painting was illuminated. Julie and Johann lifted its curtain…

The painting glowed. A girl in white lace bloomed. Face framed in black tresses, catching the afternoon sun, reflecting flowers overflowing from a wooden wheelbarrow, she was radiant. A golden yellow wall encircled the garden, twisted olive trees and stalwart cypress rose in the background, fading to hazy blue mountains into a swirling Provençal sky—a masterpiece!

Stunned, the gallery fell silent. Then gasps of "Wonderful!", "Magnificent!". The Yankees owner, as if still in the ballpark, was loudest in his approval, "Whoop! Whoop!" The art world was in love. Love at first sight.

Some eyes darted to Julie and back and forth to the painting. Not wanting to be compared to a masterpiece, she stepped from the podium and landed in Tobler Eckhart's arms as the band played Count Basie. Twirling her with suave dance steps, she had to concentrate to follow. When the next song started, Bob Bagley was waiting for her like an eager puppy and took her on a jumpy, jittery jig. Looking at his eyes, an examination, Bagley must've known what she was searching for.

"I'm back on my meds," he told her.

The Secretary of Defense was her next dance partner, the band playing *Moonlight Serenade.* Wrapping his arm tightly around her waist, she hesitantly put her hand on his dandruff-dusted shoulder. He said, "Doctor Tolle, nice to see you. How is your science fair project?"

They had first met a few months ago when her heart research had come under the scrutiny of the Defense Department, causing him embarrassment. His humiliation still stinging, he added, "My wife loves your painting. Me? I don't give a shit. Van Gogh was a whackjob." He pulled her closer. She stiffened.

Malcomb Sussman, sensing Julie's unease, tapped his way in. "Excuse me, Mr. Secretary, my turn." Rescued, Julie put her head on his shoulder.

When *Moonlight Serenade* ended with a flurry of notes, Alain Ulrich snagged her, saying, "I have a big surprise for you. Come with me." The curator led her upstairs to where Andy Warhol, Jackson Pollock, and Rothko live.

"Oh, there you are!" Julie said to Kiki. He was standing face to face with a painting. Hugging him, she said, "I've been looking for you. Where have you been?"

"Had a little dust-up. Left to get some fresh air. Too much riffraff down there. Mr. Ulrich here got me back in and showed me this…"

Together, they gazed at the only painting illuminated in the gallery.

"Wow!" Julie said. "Marc Chagall. It's beautiful." A large square canvas in every conceivable hue of dark blue showed a village in one corner smoldering in ruins, and she thought about Lech Balzec escaping the burning ghetto. A toppled white church steeple, a magical horse prancing with no rider. A man and a woman traversing green mountains carrying a suitcase and a knapsack. It was fanciful. Dreamlike. Across the cobalt night sky, a boy tumbled somersaulting over the moon and across the stars.

Julie looked at the attribution tag:

Marc Chagall
THE MOUNTAINEER 1943
On Loan—Jacob Tolle

Alain Ulrich explained, "I found this Chagall in our collection. And I found this letter from your father in our archives."

Julie read his elegant cursive:

August 5 1955

Dear Mr. Mellon,

I entrust this painting by my friend Marc Chagall to the Metropolitan Museum of Art – THE MOUNTAIN-EER. It is a loan until my situation improves. My apartment is tiny, moldy, and in a bad neighborhood. I hope your patrons will enjoy.

Sincerely yours,

Jacob Tolle

"Congratulations, Julie, you now have *two* paintings at The Met," said the curator.

Watching the boy fly across the painting, Julie said, "My father revered Marc Chagall and searched out his art everywhere we traveled. Now I know why. Think I might cry."

Back at the gala, Julie held Kiki's hand, and when they came face to face with Johann, she stood between them, feeling their anger and jealousy like a frypan simmering on the stove ready to boil over.

"You again," snarled Johann at Kiki with a curl of his swollen lip.

Johann put both hands on Julie's shoulder, searching her eyes, and said, "A shack in the woods or a villa in Tuscany? A seat at the table of the world? Julie, you and I can change the world and make it a better place. You and I. Give me a chance. Make a life with *me*."

Oblivious, Alain Ulrich twirled into the threesome, buzzing like a bothersome bee. "Come with me! Everyone wants to say 'Goodnight.'"

Feeling she was standing in a receiving line at a wedding, Julie stood with Johann and exchanged "Congratulations" and "Thank you." The Secretary of Defense came last, pushing his gracious wife; she gushed, he said nothing, fixing her with a glare that frightens four-star generals.

Johann, with his coat over his arm, said to Julie, "My jet leaves for Zurich at midnight. Wheels up. But I can hold it for tomorrow. Julie, we could celebrate this night together.

Alone. Just you and I. The Plaza Hotel is just a few blocks down Fifth Avenue."

"I don't know what to say, Johann." *I know what to say. I just don't know how to say it.* With an earnest grip on his hand, Julie told him, "We are friends, Johann. Special friends. What we have just accomplished together is monumental. Historical. Our connection is genuine. Johann, you are like a fairytale prince. Me? I'm the frog. Kiss me and I'm still a frog. You want to change the world. I just want to hop from lily pad to lily pad."

Bob Bagley butted in, holding the arm of a frail woman bent with a hump and shuffling a four-point cane. The elderly crone looked up at Johann with a sideways crook of her neck.

"Heir Imseng, this is Frau Litz," introduced Bagley, and Johann, with a politician's deft pivot, kissed her wrinkled hand. "Her family is originally from Vienna and was arrested when Germany annexed Austria in 1938. They were worked to death by Nazis at the Mauthausen camp."

"I am so sorry, Frau Litz. My condolences."

"She does not want your condolences, Heir Imseng. She wants her inheritance," said Bagley. "Her father has a life insurance policy underwritten by your bank. She has not received her benefit. Hundreds of other policyholders from the Holocaust have also been robbed. I legally represent all of them. Frau Litz has a payout due to her of 20 million francs, including decades of interest."

A man standing behind Bagely came forward, handing Johann a letter.

"This is a subpoena," announced Bagley.

Frowning and emitting a nervous cough, Johann replied, "Frau Litz, I will look into your claim personally." Giving Julie a kiss on her cheek, he whispered, "Think of me. Think of us," and he was gone.

"His bank is in real trouble," said Bob Bagley. "My clients are due payouts of billions."

Julie remembered, "I have a deposit slip of my grandfather's from a bank in Geneva. Mr. Bagley, I might need your help, too."

With the band packing, Kiki took Julie by the hand and then spoke to the pianist. With *Moon River* filling the Great Hall, Kiki said to her, "Unbelievable! In a gallery of masterpieces from around the world and across the ages... *you*... are the most beautiful. Doctor Tolle, may I have this dance?"

CHAPTER 39

The Next Day
Manhattan, New York City

Julie and Kiki had breakfast at Tiffany & Co., Dunkin Donuts doughnuts, and hot coffee while looking in the windows of the closed jewelry store. Engagement rings were on display, and each looked but said nothing, keeping their own thoughts secret.

What's Kiki thinking? Trying to do the math? Three months of my salary equals…

At MOMA, a delicate helicopter dangling from the ceiling looked like a giant art nouveau dragonfly pin. They said "Hi!" to Gustav Klimt, Andy Warhol, Mark Rothko, Georgia O'Keeffe, and her father's hero, Marc Chagall. In front of *The Starry Night*, Julie teared up. Wobbling at watching Vincent's phantasm of swirls, Kiki steadied her with his arm around her waist.

Passing Rockefeller Center, home to SNL, Julie kept an eye open for Jake and Elroy—the Blues Brothers and for

Coneheads from the planet Remulak.

Spotting the top of the Empire State Building, Kiki wondered, "Do you think Meg Ryan is still up there waiting for Tom Hanks?"

In Grand Central Station, a magnificent cathedral dedicated to transportation and saved from the wrecking ball by Jacqueline Kennedy Onassis, they stood in the middle of the cavernous hall, twirling around, looking at the constellations on the ceiling as commuters rushed like a river parting around them. Riding the subway, Kiki had Julie jump from car to car to car. Standing between speeding, shifting train cars, the track flashing underneath them, their car moving in violent jerks one way, the next car jolting its own way, earsplitting clacking in a hot, oily, smoky, smelly, tunnel, they timed their leap, like school girls gauging their entrance into a twirling jump rope, "One potato, two potato, three potato, four!..."

Out of the subway at Canal Street Station, they popped up in SoHo. Eating street pizza while looking in the window of a vintage dress store, they folded their slice of cheese pie deftly between thumb, index, and middle finger. When a long string of cheese dangled from pizza slice to Julie's mouth, Kiki made an even longer string, and the competition was on. Julie won with a string of mozzarella longer than her arm.

"Let's go inside," she said.

Not a thrift store with the smells of someone else's stale clothes from GAP or TJ Maxx, only designer labels were present, neatly organized by each designer.

"Try this on," said Kiki, hefting a full-length mink coat onto Julie's shoulders.

"Wadda ya think?" she asked, modeling the beautiful coat, its silky soft fur radiating warmth and style.

"Perfect for that Chewbacca look," he said.

Julie donned a sequined leather jacket, white gloves, oversized sunglasses, and a pouty expression. "How 'bout this? Madonna in *Desperately Seeking Susan.*" She added a couple of dance steps.

"May I help you?"

A serious woman with a British accent approached them. Tall, thin, and stylish in a dark blue suit, her glasses on a chain, spartan jewelry, smooth complexion with wrinkles only in the corners of her hazel green eyes. A brunette, still in her natural color, with red lipstick.

Probably a runway model now in her 50s?

The woman stood with a hand on her hip, ruining Julie and Kiki's campy fun.

Julie looked around the boutique—beautiful dresses, jackets, shoes, bags, belts, *Even some vintage cowboy boots for Kiki. But nothing here in my budget.* "Yes, I think you can."

Kiki raised both eyebrows.

"What are you looking for? Besides fun, which we will have as well. I'm all about having fun."

You? Fun? I don't think so.

"Something classic. From Europe," Julie requested.

Julie entered a dressing room as the woman brought her dresses.

The first dress: short and straight, shapeless in vibrant colors.

"Twiggy wore this in a London photoshoot in 1969."

"Older. More elegant and conservative."

The second dress: cream-colored, wool, a square neckline, hem below the knee—Dior.

"This dress was worn at General Eisenhower's Inauguration, 1953."

"I want something older, from the 1930s. Classy."

"Oh, now you challenge me," said the saleswoman. "We are in the Great Depression. Yet we give birth to *haute couture*. I have something special—Coco Chanel."

Julie came out of the dressing room feeling transformed, a step back in time.

"You look amazing, this dress looks as if Coco Chanel sewed this just for you!" said the saleswoman.

Kiki said, "Wow!"

"I'll take it," said Julie, looking in the mirror. When she looked at the price tag, she blanched. A small tag with a price written in fountain pen—$5000. Crestfallen, her shoulders slumped.

The saleswoman registered Julie's sticker shock. "Look, you seem like a nice couple just starting out. Saving for a house while paying off student loans? Wedding rings? I don't know. It is none of my business. My business is selling dresses. I own this shop, and the dress you are wearing has been on my rack for three years, and you are the only person to try it on. It's yours. My gift. Enjoy. See, I told you it would be fun."

Stepping out of the shop into a downpour, the streets were rivers plied by taxis spraying water everywhere, awnings were sagging waterfalls. The city was dark, the tops of buildings engulfed by clouds. Kiki tried to hail a taxi, but all were occupied by passengers warm and dry. He gave up, grabbed a pizza box from a street vendor, held it over their heads as they dashed hand in hand running towards the subway station, keeping under awnings and ducking into doorways.

In one dry doorway, guitars were displayed in the window. Stepping inside Rudy's Music, they entered a world of Fender Stratocasters, Gibson, and Les Paul. This was the store any rock guitarist visiting the city would visit. A mecca for accomplished musicians. Professionals.

"I've been practicing my guitar," Kiki said sheepishly to Julie, and he asked the guy behind the desk, "Got any Martins?"

"Back wall. Ova dare. Take these towels. Dry yourselves. My guitars donna like to get wet," he said in an accent.

Kiki chose a six-string Martin OM-45. "My dream guitar," he said in reverence, admiring its curves, finish, and structure. Honey colored wood with mother-of-pearl inlays—it was gorgeous. "Feels good." He caressed it. Fingered it. Strummed it. And ran some scales.

"This is for you," he said to Julie.

Kiki played *Blackbird* by The Beatles. Julie closed her eyes, losing herself… A mountain top in the Alps… Blackbirds… Her father… When she opened her eyes, Kiki was looking at her, looking into her, and he sang the last verse,

You were only waiting for this moment to arise…

CHAPTER 40

November 1, 2003

Asthma & Allergy Clinic

University Hospital

Salt Lake City, Utah

"Doctor, I can't breathe. I can't breathe. Can't get my air," Clyde Ekker lamented to Julie, sitting together in the bright exam room.

She thumbed through his chart and took him in—a cursory examination. Eighty-three, a rancher, clean shaven, thin and sinewy in a straw Stetson, plaid powder blue shirt with pearl buttons, Wranglers falling off his narrow hips and absent buttocks, held up by a wide, tooled leather belt with a big buckle. His newest cowboy boots. *Dressing all up for the big city doctor.* A portable oxygen tank hissing at his side ran a clear plastic tube up his nose.

"Doc, I can't saddle my horse. Can't pitch hay. Can't

climb into my tractor. Can't change sprinkler pipe. Can't go to the High Country. Can't refresh the missus. I get light-headed. Sometimes I go all the way out. Don't tell my wife LaDonna.

"But I'm whining. How are you? You look too young to be a doctor. A sprout."

Julie offered, "I have asthma too." Someone told her to always find a doctor afflicted with your same ailment: migraines, colitis, back pain. *'They know the most and care the most'. But not sure that holds for psychiatrists: bipolar mania, schizophrenia, borderline personality.* "Mine is mild and intermittent."

She asked, "Are you a smoker?"

"I fess up. We kids used to roll up cedar bark and smoke behind the barn. For one summer when I was ten or eleven, I had no eyelashes or eyebrows. Singed to a crisp."

Mr. Ekker, take off your shirt, please. I want to take a look and listen."

He was pale white, skinny, with loose skin hanging off a strong, bony frame. Barrel-chested, hyperinflated from a life of trapping air deep within his lungs. Hands, face, and neck were darkened by the sun like they had been dipped in volcanic cinder.

Julie examined her patient. Her Littman stethoscope pressed to each lung field front and back. "Take deep breaths in and out."

Pan inspiratory and expiratory wheezing. Crackles at the bases like pulling apart Velcro. A cacophony–a grade school orchestra warming up and out of tune. *My ears hurt.*

Inside his narrowed bronchial tubes, oxygen molecules—O2—fought their way into his lungs, while CO2 clawed its way out. Clambering. Elbowing each other. A catfight trapped inside his diseased airways.

"It's fall. Damn ragweed got a hold on me, Doc. I'm bad right now."

Julie went to present the case to her attending physician, the Chairman of Pulmonary Medicine—a physician scientist, with a flair for teaching, and a hard nose for administration, set to retire this year. Revered by some. Feared by others. Grandfatherly on occasion. The nurses warned her, "Julie, you'd better know your stuff."

Long white coat, unruly white hair, piercing blue eyes, an aura of intensity, he unnerved her.

"Tell me how Clyde is doing; I've known him for years."

A case presentation. My time to shine. She stood and straightened. Found her voice.

"Mr. Ekker is an eighty-three-year-old with lifelong asthma, presenting with worsening shortness of breath, hypoxemia, and audible wheezing. His Chief Complaint is: 'I can't breathe.'"Julie recited the: History of Present Illness, Past Medical History, Medications, Family History, Review of Systems, and Physical Examination. Articulate and composed, she was proud of herself.

"What about the Social History?"

Oh shit! "I forgot. I can go back and ask him."

"Let me fill you in. Clyde Ekker is from a Utah pioneer

family. They crossed the West pulling a handcart, not riding in a covered wagon. Settled in Escalante in a country too parched and poor to grow anything but a couple of cuttings of hay and a herd of Black Angus. Hardscrabble stuff. A high school wrestler. A couple of years of college. Lied about his asthma to join the U. S. Army Air Force and was discharged when he passed out in a B17 at 18,000 feet over Germany. A wife and no kids.

"He is a devout, deeply religious man. Don't get him started talking about The Atonement."

Julie filed away this information for her written note.

"Imagine the panic, Dr. Tolle, when you can't get your air. Suffocating. Do you know what he does?"

Julie shook her head.

"He brews a big pot of cowboy coffee, sticks his face into it, and inhales. Methyl xanthine and caffeine can relieve bronchospasm. Do you know what else he does?"

Julie shook her head.

"He prays. He prays, *'God help me. Help me breathe'*. Do you know what God does?"

Julie shook her head.

"God sends Clyde to you, Dr Tolle. He has no magic wand. God wants *you* to help Clyde."

The professor gave her a moment, then asked, "What is your Assessment and Plan?"

"My diagnosis. Severe asthma in exacerbation with hypoxemic respiratory failure triggered by American ragweed."

"Excellent!" said the professor and queried, "*American ragweed?*"

"That's what they call it in France."

"Oh, that's because it is an invasive species in France. A nasty pest. First introduced in the late 1800s. Now it has a foothold."

Julie's world wobbled off kilter. An unexpected surprise. A hot spell of vertigo.

"This is not adding up," she whispered and sat down, shaking her head. "This is not making sense."

The professor worried, "What are you talking about?"

"How can ragweed pollen embed itself on a canvas painted in Provence in the spring of 1889?"

CHAPTER 41

Tonight

Salt Lake City, Utah

On an evening off, out of the hospital, Julie was on her second glass of wine, and her dad's turntable was spinning Louis Armstrong with Ella Fitzgerald. She was dressed in Coco Chanel circa 1930.

A party for one, moi.

From the top shelf of her dresser, she pulled out the purple velvet Courvoisier pouch, untied the drawstring, and emptied the contents onto her bedspread. Heaped in a glittering pile, Julie stared at the gleaming jewelry, and it seemingly stared back.

What am I going to do with you?

She put on the diamond necklace, the diamond bracelet, and earrings. Only her pinky finger could accommodate the diamond ring.

Turning one way then the other, she was not the little girl playing dress-up in her mommy's clothes anymore. Her mirror reflected not only herself, but images of women in her family. Not ghostlike, these images were not scary, but welcoming, encouraging, proud, loving.

But I am the last of my family. It all ends with me.

It was a lonely feeling. Tragic. Looking in the mirror, wearing jeweled remnants of a family with origins in old Toledo, an exile to Provence, an escape to America, tears welled in her eyes.

It ends with me. And she recalled her admonishment to Malcomb Sussman: *first, stop crying.*

Out of wine, she went to the kitchen and opened a bottle of French Champagne, saved for a special occasion that never came. POP! The cork shot to the ceiling, denting it, ricocheting around her 1930s bungalow. With Ella and Louis singing, *April in Paris,* a glass of champagne as her partner, she starts to *"dance like nobody's watching."*

Then she remembered something, froze, and stopped dancing. From the velvet pouch, she withdrew the delicate parchment of the bank deposit slip:

UBCS SUISSE—GENEVA

DATE: 7 AUGUST 1939
DEPOSIT: 1,230,000 FR
NAME: PAUL TOLEDANO
ACCOUNT XXXXXXXXX

What am I going to do with **you***?*

Her mind toggled to her visit with Herr Stueben, Vice President of Accounts. And then she remembered something else, something that could not be, and she tried to shake off, dispel it, vanquish the thought.

It can't be. It's not right. It was only a glimpse.

Remembering the thin journal Herr Stueben had on his desk, the leather old but not worn, the typed label obscured by his hands, *until he stood up when I left the office…*

It can't be… But it is. I saw it. That journal is a record. A ledger. A record of Paul Toledano's bank account! The label was small but clear. A long account number. And… And a date—*1951.*

1951. That was when the account was last active. The last time someone accessed it. The last time someone made a claim *on it? 1951, after the war. But who? Who?*

Julie whispered the answer, "Eloisa? Eloisa Toledano!"

EPILOGUE

4 October 2003
Zurich, Switzerland

Why am I forsaken?
I am alone. Banished again. I weep.

Johann disrobes Moi, pulling off my linen cloak. Exposed. Stripped of my frame, I am naked for him. In the deepest vault within his bank, we are surrounded by walls of gold bullion, the warm glow casting a luster across my canvas and filling him from the inside out.

He sits and stares at Moi.

I read his expressions. His brilliant mind open to Moi even as a young boy. I know him. Always thinking, aspiring, conniving. Colluding with himself, ambition building upon ambition.

I strengthen him. Shoring his resolve. Fueling his passion. Fanning desire.

Today, I see jealousy. And you would *not* want to be the object of Johann's envy. Or his hate. And his hatred is running deep.

Yes, Johann, I know you.

But there are some things I do not know. *Why am I here? And where is Julie Tolle?*

He just stares at Moi…

I just stare at him…

He just stares at Moi…

I just stare at him…

He stands. Checks his watch. And leaves.

Johann is a busy man. He runs a bank in Zurich.

ACKNOWLEDGEMENTS

"Doug, your words are too big," from my mom, the world's most voracious reader, crossword puzzle buster, and Scrabble champion with a vocabulary larger than both Merriam and Webster. Thanks, mom. And for her parting shot, "Keep writing."

For my daughter, Mckenzie Leigh Ross, "*The Proud English Major,*" this book arose from middle school struggles, when heroes and role models were hard to find. And to Grace Vargason-Nord, my creative touchstone. You inspire me with how you live a life of art and beauty.

Tony Bell MD, my fellow Yosemite pilgrim.

Special affection and respect for my friends at Kevin Anderson & Associates, with guidance from Mark Weinstein and the editorial skill of Amanda A. Barnett. Amanda, you are a true wordsmith wizard. For Ace Silva, designer of a book cover that gave me chills when I first saw it.

A heartfelt thanks to Francine Platt for the interior design.

Hannah Rothschild, thank you for teaching me that art can indeed have a voice.

The museums: Metropolitan Museum of Art in New York City, Van Gogh Museum in Amsterdam, Musée d'Orsay in Paris—repositories of what makes us human.

And for the steadfast, unwavering support of me and our little family, and for her insightful ideas, patience, and love—Laura Marie Ross.

ABOUT THE AUTHOR

Douglas Scott Ross is a physician with a passion for medicine, history, and adventure. He grew up in Oregon, lives in the mountains of Utah, and can be found sluicing his way into desert slot canyons and deep in the Wasatch backcountry.

Read more at: douglasscottrossauthor.com